ALSO BY MICHAEL MCGARRITY

Tularosa

Mexican Hat

Michael McGarrity

Serpent Gate

A Kevin Kerney Novel

SCRIBNER

SCRIBNER
1230 Avenue of the Americas
New York, NY 10020

SCRIBNER and design are registered trademarks of
Simon & Schuster Inc.

Designed by Brooke Zimmer
Text set in Dante Monotype
Manufactured in the United States of America

1 3 5 7 9 10 8 6 4 2

Library of Congress Cataloging-in-Publication Data
McGarrity, Michael.
Serpent gate: a Kevin Kerney novel / Michael McGarrity.
p. cm.
I. Title.
PS3563.C36359S45 1998
813'.54—dc21   97–51142
CIP

ISBN 0-684-85076-1
ISBN 0-684-85345-0 (signed edition)

For Manuel "Dave" Hernandez,
Jerry Ortiz y Pino,
Miriam Brownstein,
Cathy Fernandez,
and Larry Martinez,
who helped set me on the path to
Serpent Gate.

ACKNOWLEDGMENTS

My sincere thanks go to Janette Smith, formerly of the New Mexico Department of Public Safety, Training and Recruiting Division, now retired; Michele Maxwell of the New Mexico Department of Public Safety, Office of the Secretary; Agent Bob Parsons of the New Mexico State Police; and Kathryn Jimenez of Mountainair, New Mexico, all of whom helped me during the research phase of *Serpent Gate*.

Any alteration of fact, either deliberate or otherwise, pertaining to the New Mexico State Police, the New Mexico Department of Public Safety, current state criminal statutes, and investigative procedures is my sole responsibility.

STATE OF NEW MEXICO

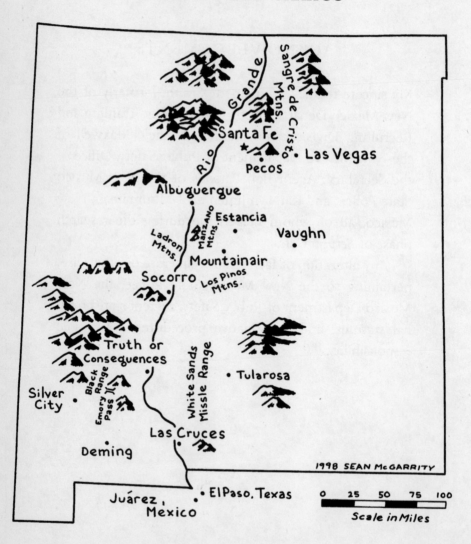

Serpent Gate

1

Kevin Kerney sat in an unmarked state police car across the street from the Shaffer Hotel in Mountainair, New Mexico, waiting for Robert Cordova to show up. Kerney had tracked Cordova to the state mental hospital in Las Vegas, only to discover that he had run off two days earlier. Cordova was a schizophrenic with a history of disappearing from the state hospital as soon as he was stabilized on medication.

A hospital psychiatrist had told Kerney that Cordova had no permanent residence and usually went back to his hometown of Mountainair after running off. Eventually he'd show up at the health clinic in town, looking for cigarette or coffee money, or he'd be found wandering the streets in a full-blown psychotic episode.

Kerney had already checked for Cordova at the clinic. The secretary hadn't seen Robert, nor had the other locals Kerney spoke with, but everybody he questioned noted Cordova liked to hang out in front of the Shaffer Hotel.

Twenty minutes into Kerney's wait, the information proved to be right on the money. A scruffy-looking man with an untamed beard and tangled dark hair came scurrying down the street around the corner from the state highway that ran next to the hotel. Filthy high-top sneakers with no laces slapped against his bare ankles as he hurried to a low fence in front of a small park and gazebo adjacent to the hotel. He stopped dead in his tracks and wheeled to face the fence.

Before the man turned, Kerney got a good look, consulted a mug shot, and made a positive ID. A runt of a man in his mid-thirties, no more than five foot four without an ounce of fat, Cordova wore tattered jeans that hung low on his hips and a soiled plaid shirt, too large for his skinny frame, that ballooned around his waist. It was a chilly early November day and Cordova wasn't wearing a coat.

Cordova interlaced his fingers at the back of his head, stuck both thumbs in his ears, did an abrupt about-face, and started marching from one end of the fence to the other in a rigid measured cadence, as though he were a sentry on patrol.

The fence bordering the park was a stunning piece of folk art. The railings, posts, and two gates were fashioned out of hand-formed concrete imbedded with an amazing array of icons depicting two-headed animals, fanciful birds, stylized fish, and human figures, all made with odd-shaped colorful stones. Smack in the center of the fence, a long serpent with an arrowhead tail writhed and coiled, its head sporting a sharklike fin, the base of its neck sprouting incongruous insect legs.

On the railing above the serpent, the artist had signed and dated his work, using pebbles and hand-cut fragments of shale to spell out BUILT BY POP SHAFFER 1931. Shaffer had also built the hotel he'd named after himself.

Kerney stayed in his unit with the motor off and the window open watching Cordova parade up and down, his thumbs jammed in his ears, shaking his head vigorously.

Cordova's bizarre behavior made Kerney hold back from making an approach. He didn't know much about Cordova's mental condition other than that the man heard voices and talked to Jesus Christ a lot. Kerney didn't want to fight his way through Cordova's delusions; he needed Cordova to be rational when he questioned him.

Six months ago, Cordova had been interviewed about the murder of Patrolman Paul Gillespie. He'd been completely incoherent at the time, in the middle of a psychotic break. After the interview, Cordova disappeared and could not be found again for further questioning. Kerney hoped he could learn something from Cordova that might help him get a handle on the case. He was running out of leads on an investigation going nowhere.

The murder had stymied the state police and the FBI. Officer Gillespie had been found shot once in the head with his own handgun at the Mountainair police station on the opening night of the annual town rodeo. Virtually every resident of Mountainair and the surrounding area had attended the event, including Gillespie, who was on duty at the time. He was seen leaving the rodeo grounds during the calf-roping finals. An hour later his body was discovered by Neil Ordway, chief of the two-man force.

A month after Kerney's friend Andy Baca had been appointed chief of the New Mexico State Police, he had reached out for Kerney, given him a badge, and sent him down to Mountainair to find Gillespie's killer. For almost four weeks Kerney had been making the eighty-mile drive from Santa Fe to Mountainair, spending his days running down every possible lead. So far, he had nothing to show for the effort.

Cordova suddenly stopped marching, pulled his thumbs out of his ears, and ran a hand over the serpent icon in the fence. To Kerney it seemed almost like a caress. Cordova turned, looked in Kerney's direction, raised his face toward the weak November sun, and smiled. His body relaxed and his face lost some of its tightness.

Kerney thought maybe the time was right to approach Cordova. He got out of the car, and as he crossed the street Cordova extended his hand like a pistol, sighted with one eye, and pulled off an imaginary round.

"Are you a cop?" Cordova called out as he walked toward Kerney in a tough-guy strut.

Kerney stopped and nodded.

Cordova smiled broadly. His teeth were chipped and badly stained. His beard had dried gobs in it, but Kerney couldn't even guess what the substance might be.

Cordova put his wrists together at his waist. "Cuff me and take me to jail. I'm hungry."

Cordova gave off a ripe odor of vomit and urine, and his breath reeked of stale cigarette smoke. Kerney forced down a gag reflex. At six feet one inch, he loomed over the man. He stepped back in an attempt to get away from Cordova's rankness.

"How about I buy you a pack of smokes and a meal?" he countered, nodding in the direction of the hotel.

"I said I want to go to jail," Cordova said crankily, craning his neck to look at Kerney. "I'm a fucking mental patient. You're supposed to take me to jail."

"Maybe later, if you cooperate."

Cordova stared in disgust at Kerney.

Behind the dirt, the beard, the unruly hair, and the chipped stained teeth, Cordova's eyes looked clear.

"How come you limp?" Cordova asked.

"I got shot," Kerney answered, thinking back to the incident that had ended his career as chief of detectives with the Santa Fe PD. An old friend and fellow officer had failed to back him up on a stakeout. The end result was one dead drug dealer, permanent damage to Kerney's right knee, and a partially destroyed gut.

"Were you a cop when it happened?"

"Yeah, I was."

Cordova threw a couple of jabs in the air at an imaginary opponent. "I'd never let that happen to me. I'd fuck somebody up if they tried that shit."

"I bet you would," Kerney replied. "Do you want that meal and pack of smokes?" He inclined his head toward the hotel.

"What do you want?" Cordova asked.

"Just to talk."

"They won't let me in there."

"They will if you're with me."

Cordova grunted and looked Kerney up and down. Kerney's jacket was open, and Robert didn't see a gun. "What kind of cop are you, anyway? You're not even wearing a *pistola*."

"Do you think I need it?"

"Of course you do."

Kerney nodded, stepped to the car, unlocked it, got his holstered sidearm, and strapped it on his belt. "Better?"

"Yeah. Now maybe they'll let me in the restaurant. Can I order anything I want?"

"Anything. I'm buying."

Robert held up two fingers, both stained nicotine yellow. "Two packs of smokes."

"Name your brand," Kerney replied as he walked Robert to the hotel entrance.

It was mid-morning and the hotel dining room was empty except for a young, round waitress who sat reading the newspaper at the lunch counter along the back wall. Kerney got Cordova settled at a table by the window that gave a view across the street of an empty single-story building and vacant lot.

"What about my cigarettes?" he asked, as he grabbed a menu, crossed his legs, and started wiggling his foot. The loose, filthy sneaker slapped against his heel with a dull smacking sound.

"After we eat," Kerney replied.

Robert grunted in dissatisfaction.

Kerney waited for the waitress to notice them. The ceiling was another folk art masterpiece by Pop Shaffer. Dark wooden beams and handmade chandeliers were painted with an intricate tapestry of Native American symbols and mythical figures, some of which looked like they came strictly from Pop Shaffer's imagination. Kerney's gaze jumped from image to image; it was almost too much to take in at one sitting.

Tired of waiting, Kerney cleared his throat. The waitress turned, glanced at Robert, nodded to Kerney, slipped off the lunch counter seat, and walked through the swinging doors into the kitchen.

"She's calling the cops," Robert predicted.

"Why would she do that?"

"Because the last time I was in here, I threw an ashtray at her."

"Did you hit her?"

"Nope, she ducked. Aren't you going to ask me why I did it?" His foot wiggle accelerated a bit.

"Do you want to tell me?"

Cordova smiled wickedly. "Nope."

The waitress reappeared and walked to the table. She stood as far away from Cordova as she could, using Kerney as a shield.

"I can't serve you," she said to Kerney.

"Yes, you can." He held out his open badge case. "This is police business."

"I know who you are," the woman said, looking over the top

of her eyeglasses. Her watery brown eyes blinked rapidly. She had stringy brown hair pinned back in a bun, most of which had unraveled against her neck. Her testy expression made her double chin more noticeable.

"I still can't serve you."

Kerney smiled pleasantly. "Tell your boss if we don't get served, I'll have every state health-and-safety inspector I can think of down here tomorrow morning, crawling all over the place looking for violations."

Cordova grinned in delight as the woman turned and walked stiffly back to the kitchen.

"That was bad," he said to Kerney. "You put her down, man. I never had a cop do anything like that for me before. They usually treat me like shit."

"No sweat, Robert. What do you want to eat?"

The waitress returned and grudgingly took Robert's order of two cheeseburgers, a double order of french fries, and coffee.

Robert didn't talk while he waited for his meal to arrive. His gaze stayed locked on the pass-through window from the kitchen. He licked his lips and tapped a finger anxiously on the table. Kerney wondered when Robert had last eaten.

When the food came, Robert wolfed down the meal, hamburger juice dribbling into his beard. His foot didn't wiggle when he ate.

Finished, Robert picked at his broken teeth with a long fingernail, belched, and smiled. "Thanks," he said.

"You're welcome."

Robert rubbed his thumb and forefinger together. "Now I need a smoke."

"In a minute. I need to ask you a few questions."

"What about?"

"How well did you know Paul Gillespie?"

"He was a motherfucker. I'm glad he's dead."

"Why do you say that?"

Robert's brown eyes turned angry. "I went to high school with him. He was always hassling me. Pushing me around, picking fights, teasing me—stuff like that. It got worse when he became a cop."

"How did it get worse?"

Robert started to respond, glanced out the window, and clamped his mouth shut. Neil Ordway was walking toward the hotel entrance.

"How did Gillespie mistreat you?"

"He didn't do nothing," Cordova said, sneering in the direction of Ordway as the cop entered the dining room.

A middle-aged man with a square face, thinning blond hair, and a pinched nose, Ordway stood over the table and looked at Kerney and Robert. He grinned without showing his teeth. It made his cheeks puff out.

"What can I do for you, Chief?" Kerney asked.

"I came for Cordova. Seems he's run away from the Las Vegas funny farm again."

"Fuck you," Robert said, his eyes hooded. "I'm not going back there. I'm never going back there."

"Don't make this hard on yourself, Cordova," Ordway said, wrinkling his nose. "Jesus, you smell like shit."

"I'll take care of the situation with Cordova," Kerney interjected before Robert could reply.

Ordway pulled out a chair and sat. "Are you going to drive him back to Las Vegas?"

"I said I'll take care of it," Kerney repeated, holding Ordway's gaze. Ordway didn't flinch.

Robert leaned across the table, cleared his throat, and spat in Ordway's face.

Ordway blinked, rubbed a sleeve across his face, and grabbed a fistful of Robert's shirt. "You're going to jail for that, shithead."

Robert grinned and nodded in agreement.

Kerney clamped down on Ordway's arm. "Let him go," he ordered.

Ordway locked his gaze on Kerney. "Whatever you say," he said with a grin, releasing Cordova.

Free of Ordway's grip, Robert tipped over his chair and scampered out the door.

Ordway laughed as Robert disappeared from sight. "Well, it seems like he's run away. Isn't that a damn shame."

"Maybe you can tell me where to look," Kerney said calmly.

"Your guess is as good as mine. But if you think Cordova can help you, you're way off base."

"I'd still like to talk to him."

"He'll turn up again. He always does."

Kerney changed his tack. "I know you gave Gillespie excellent performance reviews, but did you ever have to discipline him for failure to perform his duties?"

"No."

"He was never late for work? He never had to be corrected about policies and procedures?"

"Sure, occasionally. It wasn't a big enough deal to require any official action."

"There was no evidence of conduct unbecoming an officer? No citizen complaints lodged against him?"

"No."

"Did Gillespie show signs of having a drinking problem? Was he closemouthed about what he did on his free time? Did he have a pattern of calling in sick after his days off?"

"I never saw him under the influence, either on duty or off."

"Did he have money problems?"

"You've seen his financial records. He lived within his means." Ordway shook his head and stood up. "You know what? I think this case has got you stumped, and you're looking for a way to save face. Questioning Paul's character isn't going to get you spit or make you any friends in this town."

Kerney got to his feet. "It sounds like Gillespie was a perfect cop."

"He did his job."

"I've heard that the town council isn't very happy with your performance."

"The hometown hero, who took their high school football team to the state finals way back when, was murdered. They think I should have made an arrest the day he got shot. They don't give a tinker's damn about the lack of a suspect."

"That puts you under a lot of pressure, I bet."

"Not anymore. I've resigned. I'm out of here at the end of the week." He turned on his heel to leave.

"Chief Ordway," Kerney called out.

Ordway stopped at the door and looked back at Kerney. "What?"

The waitress stood anchored behind the counter at the far end of the dining room, tilted slightly forward, intent on every word.

"If you find Robert Cordova, don't mess with him. Tell me where he is and I'll pick him up."

"Sure thing, hotshot."

Kerney watched him leave, thinking Ordway had been a cop long enough to know that without a suspect, the victim became the prime focus of attention. But politics in small towns were played based on blood ties, and Ordway was the outsider, imported because Gillespie hadn't met the state training and experience qualifications for the chief's position. What if Gillespie had been a bad apple and Ordway had turned a blind eye to it, not wanting to fire the hometown ex-hero of the high school gridiron? It would be really stupid to admit that he let an unethical or crooked officer remain on the job in order to keep the town council placated. Such an admission would end Ordway's career in law enforcement.

From what Kerney had seen of Ordway during the past four weeks, he would be no great loss to the profession.

He dropped some bills on the table to cover Robert's meal and the tip, and smiled at the waitress. She lowered her gaze and got busy wiping down the immaculate countertop.

A RAILROAD town established in the early part of the century, Mountainair sat among the foothills to the Manzano Mountains. A state highway dissected Main Street, curved in front of the local elementary school, and continued past a gas station, motel, and some abandoned commercial buildings before making a straight run west toward the mountains. Main Street, a two-block-long strip with some retail stores, a post office, and a National Park Service building, boasted no trees, no traffic lights, and no pedestrians. Some of the buildings were vacant, and barren display shelves behind plate-glass windows created a rhythm of continual decline.

Kerney drove the strip several times looking for Robert, who was nowhere to be found. He stopped next to the post office and spotted Neil Ordway's police car parked in front of the town hall and police station.

The police station, which housed the police dispatch office and the magistrate court, had a concrete front with a thunderbird design perched above an ornamental pillar that separated two entry doors. Ordway's office took up the second floor of the adjacent town hall.

Kerney wondered if Ordway had snagged Robert in spite of his warning to leave the man alone. He switched his police radio to Ordway's frequency. If Robert was in custody, Kerney would know it when Ordway left to take him back to Las Vegas. He would keep looking until then.

Mountainair had no distinct neighborhoods to speak of, except for a string of middle-class, ranch-style houses and a few restored Victorian cottages near the high school. Even there, scattered between neat yards and tidy homes, an occasional empty lot with an old foundation or a sagging, weather-beaten house open to the elements broke any impression of a well-defined neighborhood.

Kerney did a slow patrol and checked each empty house before heading across the main drag, where the pavement quickly turned to dirt, and a string of houses, several churches, some shacks, sheds, and uninhabited cabins sputtered to a stop at a fence to an unused pasture.

Kerney kept looking, found nothing, returned to the main drag, and stopped at the grocery store to buy two packs of cigarettes. Ordway's cruiser was still parked outside city hall when he came out. He headed east on the state highway in the hope that Robert might be hitchhiking out of town. He drove to the Estancia cutoff before giving up and turning around to scout the road west of town. He shut down the hunt near the Abo Ruins National Monument and made his way back to the village.

He topped out at the hill on the outskirts of Mountainair just as a small herd of pinto horses swooped up a shallow arroyo and trotted along the highway fence. It was a pretty sight, and Kerney slowed to watch until the horses disappeared into a draw.

Mountainair had faded with the demise of dry land farming and the decline of railroad traffic. But its beautiful setting pulled tourists in and kept the place alive. It was a gateway to the wilderness that spread over the southern end of the Manzano Mountains, which were brushed at the summits with the first dusting of snow.

To the south a heavily forested mesa sheared off half of the horizon, and thick, slow-moving clouds in the blue-gray November sky rolled toward the village. Kerney had been taught by his ranching father to read the weather, and the day promised moisture sometime soon.

Mountainair was not completely unfamiliar to Kerney. After

finishing a brief stint as the interim sheriff of Catron County in the southwest part of the state, Kerney had looked at a section of land for sale in the high country outside Mountainair. It was summer grazing pasture infested with cocklebur, hound's-tongue, and prickly pear cactus—sure signs of overgrazing. It would take years to bring it back, and Kerney needed land that he could put to use immediately to produce income and make the mortgage payments, if he was ever going to get back into ranching.

With only enough money for a modest down payment, everything else he'd looked at was either way out of his price range or too small in size for raising cattle.

Kerney's parents had lost their ranch in the Tularosa Basin when White Sands Missile Range, a top-secret testing facility in the heart of south-central New Mexico, had expanded. The day they moved, military policemen and federal agents escorted the family off the spread to the Rocking J Ranch, where Kerney's father had taken a job as foreman.

That was the day Kerney's dream of owning a ranch was born. He had kept his hopes alive for almost forty years. While living on the Rocking J, during his college years, in Vietnam as a platoon leader near the end of the war, and throughout his career in law enforcement, Kerney had never let go of the dream.

He wondered if he would ever be able to achieve it. It didn't look promising.

He pulled up in front of Pop Shaffer's hotel to find Ordway using a side-handle baton in a wrist lock on Robert to force him toward the squad car. The waitress watched the action through the plate-glass window of the dining room.

"Let him go," Kerney ordered, slamming his car door to get Ordway's attention.

"Butt out, Kerney," Ordway said. "This is my business."

Kerney quickly closed the distance to Ordway.

"Move, Cordova," Ordway commanded. He applied more

force to the hold. Robert gasped in pain and lurched toward the police car.

"I said, let him go," Kerney repeated, grabbing Ordway's shoulder.

"Sure thing, hotshot," Ordway said as he pulled free, released Robert, and swung at Kerney with the baton.

Kerney kicked Ordway in the nuts. He dropped the baton, fell to his knees, and grabbed his groin.

After disarming Ordway, Kerney looked for Robert, who stood next to him, bouncing on his toes in delight.

"Kick him again," Robert said, as he threw uppercuts into the air.

"Wait for me by the fence."

"Fuck you," Robert replied, still punching the air. "You lied to me."

"What?"

"You promised me some smokes, man."

"They're in my car, on the passenger seat. Go get them. Then wait by the fence."

"Okay," Robert grumbled, moving away.

Kerney moved behind Ordway, stood him up, put the baton against his throat, and applied some pressure. "You're not a man who takes advice easily," he said.

"Fuck you," Ordway gurgled.

"I could file charges against you," Kerney said. "Unlawful arrest. Use of excessive force. Do you want that kind of grief?"

Ordway thought about it and shook his head.

"I didn't think so." Kerney released the pressure, pushed Ordway out of kicking distance, and circled around to look the man in the eyes. "Take my advice, Ordway. Find a civilian job. I don't think you're cut out to be a cop."

Ordway's expression turned ugly when Kerney locked his handgun, baton, and car keys inside the police cruiser.

"That should slow you down," Kerney said to Ordway. "Get in my car, Robert."

"Why?"

"I thought you wanted to go to jail."

Robert beamed. "Can I smoke in your car?"

"No, but I'll stop along the way so you can have a cigarette or two."

"That sucks."

"Humor me," Kerney replied.

KERNEY LET Robert sit up front wearing no cuffs. He fought off Cordova's bad smell by running the air conditioner with the window cracked, even though the cloudy late afternoon had dropped the temperature into the low forties.

"You're supposed to cuff me and lock me in the back. I'm an escaped mental patient."

"You don't like sitting up front?" Kerney asked.

"Yeah, I do. I need a cigarette."

They had just passed the Mountainair town limit sign. Kerney pulled off the road next to a cottonwood tree and got out with Robert, who quickly lit up. The cloud cover broke, and for a moment the high mesa south of the village shimmered in pale yellow sunlight.

"You were in town the night Paul Gillespie was killed," Kerney said.

Robert exhaled. "Who?"

"Paul Gillespie, the police officer."

Robert tugged at his beard. "I don't know him."

"You went to high school with him."

Robert shrugged indifferently and looked away. "I don't remember."

"Did you see Gillespie get killed?"

"I've never seen anybody get killed. But I'd like to. That would be neat."

"Do you know who killed him?"

The wind picked up and Robert started to shiver. "I'm cold," he whined, grinding out his cigarette with his sneaker. "Am I going to jail or not?"

"You're going. Get in," Kerney answered, gesturing at the car.

Kerney drove for a time without talking, keeping one eye on Robert, whose foot beat a steady tattoo on the floorboard. Kerney wondered if the habit signaled anxiety. He decided to test the theory.

"Did you see Gillespie the night he was killed?"

Robert's foot started bouncing off the floorboard. "I saw Satan."

"What was Satan doing?"

Robert's foot jiggled wildly. "Raping my daughter."

"Where did it happen?"

"Serpent Gate."

Kerney remembered the peculiar stone snake on Pop Shaffer's fence. "Do you mean by the fence next to the hotel?"

"Yeah." Robert changed his mind. "No, not there."

"Where?"

"I don't want to talk about it."

"Okay," Kerney said gently. "Tell me about your daughter." As far as he knew, Robert was childless.

"She's in heaven with Jesus," Robert replied flatly, as he gripped the back of his skull with his fingers and stuck his thumbs in his ears.

"Is that where Satan rapes her?" Kerney asked loudly, trying to get through to Robert.

Robert grunted and shut his eyes. The conversation was over.

When Kerney pulled into the sally port at the Torrance

County jail, Cordova removed his thumbs from his ears, popped out of the car, and waited at the door to the booking alcove while Kerney locked his handgun in a weapon box.

"Hurry up," Robert barked, snapping his fingers.

Kerney pressed the button to the booking alcove, and the electronic door latch snapped open. Inside, Robert immediately relaxed. He smiled at the female guard behind the glassed-in booking counter and began emptying his pockets.

The guard, a sturdy-looking woman with broad shoulders and a close-cropped haircut, welcomed Robert back with a greeting and a grin.

"What's the charge?" the guard asked, eyeing Kerney skeptically.

"Protective custody," Kerney answered. "Twenty-four-hour hold."

She nodded knowingly and pushed a form through the slot at the bottom of the glass. "Fill this out. Has he had anything to eat?"

"Lunch," Kerney replied, as he completed the paperwork. "But he's probably hungry again."

"Did you search him?"

"Pat down only."

The woman nodded.

Robert tapped Kerney on the shoulder. "I left my cigarettes in your car."

"I'll get them for you." Kerney took a ten-dollar bill from his wallet and pushed it through the slot along with the booking form. "Put the ten bucks in his canteen account. He may need a few things while he's here."

The woman smiled at him as he left to get Robert's smokes. When he returned, Robert was inside the secure area sitting calmly in a chair. Kerney passed the cigarettes through to the guard.

"Are you taking him back to Las Vegas?" she asked.

"He doesn't seem to want to go."

"Then why are you holding him?"

"He may be a witness to a crime. I'm hoping he'll talk to me. So far, I haven't gotten very much out of him."

The woman nodded. "Give him the night to settle in. Robert does real well here. He likes the structure. We'll clean him up, give him a meal or two, and he'll be a new man by morning."

"I hope you're right," Kerney said.

"He just told me you were his friend," the guard said. "I've never heard him say that about a police officer before. You might get lucky."

"I could use some luck."

Robert waved gaily at Kerney as the guard buzzed him out the door to the sally port.

SIXTY MILES east of Mountainair, Kerney waited in the gathering night outside the old Vaughn train station for the arrival of a westbound freight out of Amarillo. On it, he hoped, was Floyd Wilson, a crew chief for the Southern Pacific, who had left Mountainair the morning after the Gillespie shooting. Wilson had been transferred off a track-replacement job west of Mountainair and reassigned to a spur-line construction project in Texas.

As far as Kerney knew, Wilson had never been interviewed during the initial investigation.

Parked next to the dark station house, Kerney sat in the car with the engine running, the heater on, and the window rolled down. Robert's odor still permeated the vehicle.

At the end of a siding, barely visible in the gloom, a warning sign where the tracks ended read DERAIL. It neatly summarized Kerney's sense of futility about the case.

An occasional car rolled down the highway that paralleled the train tracks, rubber singing on the pavement. But the dominant sound came from the wind that cut across the Staked Plains, a vast, high desert plateau that encompassed thousands of square miles of eastern New Mexico.

The wind drove a light rain against Kerney's cheek, and he turned on the car wipers so he could see down the line. The flash of light from the lead locomotive showed long before the sound of the engine reached Kerney's ears. If the train blew through town without stopping, it meant Kerney would have to make the long drive to Amarillo sometime soon. On the phone, Wilson had told him he knew nothing about the case, and didn't want to lose time away from his job. Kerney had called Wilson's boss, who agreed to let Wilson make the trip to meet with Kerney on company time. He hoped Wilson was on the train.

The train stopped and a man of average height, carrying an overnight bag, climbed out of the locomotive and walked wearily toward the car. Kerney got out to greet him.

Floyd Wilson offered Kerney his hand with little enthusiasm. A man pushing sixty, Wilson had a full head of gray hair, a deeply lined face, thick, droopy eyebrows, and a condition on his neck that bleached out the pigment of his skin.

"I don't see how I can help you, Mr. Kerney."

"I'm glad you're willing to try, Mr. Wilson. Thanks for coming."

"No sweat," Floyd said.

"Let me buy you dinner."

"In this town that means the cholesterol plate."

At the only open diner in town, a cheerless establishment with Formica tables, tattered chairs, a cracked linoleum floor, and faded posters tacked on the walls, Kerney and Floyd Wilson sat by a window streaked with smoke and grease. Outside, the wind had diminished and fat snowflakes drifted against the glass, melting instantly.

"I was at the Shaffer Hotel the night that policeman got shot," Floyd said. "Me and my crew were in the game room on the second floor, drinking beer and playing pool."

"You didn't go out?" Kerney asked.

"Nope. I had a late dinner in the dining room and turned in early. I didn't even hear about the shooting until the next day, just before I left."

"Did you know Gillespie, or have any dealings with him?"

Floyd scratched his head. "Not really. I knew who he was, but that was about it. I didn't spend much time in town. Replacing track and ties on a main line is a sunup-to-sundown job."

"Did you ever see him act inappropriately?"

"You mean tough-guy stuff?"

"Yes."

"Not personally, but some of my crew said he acted like a badass when we first got to town. He settled down after we'd been there for a while."

"Did any of your crew spend time with Gillespie? Socialize with him?"

"I don't think so."

"Do you know Robert Cordova?"

"The name doesn't ring a bell."

"He's a skinny guy, about five-four. He likes to hang out by the fence next to the hotel."

Floyd nodded. "You mean the crazy guy? The one that walks around with his fingers in his ears talking to himself?"

"That's him."

"Sure, I know him. Hell, I think everybody in Mountainair knows who he is. He really gets around."

"Gets around?" Kerney repeated.

"Sometimes I'd see him when I was on the job. He liked to walk along the railroad right-of-way. I kept telling him he was trespassing, but it never seemed to sink in."

"Did you see him anywhere else?"

"Once I saw him walking up a ridge about a half mile from the tracks, west of town."

"You're sure it was Cordova?"

"Yeah. After a while, he came back and caught a ride into town with one of my people."

"When did you see him there?" Kerney asked.

"A couple of days before that policeman was killed. Do you think Cordova killed the cop?"

"I don't know what to think about Robert. Did you see him on the day of the murder?"

"Yeah, as a matter of fact I did. I was coming down the main drag after work and I saw him talking to some woman in front of the grocery store."

"Did you recognize her?"

"No. She was in a pickup truck. Cordova was standing by the driver's door, so I didn't get a good look at her."

"Did you notice anything else?"

"I think the woman was a veterinarian, or she works for one. She was pulling a horse trailer, and it had the name of a veterinary service painted on the side panel."

"Do you remember the name?"

"No. It said something about specializing in large animals. That's all I recall."

The waitress brought dinner, and Kerney picked at an over-cooked ham steak and some soggy vegetables. With part of his stomach shot away, Kerney found eating in greasy spoons to be a real chore; the food usually didn't sit well. He gave up on trying to force down the meal and made small talk until Wilson was ready to check in at the motel.

He paid for dinner, took Floyd to the motel, paid for the room, thanked Wilson for his time, and started the drive back to Mountainair. It was well into the night, and the brewing snowstorm looked like it could turn nasty, but he wanted to talk to one more person before heading back home to Santa Fe.

MARCIA YEARWOOD, the physician's assistant who ran the rural health clinic in Mountainair, promptly answered Kerney's knock at her front door.

"Yes, what is it?"

She was a pleasant-looking woman in her thirties, with big, perfectly round brown eyes accentuated by eyeglasses, and a wide mouth that hinted at an easy smile. She wore sweatpants, a sweatshirt, and slippers.

Kerney showed her his badge. "May I have a few minutes of your time?"

"It's not a medical emergency, I take it?"

"Not at all."

"Come in."

Yearwood's home, a single-story stone structure near the high school, sat well back on a heavily treed lot. The front room contained a couch with two matching chairs and a coffee table, grouped in front of a fireplace. There were some tasteful fine art posters on the walls, including a Georgia O'Keeffe print and several Gustave Baumann reproductions. Books and magazines were scattered about within easy reach, and on the floor next to the couch was a canvas bag filled with embroidery yarn. The fireplace had a crackling cedar fire going that warmed the room nicely. From the feel of the place, Kerney guessed Yearwood was unattached.

"What can I do for you, Officer?" Marcia asked, as she gestured for Kerney to join her on the couch.

Kerney obliged. "I understand that Robert Cordova gets his medication from you when he's in Mountainair."

Marcia sat at the end of the couch and turned to face Kerney directly. "Yes. I dispense it through an arrangement with the psychiatrist at the state mental hospital. Is Robert in some sort of trouble?"

She brushed a strand of long dark hair away from her face and looked at Kerney more closely. "You're the investigator looking into Paul Gillespie's murder." She stiffened a bit and crossed her legs. "Surely you don't think Robert is a suspect."

"He doesn't strike me as a killer."

Marcia answered with an agreeing smile. "He's not. Robert's normal behavior—if you can call it that—is all bravado and posturing. The onset of his illness came during adolescence. Besides being schizophrenic, he's fixated at a juvenile stage of development."

"You seem to know him well."

"Well enough. But that doesn't mean I can tell you more about him. His medical records are confidential. I've been told that he's eloped from Las Vegas."

"Eloped?"

Marcia laughed quickly. "It's a polite way of saying he escaped. After all, we don't want people to think mental hospitals are prisons."

"Aren't they?"

"Not all. Have you seen him?"

"I have him in protective custody at the Torrance County jail."

Marcia sighed. "That's a relief. Each time he disappears I'm sure he's going to be found beaten to a pulp and left to die along some roadside."

"He doesn't want to go back to Las Vegas. I thought you could help."

She nodded her head in agreement. "He never wants to go back, but once he gets there and settles in to a routine, it's beneficial. Of course I'll help. I can see him in the morning."

"I'd like to be there when you see him."

Marcia's voice became guarded. "I don't intend to help you conduct an interrogation."

"I don't plan to interrogate him, Ms. Yearwood. There's a remote chance Robert may have seen something, or may know something about what happened the night Gillespie was shot. I need him to talk about it."

"That may not be easy."

"I know."

Marcia tapped her finger against her lip. "Normally, I'd say no, but I think this time it will be okay. However, be warned: if you try to intimidate him, I'll stop you dead in your tracks."

"Fair enough."

"He doesn't like cops, you know."

Kerney smiled. "That's what I've heard. Is there some reason for it?"

"I don't know," Marcia replied with a slight shrug.

"He said he went to high school with Paul Gillespie."

"I believe he did."

"How would you characterize Gillespie?"

"He was a bit of a bully who had an eye for the girls."

Kerney had heard the same comment from several other sources, but had been unable to locate anyone who could provide specifics.

"Did he come on to you?"

"He wouldn't dare. Besides, I wasn't his type. He liked younger women."

"Anyone in particular?"

"I haven't the foggiest idea. But I'd see him chatting with teenage girls a lot after school got out."

"What makes that stand out in your mind?"

"He was always talking to the girls," Marcia answered. "The teenage boys he seemed to ignore, unless they were speeding or drinking beer at the town park after dark."

"Do you know if he was sexually or romantically involved with any of the girls?"

"No, I don't."

"Any rumors?"

Marcia waved off the question. "There are rumors floating around about everybody who lives in this town. I pay no attention to them."

Kerney tried again: "Any rumors specifically about Gillespie?"

"Rumors, no. I've made it very clear to people that I'm not part of the local gossip mill. But several years ago, one of the high school girls who came to the clinic told me she thought Gillespie was creepy."

"Creepy in what way?"

"She baby-sat for the same family on a regular basis several times a month. Gillespie would always drive by the house three or four times a night whenever she was there. But only if her boyfriend wasn't with her."

"That's creepy enough," Kerney said. "I'd like to talk to her."

"I had a fairly close relationship with the girl, and I'm sure she would have told me if anything more had happened."

"How can I reach her?"

"Not easily. She's a medical technician serving in the navy on a hospital ship."

Kerney got the girl's name for the record. He could track her down through her parents or naval authorities, if necessary. "What can you tell me about Robert's family history?"

"He was born and raised in Mountainair. The family was very dysfunctional. Robert started getting in trouble with the police when he was fairly young. He spent some time in a foster home."

"Was he sent away?"

"No. He was placed with a family here in town."

"Who were the foster parents?"

"An older couple. I never met them. I believe they're both deceased."

"Does Robert have any siblings?"

"An older sister, but she moved to Texas years ago after her parents divorced and left the state. Robert says he has no contact with her."

"Does he stay in touch with his biological parents?"

"Not as far as I know."

"Does he have any children?"

Marcia made a face and shook her head. "No. You're asking about Satan raping his daughter, aren't you? That has been Robert's predominant delusion since the onset of his illness."

"I wonder what it means."

"I have no idea." Marcia rose from the couch, signaling that the discussion had ended.

Kerney stood up with her. "Do you know any of the local veterinarians?"

"I don't think there is one. Maybe in Estancia, but not here."

"Do you know a female veterinarian, or a woman who works for a vet?"

Marcia shook her head. "Sorry, I don't. But I'm sure one of the ranchers can tell you."

After making arrangements to meet Marcia Yearwood at the jail at mid-morning, Kerney started the long drive back to Santa Fe in a snowstorm that kept pushing drifts across the highway. He wondered if he was simply spinning his wheels. He decided to give it one more day before telling Andy Baca the investigation wasn't getting anywhere. He hated the idea that the case might go unsolved.

2

In the morning, Kerney got an early start and drove the sixty miles from Santa Fe to the Torrance County jail in Estancia. The road had been plowed and a bright sun made the snow-coated range grass glisten like a sea of silver stems rolling across the Estancia Valley. At the jail, he had Robert brought to the staff conference room. He wanted time alone with him before Marcia Yearwood showed up.

Robert was brought in by a guard. He wore an orange jump-suit with TORRANCE COUNTY JAIL stenciled on the back, a pair of plastic shower sandals, and a shit-eating grin. His hair was combed, his beard trimmed, and he looked freshly scrubbed. He sat next to Kerney at the end of the long conference table and lit a cigarette.

Kerney adjusted his position so he could look squarely at Robert, and took a whiff. Robert didn't smell bad at all.

"Are you going to let me stay in jail?" Robert asked hopefully.

"I don't see how I can do that."

"Charge me with something." His foot wasn't wiggling at all, and he seemed calm.

"What would you suggest?"

Robert smiled widely. "Rape."

"Did you rape someone?"

"Of course I did. I already told you about it."

"No, you told me that Satan raped your daughter."

Robert poked himself in the chest with a finger. "I'm Satan."

"If that's the case, you'd better tell me who you raped."

Robert shook his head. "I can't. It's a secret."

"Well, it can't be your daughter. You don't have one."

"It was my sister. I raped my sister."

"The one that lives in Texas."

"Not that one," Robert said with a scowl.

"Tell me about this other sister."

"What I did to her was bad."

"Where did you rape her?"

"At Serpent Gate."

"Where is that?"

Robert waved the question away. "I'm not going to tell you."

"Did Paul Gillespie know about Serpent Gate?"

"I don't want to talk about that motherfucker."

"Okay, we won't. When did you rape your sister?"

"A long time ago."

"What's your sister's name?"

Robert put a finger to his lips. "It's a secret."

Before Kerney could ask another question, Marcia Yearwood burst into the conference room. She stood at the end of the long table, glaring at him.

"I see you started without me."

"We were just chatting," Kerney answered.

Marcia forced a smile in Robert's direction and moved down the table behind a row of neatly arranged conference chairs. She wore a dark blue turtleneck sweater and wool slacks under a long charcoal gray winter coat. She composed herself as she removed her coat, and sat down next to Robert.

"It's good to see you looking so well, Robert. What were you two talking about?"

Robert gave Kerney a conspiratorial look. "Rape."

"Really?" Marcia replied, unable to mask a hint of surprise in her voice. "I'd like to hear about it."

"No way. Women aren't supposed to hear about shit like that."

"That's not fair," Marcia responded gently.

"I can't talk about it," Robert said. "Besides, Addie doesn't want me to."

"Who is Addie?" Kerney asked as he moved to a chair across from Robert and Marcia. He wanted a clear view of Robert. He could hear Robert's heel slapping against the shower sandal.

Robert hesitated. "Somebody who talks to me."

"Is Addie short for Adele or Adelaide?" Kerney asked.

"Addie's not short for nothing."

"And you talk to her?" Kerney prodded.

"Sometimes."

"Do you talk to her in your head?" Marcia suggested.

"Yeah," Robert said, relief showing on his face. The foot wiggling stopped.

"Okay," Marcia said. "Addie is a voice you hear."

"That's right."

Marcia nodded and switched gears. "Mr. Kerney needs to ask you some questions."

"Sure." Robert glanced at Kerney. "What about?"

"Addie isn't a real person?" Kerney asked.

Robert tensed. "I don't want to talk about her. It makes me nervous."

"Okay, we won't. On the day Officer Gillespie was shot, you were seen talking to a woman in a pickup truck with a stock trailer," Kerney said. "Is she someone you know?"

"What did she look like?" Robert asked.

"I thought you could tell me. The trailer may have belonged to a veterinarian."

"I don't know anybody like that," Robert said. His foot wiggle started again. He lit another cigarette and took a deep drag.

"Do you remember talking to the woman?"

"No." He blew smoke in Kerney's direction and flicked a cigarette ash on the carpet. "Sometimes I ask people to give me a smoke or some money."

"So, it was no one you knew?"

"I don't think so." Robert swallowed hard and looked away.

Robert was lying. Kerney changed the subject again. "Several days before Gillespie was shot, you were seen outside of town on the railroad tracks."

"I like to walk along the tracks sometimes," Robert said.

"Do you go to any particular place?"

"Sometimes."

"Does the place have a name?"

"Sometimes."

"What do you call it?"

"I don't call it nothing." He turned and spoke to Marcia. "Do I have to go back to the hospital?"

"Are you hearing voices?" Marcia replied.

"Not now. Not since yesterday."

"When yesterday?" Marcia asked.

"Before lunch."

"Maybe I can get you in a halfway house in Albuquerque," Marcia said.

Robert grinned at the prospect.

Marcia turned to Kerney. "Do you have any more questions for Robert?"

"Just one. Were you near the police station around the time Gillespie was shot?"

Robert stuck his thumb out in a hitchhiker motion.

"Does that mean no?"

Robert nodded in agreement. "I hitched a ride to Estancia."

"Did you see anyone near the police station before you left town?"

Robert shook his head and looked away, avoiding Kerney's gaze.

"Thanks, Robert," Kerney said, thinking that maybe Robert had seen someone—someone he knew. But pushing Robert didn't seem to be the best way to get answers.

"We're done?" Robert asked, and stood up quickly.

"We're done," Kerney said.

Robert leaned in Kerney's direction and gave him a high five and a smile. "Later," he said.

"Take care, Robert."

After escorting him out of the room, Marcia returned and sat with Kerney.

"I expected you to wait for me before meeting with Robert."

"It was a bit sneaky on my part."

Marcia nodded. "Just so you know why I jumped on you when I came in."

In another context, Kerney wouldn't have minded the possibility of Marcia jumping on him at all. "No problem. I deserved it."

She drummed her fingers on the table. "Did he talk much about rape?"

"He had just started talking about it. He said a long time ago he raped his sister—not the one who lives in Texas."

"He doesn't have another sister. It's unusual for Robert to say anything at all about rape, other than the delusional stuff about Satan, Jesus, and his imaginary daughter."

"Do you think there's some factual basis to what he said?" Kerney asked.

"Don't count on it." Marcia took her glasses off and smiled—an amused half smile that seemed to show some personal interest in Kerney. "Robert says he likes you. That's high praise from him for a police officer."

"I'm glad to hear it."

She offered her hand to him across the table. It was warm and soft.

"I hope you catch your killer, Mr. Kerney."

Kerney let go of her hand slowly. It had been a while since he'd felt a woman's touch. "Thanks. Will you be able to keep Robert out of the hospital?"

"It's possible. I'll do a mental status exam. If he's clear enough, I should be able to swing it."

AFTER MARCIA left to evaluate Robert, Kerney stayed behind to think things through. If, as Marcia indicated, Robert never talked about rape except when he was hallucinating or delusional, why did he raise the topic in the absence of any psychotic symptoms? While Kerney was no expert in mental illness, he believed Robert had something specific on his mind.

Robert had flat-out lied about the woman in the pickup truck, with all the clumsiness of a twelve-year-old caught red-handed. And he had lied again about not seeing anyone outside the police station.

The only new bit of information Robert had provided was a name: Addie. Was she real or imaginary? Marcia thought it was part of Robert's delusion, but Kerney wasn't so sure. He stared at the freshly polished tabletop. There were smeared, sweaty palm prints where Robert had been sitting. Until Marcia suggested that Addie was only a voice in his head, Robert had nervously rubbed his hand on the table. The hand rubbing and foot wiggling started up again when Kerney pushed the issue about Addie a little harder.

Kerney smiled. Maybe Addie was real. Maybe the case wasn't as dead as a doornail yet.

Using the jail administrator's phone, Kerney called around until he connected with the state agency responsible for foster care. He had to smooth-talk a handful of bureaucrats and record clerks before he could get the names of Robert Cordova's former foster parents. An attempt to get the names of the children living with the couple during Robert's placement was unsuccessful—the juvenile records were confidential and sealed.

After confirming that Robert's foster parents, Burl and Thelma Jackson, were deceased, he got their last known Mountainair address and headed down the road.

The day had warmed up and the rangeland had shed the previous night's snow. As he drove, Kerney pondered the facts of the Gillespie murder. Gillespie's sidearm had been used to blow the top of his head off, and the gun had been wiped clean of prints. There was no sign of a struggle, and no incriminating evidence had been found at the crime scene.

How could the killer have gotten control of Gillespie's weapon? That fact alone made it highly likely that the killer was known to Gillespie. Which meant Kerney needed to find a precipitating event that could lead to a motive. The crime could have been fueled by jealousy, rage, or revenge. But was it a premeditated crime or one of passion? Either way, what did Gillespie do to make somebody want to kill him? Kerney still didn't have a hint.

Burl and Thelma Jackson's last address turned out to be a rambling adobe house with a pitched roof on several fenced

acres near a Forest Service building. East of the house an old
Santa Fe Railroad boxcar sat on masonry piers next to a working
windmill. A picket fence at the front of the house enclosed a
sandbox and swing set. Near a freestanding garage with a sagging roof, a rusted Ford Fairlane slumped on blocks with the
hood open, yawning at the sky.

Kerney knocked at the door, which was opened by an overweight woman of about forty. Dressed in a bulky sweater that
covered a thick stomach, she had a harried expression and full
lips that curved downward. In the background, Kerney heard
the voices of young children.

"Yes?" the woman asked, looking Kerney up and down. She
was holding a baby's bib in one hand. It was splattered with what
looked like applesauce or vomit.

Kerney showed his shield and introduced himself. "I'm trying to locate someone who knew Burl and Thelma Jackson."

"They were my parents," the woman replied. A child yelled
and the woman turned her head toward the sound. "Come in.
I'll be with you in a minute." She pointed at an overstuffed easy
chair in the front room and left hurriedly through a side doorway, latching a childproof accordion gate behind her.

Kerney sat, listened to the children's chatter, and looked
around. The room was meagerly furnished with a well-worn
couch, the easy chair Kerney sat in with a floor lamp next to it,
two side tables, each holding a glass vase filled with plastic flowers, and a hand-hooked oval throw rug in the center of the pine
floor. Framed family photographs hung on one wall above a
large-screen television set, and plain white cotton curtains covered the front windows.

The largest photograph was a color portrait of a smiling
elderly couple dressed in their Sunday best. The man, wearing a
cowboy hat, sat behind the woman, his arms wrapped around
her waist, both turned at an angle to face the camera. Kerney

guessed the couple to be Burl and Thelma. On either side of the portrait were high school graduation pictures of two girls. One was obviously of the woman who had greeted Kerney at the door. He could see the tendency toward heaviness in her torso and upper arms, and a hint of petulance in the smile. The other girl, a slender, pretty brunette with a faraway gaze in her eyes, had a tough little smile and a birthmark on her chin.

The noise subsided and the woman returned, closing the gate behind her. She sat on the sofa and looked quizzically at Kerney. "Why are you asking about my parents?"

"I didn't get your name," Kerney replied with a smile.

"Lurline Toler."

"I'm really interested in learning about Robert Cordova, Mrs. Toler," Kerney explained. "He was your parents' foster child."

"I know Robert. I was still living at home when he came to stay with us." A child's delighted screech followed by another child's laugh interrupted Lurline. "I do child care for some working mothers," she explained with a weary smile. She waited several beats before speaking again. All was quiet at the back of the house. "What do you want to know about Robert?"

"What other foster children were placed here while Robert lived with the family?"

Lurline shook her head. "I couldn't even begin to remember, there were so many of them. Robert was one of those who stayed the longest. Most of the others were here and gone in a matter of a few months."

"Were they all teenagers?"

"Yes. My parents only took in older children."

"Do you remember a girl named Addie that Robert was friendly with?"

Lurline blinked and hesitated. "There were no foster children staying here by that name, as I recall."

"Perhaps it was a school friend."

Lurline nodded her head. "That's possible, but Robert was pretty much a loner. I don't think he had any friends."

"Who would know?"

Lurline thought for a moment before answering. "I really can't tell you. Robert is quite a bit younger than me—about six years, I think. We didn't run with the same crowd. Is he in trouble?"

"No, he's not."

"Poor thing," Lurline said.

"He's had a hard time of it."

"Haven't we all?"

"Is that your high school graduation picture?" Kerney asked.

"Yes. I should take it down. I'll never look like that again."

"Is the other girl your sister?"

"Yes. My younger sister, Nita. Dad always wanted a boy, but he got two girls instead."

"Could she tell me more about Robert?"

"She was never close to him."

"How can I contact her?"

A child's angry shriek kept Lurline from answering. She got to her feet. "I can't talk now. Call me this evening."

KERNEY SAT in his car by the Mountainair High School and watched a group of students dressed in sweats running around a track that bordered the football field. Growing up in the Tularosa Basin, Kerney had gone to a small-town high school where the school nurse knew every student, and was the unofficial counselor, confidante, and friend to any kid with a bloody nose, scraped knee, or troubles at home. In the years that had passed, he doubted much had changed in small-town schools. He got out of the car and found his way to the health office.

Henrietta Swope, the school nurse, looked like a grandmother who brooked no silliness and expected everybody to tell the truth. She wore her gray hair pulled straight back, and her blue-gray eyes were inquisitive and lively. She had the lyrical voice of a much younger woman.

Kerney sat in her office, a small room furnished with a cot, a first aid locker, a desk with a chair, and a row of locked file cabinets. The walls were plastered with public health posters announcing the pitfalls of unsafe sex, teenage pregnancy, poor nutrition, and drug abuse. He showed his identification, told her what case he was working on, and asked about Robert Cordova.

"Of course I know him," Henrietta replied. "He haunts my memory."

"Why do you say that?"

Henrietta sighed. "Whenever I see him around town, I remember what a lonely, miserable boy he was. He acted like a whipped puppy. He would snarl when he got angry and run away when he got upset. He was such a sad child."

"Did he have any friends?"

"At best, he was always on the fringes of the social cliques. He was barely tolerated and always teased a great deal."

"Did he hang around with any of the other foster children when he lived with the Jacksons?"

Henrietta's expression brightened. "I wish Robert could have stayed with Thelma and Burl. It was the only time I saw him settle down and get comfortable with himself." Her eyes flickered and turned serious. "I think Robert has always been truly alone in the world. Isn't that enough to make a person go crazy?"

"Sometimes," Kerney conceded. "He didn't connect with anybody? Another foster child? A classmate? A teacher?"

"No. That says something about all of us, I suppose. We should have tried harder to reach him."

"Did he have a schoolmate named Addie?"

"Not that I remember."

"Someone nicknamed Addie? Short for Adele or Adelaide?"

"No, but we had a girl here until last year whose given name was Addie."

"Who is that?"

"Addie Randall."

"Tell me about her."

"Oh, I'm sure Robert doesn't know her. She would have been a senior now if she'd stayed with us."

"She moved away?"

"She's living in Socorro. I transferred her health records to the high school there during the middle of the spring semester."

"When was that, exactly?" Kerney asked.

"Sometime in March. Late March, I would say."

"Did the family move?"

"No. Her parents still live here with two younger children. Her mother works at the grocery store as a checker. I believe Addie's father is unemployed."

"Do you have any idea why Addie left?"

"Family troubles, I suspect. Addie was a popular girl at school—very pretty and outgoing—and the transfer happened quite unexpectedly."

"What kind of family troubles?"

Henrietta bit her lower lip before replying. "Confidentially, I think it's possible she may be pregnant. I've seen the pattern too many times not to have my suspicions."

"Do you know who Addie is living with in Socorro?"

"A relative, I believe." Henrietta consulted her card file. "I don't have a name. Addie's mother can tell you. I can't see how any of this has the least bearing on Paul Gillespie's murder," she added.

"It probably doesn't."

"If you see Addie, give her my best. She's a sweet girl."

"I'll be glad to."

· · ·

KERNEY PUSHED the car hard through Abo Pass at the north edge of the Los Pinos Mountains. It was a sixty-mile drive to Socorro, and a large part of the trip bordered the Sevilleta National Wildlife Refuge, which straddled both sides of the Rio Grande. With the mountains behind him, the rangeland—so vast the river was a hazy promise in the distance—opened into miles of uninhabited space colored in sepia brown and dull gray against a creamy blue sky. The only interruptions to the emptiness were a few mobile homes and camper trailers parked on small fenced lots along the state highway, most of them abandoned. West, across the river, rose the remote Ladron Mountains, accessible only by horseback or on foot.

He got to Socorro High School and checked in at the administrative offices, where he learned that Addie Randall was enrolled in a special program for teenage mothers. Through the window of the closed classroom door, he saw a group of expectant and new mothers standing around a changing table. All of them looked much too young to be having babies and rearing children.

The teacher with the students looked suspiciously at Kerney when he entered the room. A tall woman with long arms and legs, she detached herself from the group and approached Kerney quickly.

"Can I help you?" she asked.

The chatter at the table stopped and the girls, some holding infants, withdrew to a circle of chairs at the back of the room.

"I'd like to speak to Addie Randall," Kerney said quietly, displaying his credentials.

The teacher's expression remained unfriendly. "That's not possible. We're in the middle of class."

During his years as a detective, Kerney had found that teachers on their own turf were difficult to deal with. Most didn't like cops, and they jealously guarded their home ground and their students.

"I won't take much of her time," he said. "And I do need to see her now." He emphasized the last word. "I have the principal's permission."

Appealing to a higher authority, even if it was a lie, won the woman over. She nodded curtly and motioned for a girl to join her. Addie Randall moved slowly toward the teacher. She was a tall, slim girl made wide-hipped and heavy by pregnancy. Her long-sleeved pullover top had BABY emblazoned on it with an arrow pointing toward her belly. A pair of loose, floppy pants draped over the extra thirty pounds of her last trimester. No more than sixteen, she had wheat-colored hair, fair skin, brown eyes, and a worried look on her face.

"What is it?" Addie asked uneasily.

"This police officer needs to talk to you."

"I don't want to talk to him," Addie said, avoiding Kerney's gaze.

"You can talk to me unofficially now, or officially with your parents present," Kerney replied. "It's your decision to make."

Addie shifted her weight. "I haven't done anything wrong."

"No, you haven't," Kerney said. "I just need to ask you a few questions about somebody else."

"Who?" she asked suspiciously, drawing back.

"Can we talk outside? Or would you rather take a drive with me back to Mountainair?"

Addie acquiesced quickly. "I'll talk to you."

In the empty corridor, Addie stood with her hands resting on the top of her belly. Her eyes had a frosty, wary look.

"When is the baby due?"

"Soon."

"Are you going to keep it?"

"Maybe," Addie answered halfheartedly. She looked behind her to see if the hallway was still empty. It was. "What did you want to ask me?"

Kerney brushed off her question and continued, "If you keep the baby, how will you support it?"

Addie's expression tightened. "It's none of your business what I do with my baby."

"The adoption agency will want to know about the baby's father."

She gave Kerney a fretful look that quickly disappeared. "They can't make me do that if I don't know."

"Were you raped?" Kerney asked.

Addie didn't flinch at the question. "I'm going back to class now," she said, moving away.

Kerney touched her lightly on the shoulder to hold her back. "Addie."

"What is it?"

"Talk to me. Tell me what happened. Let me help you."

She grimaced, her eyes empty of emotion. "It's too late for that."

"Were you in Mountainair the night Paul Gillespie was murdered?"

"No. I've been living in Socorro since March and I haven't been back there since I left. I don't care if I never go back."

"Do you know Robert Cordova?"

"Sure. Everybody in Mountainair knows him. Why?"

"He told me you made him promise to keep a secret."

Addie shook her head. "Not me. I don't think I've ever said anything to him in my entire life. He's too weird. What secret?"

"I was hoping you could tell me."

She shook her head emphatically. "Sorry. Can I go back to class now?"

"Sure. Thanks for talking to me."

Kerney watched Addie return to her class. In spite of her unhappy predicament, the girl had spunk. He had reviewed every felony case handled by the Mountainair Police Department during the six months preceding Gillespie's death and no rapes had been reported. Had the girl been sexually assaulted by a stranger? Was it a date rape that didn't get reported? Perhaps she hadn't been raped at all but was simply covering up to protect the unborn child's father.

Kerney didn't have a clear picture, but one thing was certain: Addie was holding something back.

The bell announcing the end of the period rang and he waded through a tide of noisy teenagers who burst out of the classrooms and filled the hallway. He went back to the administration office to find out where Addie lived. She was staying with Verdie Mae McNutt, her great-aunt. He decided to pay Verdie Mae a visit.

THERE WAS no answer to Kerney's knock at Verdie Mae's door, but a four-door older Plymouth, without a dent or ding, sat under the carport. A thick band of fast-moving clouds covered the sun, and the cold afternoon air cut through Kerney's windbreaker. He zipped it up and walked to the backyard. The back porch had been converted into a greenhouse, and inside an elderly woman dressed in faded coveralls dug with a trowel in a raised planting bed.

Kerney knocked on a window and the woman glanced up with a startled look, got to her feet, stepped to the door, and opened it cautiously. She was thin, with slightly stooped shoulders and a heavily lined face that showed the wear of a good eight decades.

"Yes?" she asked.

"Are you Mrs. McNutt?" Kerney asked, showing his badge.

"I am."

Kerney introduced himself. "I'd like a few minutes of your time."

Verdie Mae let Kerney in and closed the door quickly behind him. She gestured at two Stickley oak chairs in the center of the greenhouse, positioned to look out at a birdbath, some feeders hanging in the trees, and birdhouses on posts that stood in the middle of the backyard.

"Have a seat," Verdie Mae said. "I was just about to stop puttering. Is there some problem in the neighborhood?"

"I came to ask you about Addie," Kerney replied as he sat down. The greenhouse was uncomfortably warm. Verdie Mae didn't seem to mind it at all. He unzipped his jacket and looked around. The planting beds and pots on the brick floor were filled with herbs, flowers, and vegetables. Verdie Mae was a serious gardener.

Verdie Mae put the trowel in a basket, removed her gloves, and joined him. "Is something wrong with Addie?" she asked.

"She's fine. I just spoke with her. I'd like to know a little more about her."

"For what purpose?" Verdie Mae asked, with the look of a woman not easily intimidated.

Kerney decided to see if he could get a reaction out of Verdie Mae. "Was Addie raped?"

Verdie Mae responded with an exasperated sigh. "That's why you're here. I don't know. She refuses to discuss it."

"What do you think?"

"I've known Addie all her life. She's a brainy girl with a lot of gumption and ambition. I don't think she would willingly put herself in this predicament."

"Does Addie stay in contact with her family and friends in Mountainair?"

"Not really. Her parents aren't coping very well with the situation, and Addie won't talk to them about it."

"Is she writing to anyone?"

"No."

"Has she had any visitors from back home?"

Verdie Mae hesitated. "Just one. Nita Lassiter came to visit."

"When was that?"

"Two months ago."

"Tell me about Nita Lassiter."

Verdie Mae's expression turned guarded. "What are you try-ing to discover?"

"The name of the man who raped Addie."

Verdie Mae nodded her head in agreement. "I'd try to shake the name out of that girl if I thought it would do any good. Nita might know, if anyone does."

"Why do you say that?"

"During her visit, Nita stayed with Addie in her room for several hours. When she came out, she seemed upset. I asked if everything was all right. All she said was she had to leave right away."

"What did you make of it?"

"Something Addie said troubled Nita."

"Have you spoken to Nita since then?"

"No. Nor has Addie, as far as I know. I just pray she hasn't cut herself off from Addie. They've been as close as sisters."

"Is Ms. Lassiter a family relative?"

"She's not related by blood at all. She went to school with Addie's parents. Addie's mother was Nita's best friend."

"How does Ms. Lassiter make her living?" Kerney asked.

"She's a veterinarian. Her office is in Estancia."

"Is she married?"

"Divorced."

"What was her maiden name?"

"Jackson."

"She's Thelma and Burl's daughter?" he asked.

"That's right. Do you know the family?"

"I'm beginning to. How did Addie come by her name?"

"She was named for Nita. Anita Jackson was her maiden name."

" 'Addie' was Nita's nickname?"

"Only among the immediate family."

"You seem to know the family well," Kerney noted.

"Thelma and Burl were my dearest and oldest friends."

"Is there anything else you can tell me?"

Verdie Mae clasped her hands in her lap and looked down at a planting bed. "You seem to be a very smart man, Mr. Kerney. I may have said too much already."

IN KERNEY'S mind, there really wasn't much of a difference between the towns of Estancia and Mountainair. Both had faltering business districts along a main drag, hodgepodge residential areas of mixed housing in various states of repair, and the fast-fading feel of old-time ranching communities.

But Estancia had the edge in terms of survival. It was the county seat and within commuting distance of Albuquerque. The town had gained population as old farms and ranches were carved into mobile home parks and ranchettes with prefabricated houses that served the spillover growth of city workers who wanted inexpensive land and country living.

The sprawling new developments sprinkled on the high plains and the strip businesses along the highway that connected with the interstate depressed Kerney. None of it belonged on the landscape.

On the main street of Estancia, Kerney found Nita Lassiter's office, a one-story white stucco building sandwiched between a movie theater and a boarded-up cafe. A sign on the locked office door listed business hours and telephone numbers. In the alley behind the row of buildings, he found the trailer Floyd Wilson, the railroad crew chief, had described. A painted sign on the side panel read:

LASSITER VETERINARY CLINIC
SPECIALIZING IN LIVESTOCK & LARGE ANIMALS
ESTANCIA, NEW MEXICO

From a pay phone at a convenience store, Kerney called Lassiter's office and got an answering service. Lassiter was on a call at the Von Hewett Ranch. The operator gave him directions.

He climbed back in the car wondering what Andy Baca would say if he knew the only lead that had been developed in four weeks consisted of a crazy man who had been seen on the day of the murder talking to a lady horse doctor, who happened to share the same name with a pregnant teenage girl.

If nothing materialized with Lassiter, he would turn in his commission card, thank Andy for the work, and try to figure out what in the hell he would do next, while Gillespie's unsolved murder gnawed away at the back of his mind.

Ten miles out of town and a mile off the blacktop that ran from Estancia to the village of Manzano, Kerney found the Von Hewett Ranch, backed up on the far side of a knoll, hidden from sight, with the mountains rising to the west.

The clapboard house was a two-and-a-half-story affair with five columns running the length of a porch underneath a glassed-in sunroom. Positioned between dormer windows at the roofline, two brick chimneys jutted out from the center of the house. In the front yard was an assortment of restored Depression-era farm machinery, including a spreader, cultivator, and mower, all with oversized metal wheels. The centerpiece of the display, a reconditioned buckboard wagon, was filled with terra-cotta flowerpots.

Kerney walked toward a barn, where two pickup trucks were parked by the open door. The newer truck, an extended-cab, full-size Chevy 4 x 4, had a magnetic sign on the driver's door that read NITA LASSITER, DVM. Through the open barn door, he heard two women speaking in anxious voices. He stepped inside. The women were working on a mare that was trying to foal. The animal lay on a bed of straw in a stall, her front legs tucked under her chest, straining in discomfort. An older woman dressed in work boots, jeans, and a barn jacket held the mare's head and tried to keep it still.

The other woman, in her thirties with short brunette hair, lay on her side at the mare's rump with an arm inserted in the birth canal, trying to dislodge the foal. She wore a sleeveless undershirt with no bra, blue jeans, and pair of leather work boots.

"What's the problem?" Kerney asked.

Nita Lassiter looked up from the mare and scanned the stranger. She saw a tall man somewhere in his forties, with blue eyes, square shoulders, gentle-looking hands, and an outwardly calm presence. He hunkered down next to her.

"Mama's having a hard time delivering her baby," Nita replied. "The foal is hung up." Nita sized up the length of Kerney's arms. "I can't reach in far enough to free it. Strip to the waist, slosh some antiseptic on your arm, and coat it with Vaseline. I'll walk you through what needs to be done."

"You got it," Kerney said as he hurried out of his windbreaker and shirt.

Nita tensed when she saw the badge clipped to his belt and the holstered gun. He had an ugly scar on his belly. He cleaned his hands with the antiseptic before rubbing Vaseline on his arm.

"We don't want to damage the mare's womb," Nita said, removing her arm from the canal.

She gave up her position to Kerney and watched as he slowly inserted his arm into the mare's vagina.

"Find the foal's head. Have you got it?"

"Yes," Kerney replied.

"Push it gently back toward the mare's abdomen."

"Done."

"Lift the muzzle by the chin and position it toward the vaginal canal."

"Okay."

"Now, find a hoof, cup it in your hand, and pull it forward. Careful. Don't tear the womb."

"It's free," Kerney said.

"Do the same thing with the other hoof."

Kerney felt around but couldn't find it. Nita could see the frustration in his eyes as he searched.

"Push back on the foal's head a little more," she ordered.

Kerney nodded, pushed the head back, and located the hoof with his fingertips. With his arm inside the mare up to his shoulder, he strained for another fraction of an inch to reach the hoof. Slowly, he brought it forward and the foal, no longer hung up, entered the canal before Kerney could extract his arm. At that same instant, the mare dropped a load of horseshit that hit Kerney in the face and chest. He pulled free and moved out of the way as the foal and the afterbirth came into view.

The foal was out and struggling to stand on shaky legs as Kerney got to his feet. The mare snorted once and lowered her head in exhaustion.

Horseshit dripped down the front of Kerney's jeans. "Don't say it," Kerney warned both women.

Nita tossed him a small towel. "Say what?"

"That I look like shit."

"Well, now that you mention it . . ." She waved off the rest of her comment. "Thank you for your help."

An attractive woman, Lassiter had a finely boned oval face that appeared to be almost symmetrical. Her eyebrows were straight and thick, and her lips were full. She had a small birthmark on her chin.

"I was glad to oblige."

Kerney's thoughts turned to his visits with Lassiter's sister, Lurline Toler, and Verdie Mae McNutt. Had Lurline put him off about how to find Nita? What did Verdie Mae think he was smart enough to figure out?

Nita gestured at her companion. "That's Liddy Hewett. I'm Nita Lassiter."

"Kevin Kerney."

Nita turned her attention to the foal. "It's a girl," she announced.

"Let's get you cleaned up," Liddy Hewett said, as she retrieved Kerney's shirt and jacket.

"That would be nice," Kerney allowed, blinking through the manure, and dabbing the towel around his eyes.

"We don't usually have policemen come calling," Liddy said. She walked him to a utility sink outside the tack room and turned on the faucet. "Is there a problem?"

"I came to see Dr. Lassiter," Kerney replied. Behind him, Nita Lassiter's stirring ceased and he thought he heard a sudden intake of breath.

"Well, I'm glad you came when you did," Liddy noted. "We were having a hard time of it with the mare."

"Some births don't come easy." He scrubbed his hands clean, ran the basin full, and started washing the shit off his face and chest. He dirtied one large towel and Liddy handed him another.

"Can I offer you a cup of coffee after you've cleaned up?" Liddy asked.

"That sounds nice."

She handed him the last clean towel. "I'll get the pot going. You and Nita come over to the house when you're ready."

Liddy walked off and Kerney turned to study Nita. She was bent over the mare watching the horse lick the foal clean. She straightened up and forced a smile at Kerney.

"Thanks again. I think we would have lost the foal if you hadn't shown up."

"You're welcome," Kerney said as he tucked in his shirt and put on his jacket.

"So, you're a police officer."

"I'm an investigator with the state police."

"Why do you need to talk to me?" Stiffly, Nita walked to the sink and stood with her back to Kerney. A good five foot eight, she had a slender frame, much like Addie Randall's.

"I spoke with your sister earlier today."

She splashed water on her face, cleaned her arms, slipped on a plaid work shirt, and turned to face him. "Really?"

"And Verdie Mae McNutt."

"I see."

"I also talked with Addie Randall. I understand you paid a visit to her in Socorro."

"Her mother and I have been friends since childhood. Addie is someone I care about."

"Verdie Mae made that clear. You were seen talking to Robert Cordova in Mountainair on the day Paul Gillespie was murdered."

"I've known Robert for a long time."

"He was your foster brother."

"That's right."

"What secret do you want him to keep?"

Nita's eyes narrowed. "Excuse me?"

"Where is Serpent Gate?"

"I've never heard of it."

"That's not what Robert said."

Nervously, Nita used her fingers to comb her hair. "If you've talked to Robert, you know that he's not completely rational."

"Not always," Kerney agreed. "But two thoughts seem to occupy his mind: a place called Serpent Gate and rape. Do you know why he spends so much time thinking about those two things?"

"I have no idea."

"Addie was raped, wasn't she?"

"I think that's a safe assumption."

"Did she tell you who did it?"

"Addie won't talk about it."

"Not with just anybody," Kerney said. "But maybe she would tell someone close to her. Someone who would understand what happened."

"I don't know what you mean by that."

The more Kerney looked at Nita, the stronger her resemblance to Addie seemed. He decided to roll the dice. "Does Addie know you're her mother?"

"That's absurd." Nita's voice rose several notches.

"Why would Lurline lie to me about your friendship with Robert Cordova?"

"I have no idea."

"Then lie to me again about your family nickname? It's Addie, isn't it?"

"I think I've heard enough." Nita walked to her medical bag and started repacking it. Her hands were shaking.

"I think it's more than a coincidence that you and Addie share the same name."

Nita snapped the bag closed. "I have to go now." Her eyes blinked rapidly, filling with tears, and she walked quickly past Kerney into the biting late-afternoon wind.

"Did you kill Paul Gillespie?"

"Why would I do that?" Nita opened the passenger door to her truck and put the bag on the seat, hiding her face from Kerney.

"Because he raped Addie."

Nita sagged against the door. "Who told you that?"

"Addie," Kerney lied. "Is she your daughter?"

"You'll have to figure that out by yourself." Nita closed the passenger door and walked to the driver's side of the truck. A sheen of perspiration showed on her upper lip.

Kerney followed and stopped at the front fender. "You need

to talk about this, Nita," he said softly. "You can't keep carrying it around. It's eating you up. You're sweating and shaking."

"I don't want to talk to you," Nita responded, her voice drained. She opened the driver's door, got inside, and gave him a feeble smile. "Good-bye, Mr. Kerney."

Kerney held the truck door open as she tried to pull it shut, and played his last card. "Robert did tell me one thing that may interest you."

"What's that?"

"He saw you leaving the police station the night Gillespie was shot."

Nita sagged. "Oh, poor Robert." The words came out in a whisper. "Our friendship has cost him so much. Is he okay?"

"You saw him there, didn't you?"

Nita bit her lip and nodded.

"Tell me about your relationship with Paul Gillespie."

"Paul was my classmate in high school."

"Was he a friend?"

"Hardly that."

"You didn't like him?"

"I couldn't stand him."

"You wanted to confront him about Addie. I can understand that. He raped your daughter."

Nita laughed harshly. "Addie was Paul's daughter, too, Mr. Kerney. I left town when I found out I was pregnant. He never knew about Addie and Addie doesn't know about him."

"You're leaving something out, Nita. Finish the story."

Nita's shoulders sagged further. "Paul raped me during my senior year in high school. Robert saw it happen."

"When did you decide to kill him?"

"When Addie told me what Paul had done."

Kerney sidestepped around the door so he could have a clear view of Nita. "Tell me how it happened."

"He was cleaning his pistol when I went to see him. I had a

gun in my handbag. I was just going to kill him and leave. But I got scared. He grabbed me before I could walk out and gave me this hug—grinding himself against me. I felt like I was being raped all over again. I pushed him away, picked up his pistol from the desk, and pulled the trigger."

"Get out of the truck," Kerney said softly.

"Lurline called me right after you went to see her. I knew you would find me."

"Step out of the truck."

Nita shook her head. She turned her back to Kerney and her left hand disappeared into the center console between the bucket seats.

"Put your hands in plain view and get out of the truck." Kerney unholstered his weapon and leveled the nine-millimeter at Nita.

"I'm not a very good murderer," Nita said. As she turned to face Kerney, her hand came up holding a pistol. She pressed the muzzle against her temple. "Too much of a conscience, I guess."

"Drop the gun," Kerney said.

Nita shook her head and began to squeeze the trigger.

Too far away to make a grab, Kerney fired once. The bullet caught Nita below the shoulder and jarred her arm a fraction of a second before she squeezed the trigger. The round went through the roof of the truck.

He was on her before she could recover. He yanked the gun away, pulled her out of the truck, stretched her on the ground, opened her shirt, and examined the wound. It was bleeding freely but was not life-threatening. He had never shot a woman before and it wasn't an experience he wanted to repeat.

"Why didn't you just kill me?" she asked.

"Too much of a conscience, I guess," he replied.

3

West of Santa Fe, in a subdivision exclusively for the very rich, Enrique DeLeon waited in his expansive living room. Piñon logs crackling in a stone fireplace at the far end of the room provided the only light. DeLeon watched the reflection of the flames flickering in the large glass windows, which by day afforded a stunning view of the Sangre de Cristo foothills and mountains.

DeLeon checked his wristwatch; it was twenty minutes to first light, and according to the timetable he had established, Carlos Ruiz should already have returned. He was about to become annoyed when headlights came into view at the bottom of the private road and paused briefly at the security gate. He watched the vehicle travel up the hill and turn into the driveway.

When he heard the quiet whir of the garage door opener from the lower level of the house, he smiled and closed his eyes.

CARLOS RUIZ hurried up the stairs. The job had gone well, but he was late. And the *jefe* expected his instructions to be followed exactly, no matter what got in the way. He walked through the kitchen and slowed his steps down the long gallery hall to the living room. The hand-carved doors stood open, and at the far end of the room a fireplace glow cast just enough illumination for Carlos to see DeLeon's shape in the chair.

"Shall I turn on a light, *patrón?*" Carlos asked. He spoke in English as DeLeon ordered during any visits to the United States.

"That would not be wise," DeLeon replied.

Only two other houses had a line of sight to DeLeon's property. Both were million-dollar vacation homes staffed by full-time caretakers, who, if awake, might find it unusual to see lights on at such an odd time.

"All went well," Carlos said, stepping into the room. His heels clacked on the polished flagstone floor.

"What delayed you?"

"The private elevator was small, *patrón*. Extra trips were required to move the items out of the offices to the garage. The access code to the underground garage had not been changed, so we had no trouble gaining entry to the building."

"Unseen?"

"Yes, *patrón*."

"No one was in the building?"

"Two janitors. Both were on the first floor, cleaning the rotunda. They did not see or hear us. I had Palazzi watch them throughout the operation, with orders to kill them should they become suspicious."

Carlos took a deep breath before continuing. If he left out

details, DeLeon would become displeased. The *patrón* frequently complained about the slowness of his mind. "We wore gloves, hats, and masks as you ordered," Carlos noted. "No lights were on, and we disabled the security cameras in the reception area without detection."

"Did you get everything?"

"Yes, *patrón*," Carlos replied. "The walls are bare."

"Store everything in the wine cellar," DeLeon ordered as he stood up.

"It is being done as we speak. The men will leave for Juárez as soon as they are finished."

"Have them wait."

"Yes, *patrón*. And the woman?"

"In a few minutes," DeLeon answered as he walked past Carlos.

The curtains in the master bedroom were closed and the track lights dimmed low. DeLeon looked down at the beautiful, heavily drugged face of Amanda Talley. He would remember Amanda fondly for a very long time. Her hunger had matched his own, up to a point. He lifted a strand of blond hair away from her cheek and stroked her face. Amanda did not respond.

DeLeon had promised Amanda a vacation in Belize. A pity she'd never know what she was missing. Her luggage and passport were in Belize right now, at the hotel where one of DeLeon's most trusted currency couriers—a woman of theatrical temperament who enjoyed playing roles and living well—had registered in Amanda's name. The woman would establish a fleeting presence in the midst of a great many witnesses, and then fake a drowning on a boating excursion, the body never to be found.

It was Amanda who had told DeLeon how easy it would be to steal millions of dollars of American art. Not from a museum, but from the executive suite of the governor of New Mexico, who by tradition could select any pieces he desired from

the state museums to decorate his offices. She had been bubbling over with the scheme, high on coke and champagne in this
very bedroom, fantasizing about a great art theft. She'd miss all
the headlines, too, unfortunately for her.

Amanda had offered DeLeon good sex and a great opportunity to steal from the *norteamericanos*. Enrique took full advantage of both. He turned on the lamp next to the bed. Amanda
wore only a pair of panties. In her late twenties, her body was
exactly the type that appealed most to Enrique; slender legs with
just a hint of roundness to the stomach, full breasts that were
not out of proportion to her frame, a face with a somewhat
haughty, aristocratic cast to it. And this lovely blond hair. There
was no need for her to suffer.

"Thank you, my dear," DeLeon whispered to the uncon-
scious woman.

He found Carlos waiting for him in the dark living room.
"Kill her quickly and cleanly," he ordered.

"Yes, *patrón*. And the body?"

"Have the men take it to Mexico. Dispose of it at the ranch.
No trace of her is to be found."

"As you wish."

DeLeon waited until the van left and Carlos was occupied with
removing all traces of Amanda's presence from the house before
he went to the wine cellar. The room, which was next to the
garage, contained a wet bar, built-in wine racks, recessed light-
ing, and a table and chairs for wine tasting. Stacked neatly
against the walls were almost three dozen framed paintings and
prints, but what attracted DeLeon's immediate attention were
the objects on the table.

DeLeon knew what the glass display cases in the governor's
office contained, yet seeing the bounty firsthand was still impres-

sive. Among the items were two large pottery storytellers by the renowned Pueblo Indian artist Helen Cordero, a small bronze by Allen Houser, the famous Apache sculptor, a Western Apache storage basket, a Tesuque Pueblo buffalo-head shield from the mid-eighteenth century, an old *retablo* of Saint Rita, and an exquisite hand-carved wooden *bulto* of the Virgin of Guadalupe.

Immediately DeLeon knew which piece would remain in his possession; the Guadalupe *bulto* would go in the private chapel at his hacienda outside of Juárez.

He turned to the paintings. As the museum curator assigned to select the art for the governor's office, Amanda had chosen well: three Georgia O'Keeffe oils, a Joseph Henry Sharp Indian portrait, a Maynard Dixon cowboy scene, a Henriette Wyeth still life, a Peter Hurd landscape, a Gerald Cassidy portrait of a cowgirl sitting on a fence post, and twenty-five Gustave Baumann color woodcut prints, taken from the gallery space behind the reception area to the governor's offices.

The O'Keeffes were seven-figure treasures, and the rest would fetch in the six-figure range, with the exception of the woodcuts, which were significantly less valuable but expensive nonetheless.

DeLeon did some quick mental calculations; it was an eight-million-dollar haul at the very least, and since it would eventually be sold to foreign buyers on the black market, DeLeon would add a 30 percent commission. Everything but the *bulto* of the Virgin of Guadalupe would remain in the wine cellar for six months. When the investigation into the theft cooled, DeLeon would move the collection to Mexico.

He studied the O'Keeffe paintings carefully, thinking that he might keep one, perhaps to replace the U.S. Army cavalry saber and scabbard that hung over the fireplace in the billiard room of his hacienda.

He wanted to move the sword to his library. It was the only

item DeLeon possessed from a trove of priceless American military and historic artifacts he had arranged to buy and resell on the Asian market. The cache, taken by Apaches during the Indian Wars, had been discovered in a secret cave on White Sands Missile Range and smuggled off the base. But the shipment had been intercepted by a gringo cop named Kevin Kerney before it could be delivered to DeLeon.

DeLeon had bartered with the U.S. Army for the sword, two hundred thousand dollars in diamonds, and the release of Carlos from custody in exchange for a quantity of letters written by members of the 9th U.S. Cavalry during the Indian Wars. The smugglers had given the letters to DeLeon as proof that the cache was authentic before he agreed to broker the deal.

Putting the sword in the library, where he spent the majority of his time at the hacienda, would serve as a reminder that not every venture succeeded as planned.

He adjusted the climate and humidity controls, turned out the light, and entered the security code to the door. Carlos and the team had done well.

ANDY BACA, chief of the state police for two months and counting, stood in the governor's private office on the fourth floor of the Roundhouse, the colloquial name for the state capitol. A circular structure modeled on Pueblo Indian kivas, the building had been nicknamed by political pundits while it was still under construction, and the label had stuck.

The governor's cherry-wood desk, matching sideboard, and executive chair sat in front of the only windows in the office, which were flanked by two empty, expensive brass-and-glass display cases. On the side walls were two private entrances: one connected to the chief of staff's office and the other to a large conference room.

In one corner was a leather couch, coffee table, and several oversize leather chairs. The rest of the space was taken over by two straight-backed chairs in front of the governor's desk, a small conference table with chairs, and a credenza that stood against the wall to the private bathroom.

Unhappily, Andy stared at the empty walls, fully aware the theft would draw intense public scrutiny and criticism. Failure to solve the case could damage the department and probably cost Andy his job.

Andy wasn't about to let that happen. He had retired from the state police some time ago when he realized his chances of becoming chief were nil, and moved to Las Cruces with his wife. Bored with retirement, he ran for county sheriff, won the election, served one term in office, and was asked to return to the state police as chief. It was a dream come true, the capstone to his career that he had always wanted. But not for the prestige the appointment brought. Under his calm demeanor, Andy was a reformer, and he wanted to modernize and improve the department.

In uniform, Andy wore a light gray shirt with his rank on the collars and badge over the left pocket, a black tie, black pants with a gray stripe, and highly polished black shoes. On his belt was a high-rise holster containing a .357 revolver with a four-inch barrel. It was the one personal touch he had allowed himself since taking over the job. Every other officer under his command carried the required standard-issue nine-millimeter semi-automatic.

Captain Vance Howell, the officer in charge of security for the governor, stood silently next to Andy, waiting to get his butt chewed. He had come up through the ranks junior to Andy and served under him briefly just prior to Andy's retirement as a captain. Now Baca was back as chief.

Howell knew exactly why Baca had been tapped for the

job—it was politics, pure and simple. The governor, a Republican, wanted more money from the legislature to build new prisons, and the Democrats, who controlled the legislature, wanted their man sitting in the chief's chair.

Howell had hoped to get the appointment himself, but now he would have to wait until Baca stepped down. He had the governor's promise on it, which was good enough for him. And if Baca failed on this case, Vance might get a crack at the chief's job sooner than he had anticipated.

Andy scanned the paper in his hand and turned to Howell. "Is this the complete inventory of the stolen property?" he asked.

"Yes, sir," Howell replied. "The cultural affairs office verified it."

Technically, Howell's sole responsibility was the safety of the governor and his immediate family, but that didn't mean Baca wouldn't try to lay the blame for the theft at Vance's feet, if the need arose. Vance decided to test Baca's intentions. "I guess you could say it was my henhouse that got robbed."

Andy shook his head and looked up. At six foot four, Howell towered over Andy's five-ten frame. "That's not the way I see it, Captain. But I think we need to get you out of the henhouse for a while. I'm placing you and your staff on administrative leave."

Stunned, Howell reacted quickly. "Is that necessary, Chief?"

"This job required inside knowledge. Until we get a handle on the case, everybody who works in this building is suspect."

"My people won't like it."

"And I don't like doing it," Andy replied, checking his watch. He needed to get this investigation under way pronto. "I want you and your entire unit at headquarters in an hour to meet with Internal Affairs. A temporary plainclothes detail is on the way to relieve you until the IA investigation is concluded."

"I know my people, Chief. Nobody in my unit had anything to do with this."

"We're going to cover all the bases anyway, Captain. You know the drill."

Howell nodded glumly. "Who's running the investigation?"

"Kevin Kerney."

Howell stifled a surprised expression. "Is that wise, Chief? Kerney's new to the department and he has no command authority."

"He does now," Andy replied. "When you meet with him, you'll be talking to the new deputy chief."

"Is the posting temporary?"

"No, it's not, Captain."

"You've jumped him over a lot of senior commanders."

"I'm sure I'll get an earful from all of them," Andy replied. "When the bitching is over, Captain—and it better be kept to a minimum—I expect everyone to cooperate with Chief Kerney."

Howell swallowed hard. "I'll be glad to."

"I know you will, Captain."

Vance Howell left Andy alone in the office and walked down the hall thinking that there were going to be a number of tightly puckered assholes, including his own, tiptoeing around Andy and his new deputy chief.

DOG-TIRED and not in a good mood to begin with, Kerney crawled through the early morning rush-hour traffic on St. Francis Drive, pissed off with the congestion and the yuppies in their leather-lined, air-conditioned, four-wheel-drive sport utility vehicles used for fetching children from school, shopping excursions to Albuquerque malls, and getting up to Taos for skiing. The changes in Santa Fe had turned the city into a seemingly endless array of strip malls, bedroom subdivisions, and gated communities for the rich.

The folks in places like Mountainair referred to the state cap-

ital as Santa Fake, and it rang true enough to make Kerney realize that the chamber of commerce growth mentality had won
the war over those who wanted to preserve the tradition of the
ancient city. Nothing had stopped the greed.

After dealing with the crime scene unit at the Von Hewett
Ranch and undergoing an interrogation about the shooting, Kerney had driven to the Albuquerque hospital where Nita had been
transported. Although he had a brief confession in hand, he
wanted to get a complete statement from Lassiter before the
lawyers showed up to circle their wagons.

He had waited until she was out of the recovery room, in her
hospital bed, and fully conscious before reading Nita her rights and
tape-recording her confession. She retold her story in greater
detail and with such candor that Kerney found it hard to suspend
judgment about the possibility of Gillespie's guilt. He had left the
hospital feeling slightly sickened by the ugliness of the man's
actions, and not at all happy about busting Nita Lassiter.

He got out of the traffic flow and drove into the south capitol neighborhood, an older residential area within walking distance of the downtown plaza and the seat of state government.
At the end of a paved street, a private dirt lane led to two houses.
He turned into the driveway of an adobe house almost completely hidden by a small rise at the front of the lot.

He parked at the side of the house by the door to the
attached guest quarters, dragged himself inside, stripped off his
boots, and fell across the bed, still smelling like horseshit.

IN KERNEY's dream, a soft voice told him to wake up. It sounded
remarkably like Fletcher Hartley, his host and old friend, who
had offered Kerney the use of the guest quarters.

The soft voice changed as Fletcher Hartley raised his easy
baritone several notches in volume. "Kevin, you must wake up."

Kerney opened an eye to find Fletcher standing over him. The door from the guest addition to the main house stood open. Fletcher wore a black silk kimono with brilliant orange, blue, and yellow hand-stitched flowers and butterflies. The kimono hung open to reveal a pair of boxer shorts and Fletcher's spindly but well-muscled legs.

Using the services of the best plastic surgeon in the state, Fletcher had removed a good twenty years from his seventy-five-year-old face. He was eccentric, vain, and one of the most interesting people Kerney knew.

Kerney sat up, stared groggily at Fletcher, and looked at his wristwatch. He'd been asleep for an hour.

"What is it?" he asked grumpily.

"There's a very impressive looking policeman sitting in my living room demanding to see you."

"Who is it?"

"Andy Baca. You don't smell very nice, Kevin. What in the world have you been doing?"

"Delivering a foal," Kerney grumbled as he reached for his boots. "It was a difficult birth. Both mother and child are doing fine."

"I'm glad to hear it. Policemen do such interesting work." Fletcher put his hand on Kerney's shoulder to stop him. "Shower and change first. I will not have you trailing that barnyard smell into the house."

"Don't be so picky, Fletcher. You made your reputation as an artist painting barnyard animals."

"How they look on canvas and how they smell are entirely different matters. Go shower. I'll keep the good Chief Baca entertained. Do you think he likes gay old men?"

"Andy's straight."

"Pity," Fletcher said.

"Give him your best pitch, anyway," Kerney replied as he

walked to the small bathroom. "Maybe you'll change his point of view on the subject."

"I may just do that," Fletcher said, closing the door on his way out.

KERNEY entered the living room to find Andy Baca sitting in a Mexican colonial chair while Fletcher stood in front of the corner kiva fireplace explaining the history of the twelve framed nineteenth-century Japanese fans that climbed the wall above the *banco*. On the other side of the fireplace was Fletcher's large portrait of a Holstein dairy cow bordered by hand-stenciled hearts.

Andy looked a bit nonplussed and uneasy, which made Kerney feel a little better about being yanked out of a dead sleep.

"What's up?" he asked Andy when Fletcher finished his discourse on the history and rarity of the fans.

Andy stood. "I'll tell you outside."

Kerney sank onto the Mexican colonial couch opposite Andy's chair. "Whatever it is, tell me here so I can go back to bed when you're finished."

"You don't have time to sleep, Kerney. The art collection at the governor's office was ripped off early this morning. I need you at work, now."

Kerney sat up on the couch. "The entire collection?"

"Everything."

"Any leads?"

"Not yet," Andy answered. "I figure it to be an inside job."

"What makes you say that?" Fletcher asked.

Andy eyed Fletcher uncomfortably. "By the way it was done, Mr. Hartley."

"I see," Fletcher said. "I certainly wouldn't want you to divulge confidential information, Chief Baca, but as I recall,

Governor Springer had a very valuable collection of art in his offices."

"You're familiar with the collection?" Andy asked.

"Partially," Fletcher replied. "Do you have a complete list of what was taken?"

Andy glanced at Kerney, who nodded in Fletcher's direction. He got up and gave the list to Fletcher, who read it quickly and handed it back.

"The Dixon and the Sharp paintings, I arranged to have purchased by the museum when I was director. The O'Keeffe paintings were donated to the museum by Georgia herself. Everything that was taken must be recovered. They are treasures much too valuable to lose."

"You were director of the fine arts museum?" Andy asked.

"For many years."

"Fletcher may be able to help," Kerney suggested.

"I insist upon it," Fletcher said. "First, I must contact the International Foundation for Art Research in New York and the Art Loss Register in Great Britain. I'll need photographs along with a copy of the list. I can send the information to them by computer."

"How does that help?" Andy asked.

"It alerts the international art establishment worldwide. If any queries are made to a reputable dealer offering to sell one of the pieces, it will be reported immediately."

"That could make a difference," Andy said.

"But there's no time to waste on our investigation," Fletcher added. "After the first forty-eight hours, ninety percent of stolen art is never recovered."

"That's not what I want to hear," Andy said.

"Nevertheless, it's true. Do you have an officer who specializes in art thefts? Preferably someone who knows the local dealer network and has a background in art?"

"Kerney is about as close as I can come to an expert," Andy answered.

"Thanks for the vote of confidence," Kerney said.

"That will have to do," Fletcher said. "Kevin has a good general knowledge of art." He turned to Kerney. "And I know the dealers. I will contact them on your behalf. It will save a good deal of time."

Before Kerney could reply, Andy got to his feet. "I'll draw up a consultant contract. We'll pay you for your services."

Fletcher waved off the offer. "I don't need the money, Chief Baca. Let's just say I'll assist the department in making some inquiries."

"This is real life, Mr. Hartley, not a cozy British mystery."

"I view this crime with great seriousness, Chief Baca, and have no intention of treating it lightly."

"What do you need to get started, Fletcher?" Kerney asked.

"As I said, a copy of the list and photographs as soon as possible. I'll contact the research foundation and the Brits as soon as I have it. I'll start talking to local gallery owners to see if any have been approached to buy art from suspicious characters, or have been asked for off-the-cuff appraisals on works by the artists in question."

"I'll get a packet to you right away," Kerney said as he stood up.

"Send it over with one of those handsome gay officers," Fletcher said.

"I don't think we have any," Andy replied.

"Oh, you are very much mistaken, Chief Baca."

KERNEY got in Andy's unmarked police cruiser and closed the door.

"Do I really have gay cops working for me?" Andy asked.

"Why shouldn't you?" Kerney replied. "Besides, this is Santa Fe, the city different."

Andy shook his head in disbelief. "I don't even want to think about it. How did you meet Fletcher?"

"Outrageous, isn't he? But he's sharp, talented, and a sweet guy. When I was with the Santa Fe PD, Fletcher had a California boyfriend—one of those dumb, good-looking muscle boys. Fletcher wouldn't increase his spending allowance, so he ripped off Fletcher's Japanese fan collection. It's worth a small fortune.

"I caught up with the perp when he tried to sell the fans to an Albuquerque antique dealer. The dealer sent him away, tipped me, and I picked up the suspect when he went back to close the deal. It was an easy bust. Fletcher has always been grateful."

"How grateful?" Andy asked with a grin.

Kerney grinned back. "Don't try to be funny, Andy. You know my taste in women."

Andy groaned in response. "Yeah, the type that always seems to leave you."

Kerney thought about Karen Cox, the ADA he had worked with in Catron County. "That's not true. They just don't seem to be interested in long-term relationships."

"Whatever. By the way, you did a damn fine job on the Gillespie case."

"Thanks. But it doesn't feel real good."

"Why do you say that?"

Kerney put the cassette tape of Nita Lassiter's confession on the dashboard. "Listen to the tape. I think you'll find it interesting."

"I can't wait to hear it," Andy said, reaching into his shirt pocket. "Your efforts deserve special recognition." He laid the deputy chief shield in Kerney's hand. "Put this beauty in your badge case."

Kerney stared dumbly at the shield for a minute. "What the hell is this for?"

"You've been promoted, Chief," Andy said, breaking into a grin. "I want my best man reporting directly to me on this case, with full authority to act without the bureaucracy getting in the way."

"I don't need to be a deputy chief to do this job."

"Maybe not, but I need a second-in-command I can trust to run this investigation. Most of my senior commanders were vying for my job, and they're still pissed off that they didn't get it. I can't risk the possibility of sabotage."

"Why turn over the reins to me?" Kerney said. "Handle the case yourself. I'll work with you on it."

"I don't have the time. I've got a whole department to run and two months before the next legislative session to convince the joint budget committee to give me the money I need to upgrade equipment. I want a computerized fingerprint system, a new dispatch system, onboard laptops for every patrol car, and better firepower for the field officers."

"Making me chief deputy isn't going to win you any popularity contests," Kerney said.

"Your appointment has the governor's blessing, and that's all I care about. Harper Springer knew your parents when they served together on the New Mexico Cattle Growers Association, and he knows you by reputation. Besides, he likes the idea of having a shit-kicking cowboy working for him. Said it was the one minority group he hadn't hired enough of in his administration."

"So who do I work for? You or the governor?" Kerney prodded.

"For me." Andy cranked the engine and slid into a Harper Springer twang. "But, hell, son, we all work for the people of this great state. So let's recover the goodies and catch the bad guys before the governor's opposition starts slinging mud at him."

• • •

SINCE Andy's information on the robbery was preliminary and sketchy, Kerney was up to speed in the three minutes it took to reach the Roundhouse.

"What kind of vehicle would it take to move the artwork out of the city?" Kerney asked as he opened the passenger door of the cruiser.

Andy handed him the list of the stolen items. "Nothing big; a panel truck, van, or small rental trailer would do it."

"Any idea when the break-in occurred?" Kerney asked as he scanned the inventory.

"Not more than three or four hours ago. What do you have in mind?"

"If the stuff's not airborne it's either stashed somewhere or on the road. How about telling the district commanders to have their patrol officers do some selective traffic stops? Give them a profile of what kind of vehicle to look for. We might get lucky."

"I should have thought of that," Andy said, reaching for the microphone as he drove away.

Kerney was braced for an ID by a uniformed female officer on duty in the reception area of the governor's suite. Her black uniform with gray piping had no chevrons on the sleeves and the collar insignias were silver, which identified her as a junior patrol officer.

He showed her his badge while he read the brass nameplate over her right shirt pocket. Patrol Officer Yvonne Rasmussen stiffened and pulled in her chin. No more than five-four, about twenty-five years old, with short brown hair and light gray eyes, everything about Rasmussen's bearing told Kerney that the young woman was ex-military.

"Chief," the officer said.

In spite of himself, Kerney liked the way his new title sounded. "How soon can you get someone to relieve you?"

"Ten minutes, sir."

Sending Yvonne Rasmussen to Fletcher's door would probably bring a chuckle from the old man the next time Kerney saw him. He handed the officer the list of stolen merchandise, and asked her to make a copy as soon as she was relieved, get photographs from the museum of all the items, and take everything to Fletcher's house. He gave her the address.

"I'll take care of it, sir," Rasmussen said as she folded the list and slipped it in her pocket.

"Can you have my vehicle picked up and brought to me?" he asked as an afterthought, fishing for his car keys. "It's at the same address."

"Can do, sir."

"Great," Kerney said, handing over the keys. "Thanks."

"No problem, sir."

"Who is in command of the crime scene investigation?" he asked.

"Lieutenant Marcella Pacheco, sir."

"Where is she?"

"Meeting with the governor's chief of staff."

"Have her report to me in Captain Howell's office when she's finished."

"Yes, sir."

Kerney gave Officer Rasmussen a smile and limped away, thinking his blown-out knee needed rest.

Vance Howell's office was a small room right off the reception area. Yellow crime scene tape blocked passage down the corridor that led to the governor's suite. Kerney could hear the sound of a vacuum cleaner and the voices of the crime scene technicians as they worked the area. He toured the crime scene before heading to Howell's office, where he found Lieutenant Pacheco waiting for him.

•   •   •

A BLOWOUT on the interstate just north of the Truth or Consequences exit slowed down DeLeon's men. With the Border Patrol checkpoint station only a mile up the road, it was a bad place to get a flat tire. Custom agents, state cops, and Border Patrol officers were thick as flies along this stretch of highway, and Nick Palazzi flinched every time a patrol unit cruised by.

He watched Emilio and Facundo change the tire while he stood guard at the back of the van, next to the green-and-white highway sign that announced the Truth or Consequences exit. Nick had spent many nights in local motels waiting for the Border Patrol checkpoint to shut down so he could move DeLeon's drugs safely up the pipeline, and he knew the town had been named for an old television show from the Fifties. To Palazzi's way of thinking, it was a stupid name for a town.

Emilio had been the driver, Facundo the muscle, and Nick the triggerman on the Santa Fe job. DeLeon's information and planning had been good, so nobody had gotten hurt except for the dead woman in the back of the vehicle.

Nick was nervous about the body, and he had his hand wrapped about the grip of the handgun inside his windbreaker pocket just in case a curious cop decided to stop and check them out.

He knew better than to try to hurry along the two men. An American, Nick had spent four years rotting in a Mexican prison and the past two years working for DeLeon. Both experiences had only hardened his prejudice against Mexicans, especially the mixed bloods, who were about one baby step out of the fucking Stone Age.

He stamped his feet against the cold. An Arctic low pressure system had entered the state, and the morning was dismal under a dreary sky. Creosote bushes sprinkled over the desert sand hills fluttered in a stiff breeze that swirled and lifted small dust plumes into the sky. Just as Emilio tightened the last lug nut on the spare, a state police cruiser rolled into view at the top of the hill.

Nick told Facundo and Emilio to stay put as he watched the black-and-white patrol car coast to a stop ten feet behind the van. He waved with his free hand and smiled at the officer, who waved back, keyed the handset to his radio, and started talking. Nick figured the cop was calling in the license number, which was cool since the van wasn't stolen and had valid Texas plates.

Nick started to move toward the cop car, but the officer motioned him to stop. He shrugged and complied, watching as the pig waited for a response to his radio inquiry on the van. Finally, the cop opened the driver's door and stood behind it for cover. Not a friendly sign, Nick thought as his finger found the trigger of the weapon concealed in his windbreaker.

"Just a flat, Officer," Nick called out in a friendly voice. "We've got it fixed and we're ready to roll."

Officer Jerry Rogoff kept all three men in view. There were no wants or warrants on the vehicle. "Heading home?" Rogoff asked.

"Trying to," Nick replied with a smile.

Nothing looked out of the ordinary to Rogoff, but the special bulletin on the Santa Fe art theft made a closer inspection necessary. He nodded, stepped around the open cruiser door, and walked toward the three men. The Anglo man stood near the rear door to the van, while the two Hispanics waited quietly at the rear left fender, a tire and jack at their feet.

"Mind opening the rear door?" Rogoff asked the Anglo man, stopping six paces away, out of striking distance.

Nick smiled. "Not at all." He pulled on the latch and swung the door up.

As the cop switched his gaze to the van, Nick shot him twice through the pocket of his windbreaker, the rounds punching into Rogoff's bulletproof vest.

Slammed back by the impact, Rogoff pulled at his sidearm.

Nick put a bullet in the cop's forehead before he could free the weapon.

PALAZZI studied the road map while Emilio pushed the van to its maximum down the highway. Facundo was in the backseat clutching an M16 loaded with a thirty-round banana clip. They had to get off the highway before a wolf pack of cops swarmed all over them. The best possible plan was to cut through the old mining towns of Hillsboro and Kingston, climb the mountain road through the Black Range, and swing down to Silver City. There they could lose the van, steal a car, and make a straight run to the border. After that, if they punched it hard, they could be in Mexico in an hour.

The problem was the dead woman. They had to lose the body before switching vehicles. Emory Pass at the top of the mountain range west of Kingston looked like a good place to stop. A ten-minute hike off the road should do it, Nick thought. With any luck, it could be years before the remains were found, if ever.

"Take the next exit," Nick ordered Emilio.

4

At the state police headquarters on the old Albuquerque Highway, Kerney turned Andy's conference room into a temporary office. The room had exposed brick walls, a large wall-mounted chalkboard, and three long tables pushed together to form a U. Windows provided a view of the parking lot, the highway, and a new car dealership across the road.

The word of his promotion had spread quickly throughout the building, and the range of staff reaction ran from polite congratulations to studied indifference. Kerney expected as much; cop shops were paramilitary societies, and any promotion outside of the traditional practice of rank and seniority always sent shock waves through the system.

Andy had gone back to the Roundhouse to meet with a legislative finance committee on his proposed budget, so Kerney was on his own. He selected several agents to assist him, met with the criminal investigations commander, and got busy pulling together a team. The report of Officer Rogoff's murder came in as he completed making initial assignments. He took two agents off the theft case and sent them down to T or C to take charge of the homicide investigation, and ordered field commanders in the southern part of the state to swarm their districts with patrols in an attempt to locate the vehicle and suspects.

Rogoff's murder put everyone in a foul, tight-lipped mood. By the end of the morning, all that could be done at the command level was under way. Kerney tapped more agents for field assignments to supplement the team. Almost every criminal investigator on duty was working the case one way or another.

He pushed the paperwork to one side and walked stiffly to the window. Bone tired, he stared at the traffic on the highway, trying to clean out the cobwebs in his head. As he turned back, Andy came into the conference room through his office door, dumped his briefcase on the table, and sank into a chair. Kerney joined him at the table.

"Where do things stand?" Andy asked.

"We're working from a list of all the people with access to the underground garage at the state capitol," Kerney replied. "It includes everybody on the governor's staff, the lieutenant governor and his staff, cabinet officers, legislators, and some of the state employees who work in the building."

"I hope you told our people to be diplomatic."

"Of course," Kerney replied. "We're running fresh background checks on everybody, looking for shady relationships, money problems, or indiscretions that might be suspect. I've got the two night janitors in interrogation, but neither of them seems to know a damn thing."

"Has anybody with access to the garage or private elevator turned up missing?" Andy inquired.

"No such luck," Kerney answered.

"What's the status on the Rogoff shooting?"

"No breaks yet. We've got a license number and description of the vehicle. Every law enforcement agency in southern New Mexico is looking for the van. The one bit of good news is that Rogoff had his video camera on. We've got the shooting on tape, with good pictures of the killer and his cohorts. A copy of the video has been sent to the FBI to see if they can make a match." Kerney paused.

"What else?"

"The killer opened the rear gate of the van before he shot Rogoff. There was no artwork inside, but something wrapped in a sheet was behind the backseat. Our lab people think it might have been a body. They're analyzing the videotape now."

"Do you think the shooting and the robbery are connected?"

"That's the way I read it."

Andy nodded in agreement, stood up, and reached for his briefcase.

"How are the budget hearings going?" Kerney asked.

"I'm due back tomorrow morning. The committee wants me to cut ten percent from my request for new money for equipment."

"Will that ding the department?"

"Not really," Andy said, walking toward his office. "I padded the budget by twenty percent, figuring I'd have to take a cut somewhere down the line." He stopped at the door. "Catch Rogoff's killer, Kerney."

"That's the plan."

During the remainder of the day, Kerney kept in touch with the field investigators as they worked their lists and conducted initial interviews. He didn't expect anything interesting to pop up at the information-gathering stage, and nothing surfaced. Likewise, the background checks were raising no red flags.

Night had settled over the city by the time Kerney left headquarters and walked to his car. Going thirty-six hours on an hour's sleep had drained him, but his day wasn't finished. Nita was about to be discharged by the doctors, and she'd have to be booked into the Torrance County jail.

NITA HAD been moved by the deputy sheriff guarding her from the hospital room to an office in the administrative wing, which got her away from family and friends who had congregated throughout the day. Grateful for the deputy's good sense, Kerney thanked the officer.

"She doesn't act like a cold-blooded cop killer," Deputy Henry Delgado said as he nodded at the open door to the office where Nita waited. "In fact, she's been so damn easy to guard, I've had a hard time believing she killed a cop."

"She had her reasons for doing it," Kerney replied.

"They better be damn good ones," Delgado noted.

An older officer, probably near retirement, Delgado still looked like he could mix it up with the bad guys and come out on top. He had short-cropped hair, a high forehead, and a chunky face with deep-set brown eyes. Kerney liked the man immediately.

"Has she spoken with an attorney?" Kerney asked.

"Yeah. A lawyer was in to see her. He wasn't anybody I knew."

"Did you get a name?"

"He gave me his card." He passed it to Kerney and smiled apologetically. "I don't mean to rush you, but am I done here? My grandson is the point guard on his junior high school basketball team. He's got a game tonight. I try not to miss any of them."

"Take off. And thanks again."

Kerney entered the office to find Nita Lassiter sitting on a small couch. She stood up quickly. She wore a black tailored jacket that broke just below her hips, a pair of double-pleated gray trousers, and square-toed black pumps with low heels. The sophisticated outfit favored her good looks. Her right arm was secured against her side by a sling.

"Ms. Lassiter," Kerney said, waiting for a reaction.

Nita nodded silently in response.

"I understand from the doctor that there is no permanent damage."

"That's what I've been told. My lawyer tells me that I'm probably going to spend the night in jail."

"That's true," Kerney said.

Nita glanced at the door. "Let's get it over with."

"I'd like to talk to you for a minute."

"My lawyer told me not to say anything more to the police unless he was present."

"That's wise advice. But I wasn't planning to interrogate you, just ask a question or two that you may find helpful."

Nita looked Kerney up and down. "What are your questions?"

"Has your lawyer discussed the possibility of bail?"

A worried look crossed Nita's face. "We didn't talk about that."

"Has he ever practiced criminal law?"

"I don't think so. Just real estate and tax law."

Kerney shook his head. "You'll need a criminal defense lawyer. I'm going to book you on a murder-one charge, Ms. Lassiter, and with your confession, a judge or grand jury will most likely find there is sufficient probable cause to go to trial. You'll be facing a pretty stiff bond for your release, if the court agrees to let you make bail at all. Do you have property to put up as security?"

"My home and my practice," Nita replied. "I should talk to my lawyer. Is that possible?"

"Of course. You'll be allowed to call him from the jail." Kerney took out a business card, wrote quickly on the back of it, and held it out. "But in case he doesn't know who to use as a bail bondsman, the name of this gentleman might do. He's honest and reliable."

Nita took the card. "I'll pass the information along."

"Have your lawyer call me if he wants the name of a good attorney."

"Do you have any more helpful questions to ask?" There was a challenge in Nita's voice.

Kerney sensed that Nita's mistrust of police officers ran deep. He let the question go unanswered. "There are some reporters at the front of the building. To avoid them, we'll leave by way of the rear loading dock." He stood to one side of the door to let Nita pass.

"Shouldn't I be handcuffed?"

"Are you planning to escape?"

"No."

"Handcuffs won't be necessary until we get to my unit. Then regulations take over."

A thin smile crossed her lips. "How very thoughtful."

Without giving Kerney the opportunity to respond, Nita Lassiter walked into the hallway.

KERNEY ushered Nita into the booking area of the jail. When the electronic lock of the security door clicked shut behind them, Nita stiffened. Kerney could see panic building in her eyes, so he stayed after the booking process and waited until she returned from a strip search and change-out into a jail uniform. Even with a stiff upper lip, she looked frightened.

He arranged for Nita to be kept in a seclusion cell away from the general population. She gave him what may have been a weak, thankful smile when he left.

He called the on-duty assistant DA and told him that Lassiter was in jail. Wesley Marshall, the ADA—a man Kerney didn't know—asked Kerney to meet him at the county courthouse.

In Marshall's office, Kerney sat quietly while the ADA read the criminal complaint, the transcribed copy of Lassiter's tape-recorded confession, and Kerney's case report on the events leading up to the shooting incident.

A young man in his late twenties, Marshall had dark curly hair, thick eyebrows, and a bushy mustache. He looked up from the documents and stared intently at Kerney.

"You didn't read her rights to her prior to her first confession," Wesley noted.

"She wasn't in custody at that point," Kerney answered.

"Did you have the intent to arrest her at that time?"

"No. She was in her truck when she confessed to killing Gillespie. I arrested her after she attempted suicide. I read her the Miranda rights, placed her in custody, and explained the charges against her."

"Was she coherent at the time?"

"She was."

"Was shooting her necessary?"

"It was. I had no other option. If I hadn't fired, she would have killed herself."

"The level of force may have been excessive." Marshall thumbed through the paperwork. "Did you perceive a risk to yourself?"

"Facing a loaded weapon is always a risk."

"When you taped her confession at the hospital, was she in full possession of her faculties?" Marshall asked.

"She was."

"Who made that determination?"

"The attending physician," Kerney replied, flipping over a page in the notebook. He read the doctor's name.

The ADA nodded, wrote down the name, scrawled his signature on the documents, and glanced up at Kerney. "That should do it. It looks like a solid, legal bust to me."

"Are you taking Lassiter before the grand jury?"

Marshall shook his head. "Nope. We'll do a probable cause hearing before Judge Ross-Gorden sometime tomorrow. My boss wants to move fast on this one."

"Has the DA told you to go for no bail?"

"Damn right he has. A murder-one defendant has never made bail since he took office. I doubt we'll have a problem with the request." Marshall stuffed the paperwork into a folder and stood. "We're going to push to go to trial as soon as possible. The defense will probably want to depose you in a day or two. I'll let you know when the request comes through."

"Good enough," Kerney said as he pushed himself out of the chair. The bum leg had locked up on him again.

Marshall's office was near the sheriff's department at the back of the building. Kerney knew Judge Willene Ross-Gorden, who had served on the bench for over twenty years. He called her at home from the receptionist's desk in the sheriff's office. After an exchange of pleasantries, he asked the judge if she would have her clerk notify him when Lassiter's hearing had been set.

"Of course," Ross-Gorden replied. "I was surprised when I learned that you were the arresting officer in this case, Mr. Kerney. I thought you were retired."

"I can't seem to stay that way, Judge."

Ross-Gorden chuckled. "I look forward to seeing you tomorrow. My clerk will call you."

•   •   •

A HAND shook Kerney awake.

"Get up," Fletcher commanded. "It's time for our morning run."

"Hump," Kerney said into his pillow.

Fletcher shook him a little harder and Kerney turned to see Hartley standing over him, dressed in sweats and running shoes. In the few weeks Kerney had been bunking with Fletcher, he had joined him on an early morning two-mile jog around the quiet streets when his schedule allowed.

Kerney enjoyed Fletcher's company on the morning runs. Before returning to Santa Fe, he'd lived alone in a borrowed house in Reserve, New Mexico, while serving as the interim sheriff. Breaking up the local militia's plans to assassinate Forest Service employees hadn't won him any popularity contests among many of the residents of Catron County.

"If you want to become an ageless beauty like me, you must remain fit," Fletcher said.

"What time is it?"

"Six."

"It's too early."

"Then I simply won't tell you what the very nice art theft investigator I spoke to in London told me."

"I'll get up," Kerney said. "Give me a few minutes to get dressed."

Kerney dressed, met Fletcher outside, and the two men ran together in silence, trotting past Victorian cottages, sprawling flat-roofed adobes, and two-story homes reminiscent of Mid-western farmhouses.

Halfway into the run Kerney broke the silence. "What have you learned?"

"It's mostly a rehash of what I mentioned yesterday. We should be talking to gallery owners who deal in the works of the artists on the list," Fletcher explained. "Particular attention should be paid to recent new clients looking to either buy or sell. Some of the more intelligent thieves will approach dealers before they pull the job to get a feel for what the market will bear once the objects are in hand. Others, who have no idea what they have stolen, will do the same after the fact."

"I'll put somebody on it," Kerney said, slowing down a bit to accommodate Fletcher's pace. In the cold morning air, his breath turned to frost.

"No need," Fletcher said. "I've been doing it myself. I've spoken to a number of dealers by phone, and left messages for others to call me."

"Has anything interesting come up?"

"Not as it pertains to the investigation. This morning I plan to visit a number of galleries. Fortunately, whoever chose the collection for the governor's office had good taste. I won't have to go into those vile places on the plaza and Canyon Road that sell romanticized cowboy and Western sleaze art."

"You don't like cowboys?"

"I love cowboys," Fletcher responded as he turned the corner, keeping a steady, slow pace. "But I hate bad taste. By the way, you need to be more attentive to my wishes."

"How so?"

"That young officer you sent over with the inventory and photographs had the right sexual orientation, but she was the wrong gender."

"I'll keep that in mind next time. Did you get any additional feedback from the research foundation and the Art Loss Register?"

"Yes, indeed. It could be that the works were stolen to fill an order, but that's considered unlikely. Most thefts are done by uneducated crooks who have no appreciation of what they've stolen. In other situations, it may be a curator who can't resist an opportunity to steal, an art lover who is obsessed with a certain work, or a professional criminal who knows how to sell the item."

"That's not much help."

Fletcher shrugged a shoulder as he ran comfortably at Kerney's side. For a man in his mid-seventies, he was in remarkably good physical shape. "Over two hundred and fifty works by Picasso are listed as stolen. Signed paintings, prints, etchings, and lithographs—worth a fortune. Art theft is not an easy crime to solve."

"Anything else?" Kerney asked, thoroughly discouraged by Fletcher's report.

"The market in stolen fine art is global. What was taken from a church in Spain might wind up in a Brussels gallery five years later. Georgia O'Keeffe's work is admired worldwide, and much in demand. Certain collectors are not terribly concerned about the legality of the purchases they make."

"Did you get any names of potential local buyers?"

"Not yet," Fletcher answered, slowing to a walk. His face was rosy from the exertion of the run. They were within sight of the dirt lane at the end of the street that led to the house. "However, people who buy high-quality stolen art are typically rich, influential, and usually avoid prosecution."

"We need something to break soon," Kerney said.

"According to the newspaper, this mischief has put some egg on the governor's face. Is it trickling down to you?"

"Not yet, but I'm sure he'll pass it on soon enough," Kerney predicted.

CAPTAIN Vance Howell slouched down in the chair across from Kerney, reached for a coffee cup on the conference table, picked it up, and took a sip. The call to meet with Kerney early in the morning forced Howell to dress hurriedly and miss his second cup of coffee. In civilian clothes while on administrative leave, he wore a pullover crew neck sweater that made him look big and beefy, a pair of blue jeans, and work boots. His long legs were stretched out under the table.

Howell studied Kerney as he took another sip. Kerney's congenial expression gave nothing away. Howell smiled back at the new deputy chief, took one last sip, and put his cup down.

"Has Internal Affairs finished their investigation on my team?" he asked. For ten fucking hours yesterday, he had been put through the wringer by two hotshot, button-down IA agents, and he didn't relish undergoing a repeat performance with Kerney.

"Not yet," Kerney answered.

"Is there a problem?"

"None that I know of. I'm more interested in some crime scene evidence I'd like to ask you about."

"Ask away," Howell said.

"The technicians discovered female pubic hairs in the governor's suite. Would you consider that unusual?"

"I don't think so. A lot of staff members use the governor's bathroom when he's out of the office. The door stays unlocked most of the time. It could be the first lady, for all I know."

"The first lady isn't a blonde," Kerney replied.

"That's right, she isn't," Howell said. "But blond pubic hairs found in the bathroom don't seem like substantial crime scene evidence to me."

"Evidence is evidence," Kerney said, wondering why Howell seemed to think that pubic hairs were only found in bathrooms. "Governor Springer was out of the office for a week until yesterday."

"That's correct."

"How frequently are his offices cleaned when he's away?"

"When he leaves town, the janitors will shampoo the rugs, wash the walls, and clean the place top to bottom. After that, it's just a quick wipe down until he gets back."

"Was that done last week?"

"Yeah, the day after the governor left. Why all the cleaning questions, Chief?"

"The pubic hairs we found were from the carpet in front of Governor Springer's desk."

Howell tried to stifle his reaction, but grinned anyway. "I'll be damned. Somebody's been getting their rocks off in the old man's office."

"Possibly," Kerney said. "Work up a list of names for me, Captain. I want to know the identity of every blond female who might have had access to the governor's office last week. That includes staff members, any visitors, girlfriends, wives, or friends. Everybody."

"I'll do what I can, but it won't be inclusive," Howell said. "I have no idea who comes and goes when he's not there."

"Ask people," Kerney said flatly, thinking Howell needed to stop worrying about covering his ass and get with the program.

Howell nodded and got up from his chair. "Am I back in harness, Chief?"

"This is a special assignment, nothing more. I'll let you know when you're cleared to return to regular duty."

The conference room telephone rang as Howell made his exit. Kerney picked up the receiver to find Judge Ross-Gorden's clerk on the line. Nita Lassiter's arraignment had been set for one o'clock. He hung up and went into Andy's office.

"What's happening?" Andy asked hopefully.

"Nothing. I'm grasping at straws, or pubic hairs, to be more exact."

"Is this a Clarence Thomas joke?" Andy asked.

Kerney explained his comment.

"This could create a bad news day for the governor if word of it leaked out," Andy said.

"It won't. But I'll bet even money Springer will hear about the pubic hairs from Captain Howell."

"Why do you say that?"

"I put a tail on Howell yesterday evening after IA finished interviewing him. He went straight to the governor's ranch. I believe the captain may have divided loyalties."

Andy pressed his lips together tightly before responding. "Let's see what plays out before we jump to conclusions. But if Howell does tell the governor, Springer won't like it. He's a conservative Republican who beats the family values drum every chance he gets. He may want me to put the brakes on the inquiry."

"What do you want me to do?" Kerney asked.

"Keep at it. I'll take the heat, if it comes."

DeLeon was not an early riser, nor did he have a sunny disposition upon awakening. At ten o'clock in the morning, Carlos waited in the library for DeLeon to appear. The room had floor-to-ceiling bookcases, and the centerpiece was a reproduction of the last Mexican viceroy's desk positioned to take full advantage of the view of the mountains. There were whitecaps of snow on the peaks, which Carlos found uninviting; he didn't like snow.

He sat in a reading chair next to a wall of first editions and rare books, with the morning newspaper in his lap. In spite of the fact that his upper false teeth fit perfectly, Carlos adjusted the plate with his thumb. It was an old habit hard to break. His new plate had been provided by the U.S. Army after he'd been beaten by Kerney in the El Paso railyards, dragged along the tracks tied to the bumper of the gringo's truck, and stripped naked, bound, and left in the dirt to be arrested by military police.

It had happened eighteen months ago, but Carlos would never forget it.

Kerney had come thundering back into his mind as soon as he saw the newspaper article announcing the gringo's appointment as deputy chief of the state police. Carlos wanted the *patrón* to wake up, read the paper, and order him to kill the motherfucker.

DeLeon came into the room just as the telephone rang. Carlos started to rise but the *jefe* waved him back down, picked up the receiver, and sat in the high-backed antique Spanish Colonial chair behind the desk.

"What is it?" DeLeon asked in Spanish, not waiting for the caller to identify himself. Anyone with access to the phone number was an employee.

Carlos watched DeLeon's eyes harden as he listened to the caller. When he finally spoke his voice was cordial but his jaw tightened.

"You did what was necessary considering the circumstances," DeLeon said, switching to English.

DeLeon listened some more. "Is the body well hidden?" he asked.

Carlos immediately became more attentive.

"No, stay where you are," DeLeon ordered. "I'll get back to you."

He replaced the receiver and glared at Carlos.

"*Patrón?*" Carlos asked.

"It seems that Nick Palazzi decided it was necessary to kill a state policeman on his way to Mexico. He was reluctant to tell me about it until today. He also felt it necessary to bury Amanda Talley's body and steal a car before he crossed the border."

"What do you wish done?" Carlos said, remembering to respond in English.

"Visit with Nick, Carlos. Have him tell you exactly how to locate Amanda's remains, and when he's told you everything, kill him. Make all traces of Amanda vanish, and get the vehicle safely across the border. Take the Range Rover. You may need it in the mountains."

"Emilio and Facundo?" Carlos inquired as he stood.

"They are blameless in the matter." Enrique waited for Carlos to depart. Instead the man stood rooted to the floor. "Are my instructions unclear?"

"No, *patrón.*" Carlos stepped to the desk and placed the newspaper on it. "There is news which might interest you."

"What is it?"

"An article on the inside page announcing an appointment to the state police."

"Why would that hold any interest for me?" DeLeon inquired, opening the paper to find the article.

Carlos held back a smile. When DeLeon finished reading, his eyes flashed at Carlos.

"Go now," DeLeon said. "We will deal with Señor Kerney when you return."

DeLeon reread the article after Carlos departed. Kevin Kerney, the man who had thwarted the sale of the military artifacts smuggled from White Sands Missile Range, was in Santa Fe.

Enrique pushed the paper aside and looked at the sweeping view of the Sangre de Cristo Mountains. Northern New Mexico was one of the few places in the United States where he felt completely at home. With a rich Hispanic heritage, flourishing Spanish arts, and a culture tied closely to his own, the area deeply appealed to him.

He switched his thoughts back to Kerney and smiled as he contemplated the police officer's death.

"THIS IS A preliminary hearing to determine if there is probable cause to believe that the crime of murder may have been committed by Anita Lassiter," Judge Ross-Gorden announced.

She had delayed the hearing ten minutes waiting for Kerney to arrive. He was still a no-show. She looked out over the top of her reading glasses at the nearly empty courtroom. In her late fifties, Ross-Gorden had a high forehead, narrow cheeks, and a slightly pointed chin. She wore her gray hair pulled into a bun at the nape of her neck. The occupants in the courtroom included the defendant, her attorney, the ADA, Wesley Marshall, a court stenographer, and the deputy sheriff guarding Lassiter.

Anita Lassiter was an attractive, well-dressed woman with an intelligent face who looked frightened. Judge Ross-Gorden wondered if the defense counsel had taken the time to prepare her for the hearing.

"Does your client understand the purpose of these proceedings?" Ross-Gorden asked Lassiter's attorney, a pudgy man the judge knew only in passing. He was not a criminal trial attorney, and Ross-Gorden wanted to make sure Lassiter had been adequately advised by counsel.

Bradley Pullings stood next to Nita Lassiter at the defendant's table. "She does, Your Honor."

"Very well," Ross-Gorden said, deciding to be a bit more explicit for Lassiter's sake. "I have reviewed the arresting officer's written report, and the transcript of Ms. Lassiter's tape-recorded confession. I find that there is sufficient evidence to proceed to trial on the charges of first-degree murder. How does your client plead?"

"Not guilty, Your Honor," Pullings said.

"Do you plan to engage a co-counsel with criminal defense experience?" Ross-Gorden asked Pullings.

Bradley blushed. "Yes, Judge."

"That would be wise." Ross-Gorden inclined her head at ADA Marshall, who took the cue and stood.

"We ask the court that Ms. Lassiter be held without bail, Your Honor. She has confessed to the premeditated murder of a police officer, which is a crime punishable by death if the defendant is found guilty. We believe, based on the serious consequences to the crime, she might be a flight risk."

"Mr. Pullings?" Judge Ross-Gorden asked.

"Ms. Lassiter is a doctor of veterinary medicine, a professional woman of excellent reputation, a businesswoman, and a property owner," Pullings replied. "Moreover, this is the first time Dr. Lassiter has ever appeared before a court of law as a defendant in either a criminal or civil matter. She is not a flight risk, nor is she a danger to society. I ask the court to release Dr. Lassiter on her own recognizance."

The door at the rear of the courtroom opened and Kerney slipped inside.

Ross-Gorden nodded slightly in his direction and spoke directly to Pullings. "You are new to my court, Mr. Pullings. I have made it a practice since assuming the bench to allow investigating and arresting officers to make a statement at preliminary hearings, if they so choose."

"May I ask for what purpose, Your Honor?"

"Frequently their impression of the defendant is helpful to me."

"I have no objection, Your Honor."

"It is not a decision you can object to, Mr. Pullings," Ross-Gorden replied gently.

Pullings blushed again. "Sorry, Your Honor."

Ross-Gorden turned her attention to the back of the room. "Mr. Kerney, you are the investigating officer in this case. Do you have something to say for the record?"

"Yes, Your Honor."

"Come forward."

Nita Lassiter swung her head around as Kerney moved to the railing. She bit her lip and dropped her gaze when he looked at her.

"What is it you would like to say to the court?" Ross-Gorden asked.

"I don't think Ms. Lassiter will flee your jurisdiction, Your

Honor," he said. "I believe she is a woman with a strong sense of right and wrong who feels a great deal of guilt about what she did. If I may, Your Honor, I suggest that reasonable bail be set."

"That recommendation will not make you very popular with your fellow officers," Ross-Gorden noted as she watched Wesley Marshall glare at Kerney. "Or with the prosecutor, for that matter," she added.

"I realize that, Judge."

Before Marshall had a chance to react, Ross-Gorden swung her attention back to Pullings. "Your client's attempted suicide troubles me, Counselor. Therefore, I order that she be held in custody pending the results of a psychiatric evaluation. Should the evaluation show that Ms. Lassiter is not a danger to herself, bail is set in the amount of three hundred and fifty thousand dollars, cash or property. This hearing is closed."

Kerney turned to leave.

"Mr. Kerney," Judge Ross-Gorden called out.

"Ma'am?"

Willene Ross-Gorden smiled. "The morning newspaper noted your promotion. Congratulations, Chief."

"Thank you, Judge." He watched Nita, Pullings, and the deputy sheriff move to a side door. Before Lassiter stepped through the doorway, she stopped and looked back at him. Kerney couldn't read her expression.

THE DISTRICT courtroom ate up the center core of the courthouse. From the main lobby, two hallways ran along both sides of the courtroom, leading to various county offices. In the lobby, a large plate-glass window separated two entrances at the front of the building. Through the window, Kerney could see Wesley Marshall surrounded by a group of reporters and camera crews, eager for the prosecutor's latest pronouncement. Three television station vans equipped with satellite antennas were parked in the lot, sending live feeds back to the studios in Albuquerque.

Without being noticed, Kerney walked to his car parked on the side of the building. Robert Cordova leaned against the driver's door, wearing clean jeans, running shoes without laces, and a worn but serviceable navy pea coat.

Kerney was surprised to see him. Marcia Yearwood had supposedly arranged for Robert to stay at a halfway house in Albuquerque. Before he could ask Robert what he was doing back in Torrance County, Cordova stood on his tiptoes and punched Kerney in the jaw.

Kerney picked Robert up by both arms and held him against the side of the car. Robert's feet flailed at Kerney's shins.

"What are you doing here, Robert?" Cordova's punch had a sting to it, and Kerney held him tight to avoid another blow. "Why aren't you at the halfway house?"

"I ran away. I came back to kick the shit out of you."

"Why?"

"Because the television said you shot Nita," Robert answered, trying to butt his head against Kerney's face.

Kerney kept him pinned against the car at arm's length. "Calm down."

"Fuck you, calm down. Put me down, dammit."

"Will you behave if I do?"

"Did you shoot Nita?"

"I had to," Kerney explained. "She was trying to kill herself."

"Nita would never do that."

"I swear it," Kerney said solemnly. "She's going to need your help, Robert."

Cordova squinted at Kerney with one eye and stopped thrashing his feet. "What do you mean?"

"You know why she killed Paul Gillespie. You need to tell me what happened."

"I saw the asshole rape her, man."

"Will you tell me exactly what you saw?"

"What good would that do?"

"You're a witness, Robert. What you say can help Nita."

"You're just trying to fuck her over some more."

"No, I'm not. But you'll fuck her over if you don't help," Kerney shot back.

"Nobody's gonna believe a crazy fucking mental patient."

"I thought you were a stand-up guy, Robert. Somebody who would take the heat for his friends. Maybe I was wrong." Kerney dropped Robert on his feet and pushed him away from the car.

"What are you doing?"

"I'm leaving."

"Wait a minute," Robert said anxiously.

"Will you help Nita? Yes or no?"

Robert struggled with the decision, shifting his weight back and forth on each foot. "I'll tell you," he finally said. "But just you."

"Get in the car and we'll tape-record it," Kerney replied, opening the car door.

Robert balked. "I want to see Nita first."

"You can't see her now. She's going back to jail."

Robert stuck his chin out defiantly. "That's where I want to go."

"It's a deal," Kerney said. "I'll put you in protective custody as soon as you tell me what you saw Gillespie do to Nita. Just don't try to hit me again. Okay?"

"Did it hurt?"

"Damn right it hurt."

Robert swaggered around the front of the car, looked at Kerney over the roof, and cocked his head. "I told you I could fight, man."

"You're one hell of a tough dude," Kerney agreed. "Now, get in the car."

5

Kerney tape-recorded Robert's statement, put him in protective custody at the county jail, and headed back to Santa Fe. He called in his ETA to headquarters and was asked to report to Governor Springer at his ranch. Harper Springer rarely stayed at the governor's mansion in Santa Fe, instead favoring his ranch thirty miles outside of the city near the small village of Pecos. Nestled behind the mesas and foothills of the Sangre de Cristo Mountains, the ranch headquarters was several miles down a dirt road from the interstate highway.

Kerney parked in front of a hundred-year-old double adobe hacienda surrounded by a stand of mature cottonwood trees. At the edge of a wide acreage of fenced pasture were a cluster of buildings consisting of equipment sheds, barns, corrals, and staff living quarters, all painted white. Thick stands of evergreens along the base of the hills confined and sheltered the ranch, giving it a sedate feeling of isolation. The east slope of the mountains, snowcapped and charcoal gray, towered above a mesa shaped like the prow of a sailing ship.

An unmarked state police unit was parked next to the governor's Cadillac. A thin, middle-aged woman answered Kerney's knock and ushered him into a vast living room that could easily accommodate a dance band and a hundred party guests. Large hand-carved beams spanned the high ceiling, and long windows ran down two lateral walls. On the walls were oil paintings of ranching scenes and Western panoramas. None of them paintings Fletcher would approve of, Kerney decided.

On the back wall above a fireplace was a portrait of the governor's father, the man who had bought scrub rangeland in southeastern New Mexico that eventually yielded a fortune in gas and oil royalties. In the center of the room, oversize leather chairs and couches were grouped around a massive coffee table. Governor Harper Springer sat on a couch with his jacket off and his cowboy boots propped up on the coffee table. Vance Howell slouched in a nearby chair, looking relaxed and perfectly at home.

Kerney sized up the governor as he moved across the room. In his late sixties, Springer was a stocky man of average height with a large head and a full mane of gray hair. He had round cheeks that sagged a bit, and close-set eyes beneath a high forehead.

While Springer fancied himself a rancher, he was mostly a politician who had worked hard over the years to gain the governor's office. He had a down-home style that put just about everybody at ease, and a shrewd mind for cutting political deals.

"Chief Kerney," Governor Springer said as he rose and extended his hand across the coffee table with an amiable smile.

Howell grudgingly got to his feet.

"Thanks for stopping by," Springer said.

"Governor," Kerney replied. Springer's grip was firm.

"Take a seat. You know Captain Howell."

"I do." Kerney settled on the couch opposite the governor and smiled at Howell, who nodded stiffly and quickly sat.

Springer continued to smile, resumed his seat, and plopped his boots back on the coffee table. Handmade, they probably cost no less than a thousand dollars.

"I knew your parents," Springer said. "Served with your daddy on the state cattle growers board. They were fine people."

"I'm glad you feel that way about them, Governor," Kerney replied.

"I do," Springer said somberly. "The fact is, I talked to your father just before you came back from Vietnam. He was proud of you, and damn happy you were coming home alive and in one piece. It about broke my heart when they got killed in that traffic accident on their way to meet you at the airport. It was a terrible thing." Springer shook his head and smiled sadly.

"Yes, sir, it was," Kerney replied, waiting for more.

"And a terrible loss for you."

Kerney nodded in agreement, but he doubted that Springer knew the depth of his loss. His parents had been his best friends.

"My foreman tells me you helped out on a couple of our roundups when you were caretaking a spread down in Galisteo. You should have stopped by and introduced yourself."

"I didn't have the opportunity, Governor."

"Roundup is a busy time," Springer agreed. "Well, no matter. Here you are now, and I'm glad to have you on my team. Andy Baca said he had to strong-arm you into taking the job as his deputy."

"I didn't put up that much of a fight," Kerney said.

Springer chuckled. "That's good to hear. Where do we stand with the investigation?"

"It's just getting under way," Kerney answered. "We've made contact with organizations that track stolen art on the international markets, and have conducted a series of interviews with your staff and others who work at the Roundhouse. So far we have no suspects."

"Andy Baca said it had the look of an inside job."

"I'm inclined to agree. But if we don't develop a suspect fairly soon, we'll have to rethink that hypothesis."

"It doesn't sound promising," Governor Springer said.

"It's going to take a lot of legwork. We might get a break if we can find the man who killed Officer Rogoff."

Springer stroked his chin. "You think the two crimes are related?"

"I do. Based on an analysis of the videotape from the camera in Officer Rogoff's unit, there's a good chance the vehicle contained a corpse wrapped in a blanket."

"That doesn't tie the crimes together," Springer said, still smiling warmly.

"I'm hoping that the vehicle and the corpse will provide that link, once we find them. According to our analysis, the van could have been used in the heist. It fits the profile exactly."

"Aren't you dismissing the possibility that Officer Rogoff's murder occurred because he stumbled upon a completely separate crime?"

"You're right, Governor, except for one additional fact. Rogoff's killer is a man named Nick Palazzi. He's got a long rap sheet that includes arrests for contract killings, armed robbery, and drug smuggling. Palazzi is a hired hand and a career criminal. He's not stupid, but on the other hand, he's not a master crook either. Our thinking is that Palazzi, along with the two men who were with him, were operating under orders."

"That sounds like pure speculation."

"Our profile analysis of Palazzi should be fairly accurate. We have a good deal of background information on him."

"We need an arrest here, Chief, not an analysis."

"Every available officer is working the case, Governor. We'll chase down any leads that surface."

"That's what I want to hear. I understand you've asked Captain Howell to find out who left female pubic hairs on my office carpet." Springer's friendly smile turned icy.

"Captain Howell may have misunderstood my request."

Howell shook his head in disagreement. "I don't think I did, Chief. When the governor asked me what you wanted me to do, I told him exactly what the assignment was."

"That's good to know," Kerney replied, turning back to Springer. "But just to keep the issue clearly understood, I asked Captain Howell to identify any blond females who had access to your office last week while you were out of town."

Springer shook his head in disagreement. "I don't see the sense to it."

"We have physical evidence that may or may not lead us to a suspect or a witness, Governor."

"I don't want anybody playing up some nonsense of sexual indiscretion among my staff."

"I'm confident Captain Howell has been discreet in his interviews," Kerney replied.

"I asked Vance to hold up until I had a chance to talk with you," Springer said, studying Kerney's face. Kerney didn't react. "I don't want this investigation sidetracked into an imbroglio that could damage my administration."

"That is not the intent."

"That's what I want to make sure of. I expect the matter to be handled sensitively."

"May Captain Howell proceed?" Kerney asked.

Springer nodded. "But if Vance does find that somebody on my staff has been getting their meat where they get their potatoes, I don't want to read about it in the newspapers."

"I'm sure Captain Howell will share that information strictly on a need-to-know basis, so that you can deal with the matter confidentially, as you see fit," Kerney answered.

Harper Springer eyed Kerney for any hint of sarcasm, but all he got was a strong feeling that the man didn't intimidate easily. He didn't like too much of that trait in the people who worked for him.

"I want daily progress reports sent to my chief of staff. Tell Andy Baca if he needs money to pay for any overtime to let me know."

"I'll pass your message along." Kerney stood.

Harper Springer got to his feet. His friendly smile came back as he looked up at Kerney. "Keep up the good work, Chief."

"It was a pleasure to meet you, Governor. When can I expect your report, Captain Howell?"

"I'll get right on it, Chief."

FOR HIS role as a detective, Fletcher Hartley had dressed carefully. He wore a blue oxford shirt over a white turtleneck, a black wool sport coat, and gray slacks. As a concession to the unpredictable November weather, he carried an umbrella.

In the window of the two-hundred-year-old building on Canyon Road that housed the Frank Bailey Gallery, Fletcher inspected his reflection. All in all, it was an ensemble that would have made Noël Coward proud. To complete the picture he needed a cigarette to hold carelessly in his hand. For a moment, Fletcher regretted that he'd stopped smoking.

He made his entrance, breezed past the gallery manager and the nicely hung, perfectly lit art, and walked to the office at the rear of the building.

Bailey's office had a wall of windows that looked out on a remnant of vacant land that two hundred years ago had been part of a sheep pasture.

Frank Bailey stood behind a tall antique clerk's desk that had been salvaged from the basement of a nineteenth-century New England textile factory. Stacked against the walls were shipping crates, framed paintings, and piles of art books.

Bailey nodded at Fletcher and kept talking on the telephone as he scribbled notes to himself on the slanted desktop. Bailey sold high-end Western artists, specializing in Charles Russell, Frederic Remington, Joseph Henry Sharp, and Maynard Dixon. Most of his business came from wealthy out-of-state collectors. There simply wasn't any other way to run a successful gallery in Santa Fe.

Content to wait for Bailey, Fletcher settled into one of the two overstuffed chairs positioned to give the most pleasing view of the pasture. He unbuttoned his jacket and adjusted his cuffs. So far, Fletcher's efforts had yielded nothing, but gossiping with old friends had been entertaining nonetheless.

Bailey hung up the receiver and joined Fletcher. He had long, prematurely gray hair that he wore in a ponytail, green eyes, high cheekbones, and an angular face. In his early forties, he was considered very attractive by the ladies from Dallas and Houston who shopped Santa Fe. His appeal had cost him two marriages.

"It's been a wasted day, Fletcher," he said. "The rich just don't seem to be practicing trickle-down economics right now. What brings you out to see me?"

"I'm assisting the police with their inquiries," Fletcher replied.

"Really?"

"Yes. The art rip-off at the governor's suite." Quite pleased with his use of the correct slang word, Fletcher decided he had to learn more cop jargon from Kerney.

"Wasn't that something?" Frank said, shaking his head in disbelief.

"Have you had any recent inquiries to buy or sell a Sharp or a Dixon?"

"Unfortunately, no."

"Has anybody asked for a market appraisal of either artist's work?"

"Not recently."

"Have you had any walk-in browsers who seemed a little peculiar or out of place?"

"This is Santa Fe, Fletcher. Everybody's peculiar."

"Have you heard any gossip?"

"I've heard a rumor that you have a cop living with you. Have you snagged a hunk to comfort you in your old age?"

"If only that were true." Fletcher sighed. "He's a friend, not a lover, and he's staying with me, not living with me. He's very straight and not at all homophobic.

"Now," Fletcher continued, "no matter how interesting I might be, I am not the subject of this conversation. Have you heard any chitchat about the robbery?"

"No."

"It's not the response I was hoping for," Fletcher said as he started to rise from the chair.

"But I can't wait to tell Amanda Talley that she was right," Bailey added.

Fletcher settled back. "Isn't she that leggy young woman who works at the fine arts museum?"

"That's her. She predicted the robbery would happen," Frank replied. "She went on and on about how easy it would be to walk off with the collection."

"When was this?"

"During the Georgia O'Keeffe Museum fund-raiser last month at the Rancho Caballo clubhouse. I fully expected to see you there."

"I was hanging a show in Seattle. Mostly my smaller pieces. It did very well. What exactly did Amanda Talley say?"

"Just that she had misgivings about the lack of security. She didn't think the works were properly protected."

"Did she share her concerns with others besides you?" Fletcher asked.

"The subject came up while a small group of us were having a drink in the bar."

"Who was there?"

"Bucky Watson, Henry and Carol Jergerson, Roger Springer, and a couple of Rancho Caballo homeowners. I don't recall their names. Bucky knew this one guy who hung out with us. A Spanish or Mexican fellow who seemed interested in Amanda."

"Anyone else?" Fletcher asked.

"Not that I recall. We had one drink together and then everybody went their separate ways."

"How well do you know Amanda?"

"We dated briefly when she first came to town. She's a knockout. She has brains, a great body, and likes to party. I think she's looking for a rich husband so she can quit her day job and be a trophy wife. She'll do it with style, too."

"Would you say she has a criminal mind?"

Frank laughed. "Amanda? I don't think she weighs herself down with scruples, but I don't think she'd go that far, either."

"Is she your garden-variety gold digger?"

"Not at all. Amanda's hard to pigeonhole. She's tough-minded, very clear about who she is, and doesn't play any dumb games. Whoever corrals her gets a prize."

"You sound smitten."

"I'm just one of many strewn in her path."

"Would you mind writing down the people you just mentioned?" Fletcher asked, holding out pen and paper. "I'm terrible with names."

"You're such a damn princess, Fletcher," Bailey said, taking the proffered items.

Fletcher smiled broadly. "Someone has to set the standards for the common folk to emulate."

•　　•　　•

CARLOS RUIZ was glad to be back in Mexico. Santa Fe's wintry November weather didn't suit him, and the late-afternoon Juárez sun warmed his bones. Little more than three hundred miles separated the two cities, but they were worlds apart in climate.

There was no answer when he knocked at the door of the Juárez apartment Nick Palazzi shared with his Mexican girlfriend. That suited Carlos just fine. Inside the apartment he could hear the two chattering monkeys Palazzi's whore kept as pets. He hated those fucking monkeys; they were always climbing all over him and sitting in his lap whenever he had to stop by on business for DeLeon. Before he turned away, he thought about breaking in to shoot the ugly little fuckers just for the hell of it.

At the Little Turtle, DeLeon's nightclub and gaming establishment, Carlos scanned the room looking for Palazzi. The crystal chandeliers above the gambling tables were dimmed low and a full house of players spilled over to the long antique bar and the nearby dining tables under the mezzanine. Carlos looked up at the mezzanine. Palazzi and his whore sat at a table near the railing, engrossed in conversation.

Before Carlos could move to the staircase, he was stopped by three of DeLeon's friends, who wanted to know if Enrique was back in town. He answered politely, keeping an eye on Nick, who caught sight of him, waved, and came down the mezzanine stairs to meet him.

"What's up, Carlos?" Palazzi asked, studying Ruiz carefully. Even with DeLeon's reassurance on the phone that everything was all right, Ruiz's unexpected appearance made him uneasy.

"The *patrón* wants the body moved to Mexico and the van recovered, if possible."

"No problem," Nick said. "I can take you to both."

"Don Enrique wants you to stay put," Carlos said. "It would be too much of a risk for you to go back right now. Tell me where they are and I will do it."

"Is DeLeon pissed?"

"No," Carlos answered. "He understands that you had no choice in the matter."

"You'll need a driver for the van," Nick said hopefully.

"I can't take you with me, Nick," Carlos said with a smile as he led Palazzi through the back door to the old stone warehouse at the rear of the Little Turtle. "You killed a gringo cop. You have to stay in Mexico. Just tell me where I need to go, and enjoy yourself with your *chicha.*" He closed the soundproof door and walked Nick to the loading dock.

"The van is parked at a Wal-Mart in Silver City, on the side of the building," Nick said.

"And the body?"

"In the Black Range on State Road 152 there's a big sign that says Emory Pass. You can't miss it. Walk straight behind the sign about a hundred yards. I stashed the body there and covered it with rocks. Facundo helped me carry it. He knows exactly where it is."

"I'll take Facundo with me," Carlos said. "*Gracias,* Nick. Go have a good time."

When Palazzi turned to leave, Carlos reached out and broke his neck.

AT QUITTING time, Andy's secretary brought Kerney the typed transcript of Robert Cordova's statement. He stood by the conference room windows watching the last brush stroke in a red sky change to twilight, and thought about Robert's account of the rape of Nita Lassiter. Robert's recall, while disjointed, had been fresh and detailed, as though it had happened days instead of years ago. Kerney stayed at the window and read through the meat of Robert's statement.

KK: *"Robert, tell me what happened on May 18, 1980."*

RC: *"Addie and I—"*

KK: *"Can you identify Addie more precisely?"*

RC: *"Anita Lassiter. Her nickname was Addie when I lived with her family. That's what I call her."*

KK: *"Go on."*

RC: *"It has a big head with round spots for the body. And ears and little feet."*

KK: *"Back up, Robert. What are you talking about?"*

RC: *"The snake, man."*

KK: *"Let's start over. Were you with Addie—Nita Lassiter—on May 18, 1980?"*

RC: *"Yeah. After school, Addie and me went snake hunting. I wasn't crazy then. I was pretty cool. Had a lot of friends. Everybody liked me."*

KK: *"Where did you and Addie go?"*

RC: *"Serpent Gate."*

KK: *"Tell me about Serpent Gate."*

RC: *"I already told you. It has ears and little feet, just like the one on Pop Shaffer's fence."*

KK: *"Where is it?"*

RC: *"Out of town. Snakes live there. Addie says it's because of the gophers and mice. Snakes eat them."*

KK: *"And there's a serpent like the one on Pop Shaffer's fence?"*

RC: *"It's identical. Some Indian put it there hundreds of years ago. It's on a big boulder. There's lots of other stuff scratched and painted in the rocks."*

KK: *"Rock art?"*

RC: *"Yeah."*

KK: *"What happened at Serpent Gate?"*

RC: "He kept saying, 'Do you like my snake, Addie? Tell me you like it.' Stuff like that."

KK: "Slow down, Robert. Who are you talking about?"

RC: "Paul Gillespie. He fucked her, man. Had her pinned to the ground. Raped her, man. Her panties were down at her ankles. Kept saying 'Jesus Christ, you have a tight pussy.' He beat me up, man. Bad. I passed out for a minute or two."

KK: "Was he alone?"

RC: "Yeah. He had a rifle. I should have killed him. Addie made me promise not to tell anybody."

KK: "Maybe Addie wanted to have sex with Gillespie."

RC: "Fuck you. Addie isn't like that."

KK: "How do you know?"

RC: "He held the rifle under her chin. Said she had to fuck him or he'd shoot both of us. Then he slapped her. He was drunk."

KK: "How drunk?"

RC: "Well, maybe not drunk. But he had a six-pack of beer with him."

KK: "Can you remember anything else?"

RC: "No. Will you take me to jail now like you promised?"

KK: "In a minute. Nita means a lot to you, doesn't she?"

RC: "She's my best friend. She doesn't let anyone but me call her Addie."

KK: "Is that why you didn't want to tell me you saw Nita outside the police station the night Gillespie was killed?"

RC: "Who says I saw her?"

KK: "Nita does."

RC: "She's lying. I didn't see nothing."

KK: "You need to tell me the whole truth, Robert."

RC: "I want to go to jail now."

KK: "Nita wants you to tell the truth."

RC: "Satan killed Paul Gillespie."

KK: "Try to remember what you saw outside the police station."

RC: "Crazy people don't have to remember."
KK: "We're going to have to talk about this again."
RC: "No way."
KK: "You're one tough customer, Robert."
RC: "That's right."

Kerney stared out the window, thinking about Nita Lassiter, her pregnant daughter, and Robert, wondering how many other victims Paul Gillespie had left behind.

SERGEANT Gilbert Martinez, the lead agent on the art theft case, stood in the open doorway of the conference room waiting for the new deputy chief to notice him. Chief Kerney stared out the window with a sheaf of papers in his hand, apparently lost in thought.

For ten of his fifteen years on the force, Martinez had been assigned to the criminal investigations unit in Albuquerque with officers and supervisors he knew well. His promotion to sergeant and transfer to Santa Fe had come through two months ago. Now he had a new boss he didn't know, responsibility for a case that could turn into a political time bomb, and information that made him believe the bomb might be ticking.

Over the years, Gilbert had watched some damn fine agents and investigators get demoted back to patrol duties or dumped at a desk job because they pissed off a department bigwig or politician. And while the brass bragged about having the best cop shop in the state—which wasn't an exaggeration—it was still a bureaucracy, where people covered their asses and shit flowed downhill.

Two brief meetings with Kerney had not yet told Martinez what kind of cop the deputy chief would turn out to be when faced with the tough decisions. He was about to find out.

Tired of waiting to be noticed, Gilbert cleared his throat to get Kerney's attention.

"Come in, Sergeant," Kerney said as he turned, spotted Martinez, smiled, and walked to the conference table. "Grab a seat."

The chief looked tired and his limp seemed more pronounced.

"Thank you, sir."

Tall, slender, with blue eyes and light brown hair graying at the temples, Martinez didn't fit the popular stereotype of a Hispanic. An unruffled man with a gentle way of speaking, Gilbert looked more like a college professor than a cop. He sat across from Kerney and opened a thick file.

"We've got a potential hot potato on our hands, Chief."

"What's the problem?"

"I talked to a journalist with some reliable sources. He relayed some rumors floating around about Roger Springer, the governor's nephew, that may be of interest."

"What kind of rumors?" Kerney asked.

"Springer's marriage fell apart midway during the governor's first term. Springer is a lawyer. He was serving as deputy general counsel on the governor's staff at the time. Rumor has it that Springer was screwing around with some of the women in the governor's office. Springer left his position to enter private practice with a firm here in town. According to my source, the governor called in a few favors to keep the situation hushed up."

"How did he do that?" Kerney asked.

"The two women in question got promoted into jobs at state agencies. One now works in the health department and the other one has a position at the state library."

"Go on," Kerney said.

"From what I've been told, it's like Springer never left his uncle's staff. His law firm has a consultant contract with the governor's office. He's handling litigation with Texas over the apportionment of water rights in the Pecos River. He has free and unrestricted access to the governor's suite."

"Does that include underground parking and use of the private elevator in the Roundhouse?" Kerney asked.

"According to the night janitors, it does. Springer sometimes shows up late at night, with different women in tow. It has happened three or four times."

"Are any of them blondes?"

"I don't know," Martinez replied.

"Is he currently dating anybody on the governor's staff?"

"If I can believe what I've been told, he's not."

"What else have you learned about Springer?"

"He runs with a fast crowd of thirty-something yuppies. He drinks at the best watering holes, gets invited to the most prestigious gallery openings, has opening night tickets to the opera, dates a lot of different women—that sort of thing. He lives high off the hog, but supposedly can afford it."

"Have you verified his financial status?"

"Not yet," Gilbert replied. "One more thing, Chief. Some of the people Springer hangs with are known recreational drug users. Mostly cocaine, hashish, and marijuana."

"Is Springer a user?"

"Not as far as I know."

"When is the last time Roger Springer was seen at the Roundhouse with a woman?" Kerney asked.

"I don't know."

"You've read the lab report on findings from the crime scene?"

"I have," Gilbert answered.

"Maybe we should find out if Springer's been dating any blondes."

Martinez nodded.

"Meet with Springer personally, Sergeant. Tell him we have

reason to believe that he's been using the governor's office for late-night romantic rendezvous. Reassure him that his conversation with you is strictly off the record, at this point. Let's see where it takes us."

"This could get me reamed, Chief."

"That's not going to happen," Kerney replied. "If you catch any flak from Springer, bail out and dump it back in my lap. I'll take the heat. If he's sharp, he'll put up a smoke screen to protect his uncle, but you still might learn something."

Martinez studied Kerney, who looked him dead in the eye without flinching or fidgeting. Cops were no better than anybody else when it came to telegraphing lies, and Kerney was playing it straight with him. That was good enough for Gilbert.

"You've got a deal, Chief."

"One more thing, Sergeant," Kerney said. "I don't think the governor personally selected all the artwork for his office. From what I saw at his ranch, his taste doesn't include Georgia O'Keeffe. Her works were the most valuable of the lot. Worth almost half of the total haul. Send somebody to the fine arts museum in the morning. I want to know who put the collection together and when it was installed. Talk to that person."

"What are we looking for here, Chief?"

"Clues, Sergeant. I've been told that occasionally curators decide to appropriate art for themselves. If that's the case, wouldn't it be smart to move the works you wanted to steal to a less secure setting before you swiped them?"

"I'll get on it."

CARLOS sat in the Range Rover across the street and watched a tow truck back up to the van parked at the side of the Wal-Mart in Silver City. Two city police units were stationed in the parking lot to keep curious people away, and a cop in civilian clothes stood next to the van directing the tow truck. His unmarked police car idled nearby.

"We got here too late," Facundo said indifferently.

Carlos shot him a dirty look, but in the darkness Facundo missed it.

"Do you want to leave?" Facundo asked.

"Not yet," Carlos answered. DeLeon had told him to retrieve the van, which now appeared impossible. What would DeLeon want him to do? "We'll wait," Carlos added.

The van couldn't be traced back to DeLeon, of that Carlos was certain. But the *patrón* was a man of exacting standards, who viewed an inability to carry out orders as negligence, regardless of the circumstances.

Carlos stopped grappling with the problem. It was too confusing. His best bet was to call DeLeon and ask for instructions. But he would wait until he knew exactly where the police were taking the vehicle before disturbing the *patrón*.

The tow truck pulled away with the van and Carlos nudged Facundo. "Stay at a safe distance behind the police car," he ordered.

Facundo waited until the tow truck was a block away before he pulled onto the street. The flashing blue lights on the truck made it easy to follow. At the police station, the truck turned and disappeared behind the back of the building. Facundo continued on to the next intersection before doubling back and coasting to a stop at the curb.

"Wait here," Carlos said as he got out of the vehicle.

He walked behind an adjacent building and stood in the shadows. The tow truck operator was winching down the van at the back of a parking area inside a vehicle impound lot. No one else was in sight. Three empty police cars, including the one that had followed the truck to the station, were parked near the rear entrance.

Carlos took the cellular phone from his jacket pocket,

flipped it open, and dialed DeLeon's private Santa Fe number. As soon as DeLeon came on the line, he explained the situation.

"You did well to call me," DeLeon said when Carlos finished. "Is there any way you can safely get to the vehicle without being seen?"

"Yes, *patrón*. It is not under guard. But I believe the police will search it soon."

"Can you drive it away?"

"No, *patrón*. It is parked in an impound lot behind a locked gate."

"Burn the van," DeLeon instructed. "Do not allow yourself to get caught. Do not allow the police to see the Range Rover."

"Yes, *patrón*."

Carlos rang off and studied the layout. He would climb the impound fence at the rear of the lot, and use darkness for concealment. He went back to the Range Rover, took the road atlas away from Facundo, and tore out a handful of pages.

"Drive away when I leave," Carlos ordered. "Do not come back here. I will meet you at the all-night convenience store on the main street in one hour. We passed it on our way here."

"I know where it is," Facundo answered, as he slipped the vehicle into gear and pulled away.

Carlos waited until Facundo was out of sight before returning to the back of the building next to the station. The tow truck was gone and no one was in sight. Staying in the shadows as much as possible, he made his way quickly to the rear of the impound lot, climbed the fence, and moved in a crouch to the van.

He reached under the fender near the fuel tank, found the flexible hose to the tank, and slashed it with a knife, opening a wide, deep cut. He stuffed some twisted pages from the atlas down into the tank until they were saturated with gas. He pulled them out and repeated the process until he had enough to make a fuse that ran from the tank to the ground.

Maybe he had three or four seconds to get away once he lit

the paper. He judged the distance to the back fence. He could just reach it before the van blew up. Somebody might catch a glimpse of him, but he would be too far away to be identified.

He lit the fuse and started running at full tilt. The van exploded into flames and heat seared the back of his neck. He was safely over the fence and in deep shadows when the first cop burst out of the back door of the police station, carrying a fire extinguisher.

Carlos turned down an empty side street and trotted away.

6

Kerney was two blocks away from Fletcher's house and some much needed sack time when he got the news that the van used in the shooting of Officer Rogoff had been found in Silver City. He hit the siren and ran Code Three back to headquarters. Within minutes of his arrival the Silver City PD dispatcher called to report that the van had been torched and heavily damaged by persons unknown.

Kerney reviewed the background information on Nick Palazzi. While serving time in a California prison, Palazzi had joined the American Nazi Party. Any known party members in the Silver City area needed to be identified and interviewed immediately. His arrest for a contract killing had been tied to a territory dispute among drug traffickers in Southern California. Intelligence information needed to be updated on trafficking in southwestern New Mexico. Street dealers had to be rounded up and grilled. Palazzi was known to favor prostitutes as girlfriends. Local hookers should be contacted and interviewed.

He put together a few more facts on Palazzi, assembled the response team, sketched out the information, and fielded some questions before sending them on their way. A plane waited at the airport to fly the team on the forty-minute hop to Silver City.

He sank into a chair, thinking it was more than likely that—assuming Palazzi torched the van—he would be across the Mexican border before the plane touched down at the airport. But unless crime scene techs could develop some solid evidence from the van, searching for Palazzi was the only card he had to play.

He fleetingly thought about a good night's sleep, pushed himself upright, and went to make a pot of coffee. His patched-together gut wouldn't like it, but the caffeine would keep him awake.

As he watched the coffee brew, Kerney brooded over the fact that tying Officer Rogoff's murder in with the art theft could have been a mistake on his part. If the two crimes weren't connected, it would mean starting over from square one. He carried a coffee cup back to the conference room and stared at the telephone. He doubted the team would have anything to report for at least several hours.

He sat and read through the agents' field interview reports, looking for anything out of the ordinary. Nothing jumped out at him. He put the reports aside, picked up a clean sheet of paper, drew a line down the middle, and started separating out the facts of the two cases. If he had to give up the theory of connecting Palazzi to the theft, he needed to be ready to move as quickly as possible.

• • •

KERNEY caught a quick nap on Andy's couch and at dawn went outside to clear his head. The reports from Silver City had been encouraging. The interior of the van had been badly burned, but fingerprints had been lifted from the vehicle and some human hairs had been found on a piece of unburned carpet.

On the lawn next to the law enforcement academy, a class of new recruits were preparing for an early morning run. A light dusting of snow covered the ground and the temperature hovered near freezing. High in the Sangre de Cristo Mountains, snow clouds masked the peaks, but the foothills were glistening pale pink in the early morning light.

Kerney walked to the memorial for slain police officers. The state and national flags bracketing the monument flapped lazily in a slight gust. Paul Gillespie's name had been chiseled into the marble. He wondered if it truly belonged there.

He walked back to headquarters thinking about the evidence found in the van. The discovery of human hair was particularly intriguing. But until he could identify a blond-haired woman who had access to the govenor's suite, he wouldn't be any closer to solving the crime.

GILBERT MARTINEZ waited in the reception area of the law firm Roger Springer had joined after leaving his post at the governor's office. The building, two blocks from the plaza, had a brass plaque listing the names of the partners. All were prominent Anglos connected to the state's political machinery.

Born and raised in Santa Fe, Gilbert had been weaned on family accounts about Dawson Cobb, the founder of the firm; how Cobb had screwed Gilbert's ancestors out of a Spanish land grant after the Civil War with a court decision by an Anglo jury in Cobb's favor. Only a few thousand acres remained in the family after Cobb took possession of the huge grant and the water rights that went with it. Even those acres had been sold to pay the legal fees of the family's Anglo lawyer, who soon became Cobb's partner.

With no land to hold them, the family scattered. But the story of Dawson Cobb stuck in the minds of the Martinez family like a cactus thorn festering for over 130 years.

Wasn't it Balzac who said behind every great fortune was a great crime?

Gilbert had done some additional research on Roger Springer. A Big Ten graduate with an Ivy League law degree, Springer had worked for one of the New Mexico senators in Washington before returning home with a new bride. He and his ex-wife, an architect, had no children, and the divorce settlement appeared to be amicable. However, a domestic court clerk told Gilbert that Springer and his wife had squabbled like brats over the division of the joint property, and the judge had privately chewed them out in his chambers.

Twenty minutes past the time of the appointment, Springer made his appearance, striding out of the double doors that led to the inner sanctum. He gave Gilbert the family glad hand, flashed his teeth in a winning candidate's smile, and added an apologetic shrug.

"Sorry to keep you waiting so long, Sergeant," Springer said. "I just finished a telephone conference with the governor's chief counsel. It went on much longer than I thought it would."

"I hate to bother you, Mr. Springer. I know you're a busy man." Gilbert studied Springer's eighty-dollar haircut and expensive Italian suit. "Do you have time for me now?"

"Of course," Springer replied, gesturing toward the double doors. "Are you making any headway with the investigation?" He took Gilbert down a wide hallway filled with framed photographs of old Santa Fe at the turn of the century.

"It's still in the preliminary stage," Gilbert replied.

"I thought it might be," Springer said, standing aside his open office door to let Martinez enter. "No leads?"

"We're working on it," Gilbert answered.

The office, bigger than Chief Baca's, was uncluttered and functional, with expensive furniture and nice art on the walls. An older man sat in one of four chairs placed in front of a large window.

"Make yourself comfortable," Springer said. "I'd like you to meet Sherman Cobb. Mr. Cobb is the senior partner in the firm."

Cobb smiled a greeting and Gilbert nodded in return.

"I don't have any questions for Mr. Cobb," Gilbert said.

Springer laughed. "I didn't think you would. The firm likes to have another lawyer present whenever the police meet with an attorney. It helps avoid misunderstandings."

Springer dropped into a chair and gestured for Martinez to do the same.

"I had hoped to speak with you on a confidential basis," Gilbert said as he sat.

Springer flashed a smile. "Feel free to do so."

"On matters of a personal nature," Gilbert added.

Springer raised an eyebrow. "And what might those matters be, Sergeant Martinez?"

Gilbert shifted his weight. "Issues which could create political repercussions for your uncle."

"You have my full attention," Springer said.

"Since leaving the governor's staff, have you ever made a visit to your uncle's office that was not either of a business or family nature?"

Springer's expression turned quizzical. "I'm not sure I'm following your question, Sergeant."

"Several times you've been seen at the Roundhouse late at night accompanied by different women."

Springer laughed. "Oh, that. Yes, I've taken some dates on impromptu tours of the governor's offices."

"Did you take anyone there last week?"

"No."

"Can you tell me the names of the women you took there in the past?"

"How can that information have any value to your investigation?"

Gilbert chose his words carefully: "It's possible that a man and a woman had a romantic interlude in Governor Springer's office last week while he was out of the state."

"A romantic interlude?" Springer repeated.

"Of a sexual nature. It would help if you could remember the names of the women who went with you on the tours, Mr. Springer."

"You're joking."

"No, I'm not," Gilbert replied. "We need to talk to everybody who has had access to the governor's office, no matter what the circumstances."

Springer clasped his hands and tapped his index fingers together several times. "Of course you do," he finally said. He got up, walked to his desk, opened a leatherbound appointment book, flipped through the pages, wrote a note, and brought it to Gilbert.

Gilbert read the names. "Do either of these ladies have blond hair?"

"No."

"Are you presently dating any blondes?"

"No, I'm not dating any blondes."

Gilbert slipped Springer's note into a pocket and looked over at Sherman Cobb, who had been as quiet as a church mouse. "Do you have any questions for me, Mr. Cobb?"

Cobb smiled cordially. "I know you'll do your very best to bring the investigation to a successful conclusion," he said.

Gilbert decided he couldn't tell Cobb to stuff the patronizing attitude, and stood up. "Thank you for your time."

"Not at all," Springer replied with a smile that seemed a little wary.

Outside Springer's office, Gilbert buttoned up. The snow-storm had moved off the mountains and into the city. The air was still, and a thick curtain of wet, fat snowflakes drifted slowly down from a low blanket of clouds. There wasn't much traffic and few people were out. The city had a quiet, sleepy feel to it.

Gilbert walked to the corner, crossed the street against the light, and headed for the plaza. In the lobby of the La Fonda Hotel he used a pay phone and tried without success to reach Springer's lady friends. He left messages on their answering machines and went back outside. He crossed through the plaza to the fine arts museum and stood for a moment by the old Spitz Clock on the corner.

All the old stores where the locals once shopped were gone, replaced by tourist shops and galleries. The lovely plaza and the beautiful old buildings surrounding it no longer served as the heart of the city for the citizens. Instead, it had become nothing more than a charming, high-priced outdoor mall for the thousands of visitors pouring into the city to shop, vacation, and sightsee.

Gilbert let his resentment over the change surface. But his irritation was really with Cobb and Springer, and their air of superiority and condescension.

He shrugged it off and went into the museum. It was time to find out who put the art collection together for the governor's suite.

KERNEY had kicked off his blanket. Stretched out on his back on the twin bed in the guest house, his feet dangled over the edge. He wore only boxer shorts, and while the scar from the gunshot wound and the surgery on his stomach looked ghastly, Kerney's body was lean and muscular.

Reluctantly, Fletcher shook Kerney awake. His eyes opened instantly.

"You again?"

"With my deepest regrets," Fletcher answered with a smile. "A very cranky prosecutor named Wesley Marshall gave me an urgent message for you."

Kerney sat up. Fletcher wore a paint-splattered apron over blue jeans and a shirt. He had obviously been at work in the studio.

"What was it?" Kerney asked.

Fletcher consulted the piece of paper in his hand. "Mr. Marshall said that you are to be deposed by defense counsel at three this afternoon, and to meet him at his office."

"What time is it now?"

"Noon."

Kerney got to his feet. Three hours sleep was better than none, but he still felt stiff and groggy.

"Aren't you overdoing it a bit?" Fletcher asked. "You look haggard and wrung out."

"It was a long night."

"So I gather. I tried to wait up for you. I have information that might be of value to our investigation."

Kerney walked toward the bathroom. "First things first, Fletcher. Do you have any food in your refrigerator?"

"Would a nice omelette do?"

"Perfect. I'll be there in five minutes."

The kitchen, a wide room at the front of the house, had an arched entryway leading to the dining room, and a cobalt blue Mexican tile splash guard on the wall behind the sink, stove, and countertops. There were no cupboards in the kitchen. A series of open shelves held glasses, plates, canisters, and jars. Pots and pans hung from suspended racks, and a huge pantry enclosed by hand-carved doors filled most of the far wall. In the middle of the kitchen sat an antique Spanish Colonial table with thick hand-turned legs, big enough for a family to eat at one end after the meal had been prepared at the other.

In front of a woven place mat was a small Waterford vase containing a single, showy bronze chrysanthemum. Fletcher's best silverware and a fresh linen napkin completed the arrangement.

Kerney sat as Fletcher eased the omelette onto a plate and brought it to him.

"All this for me?" Kerney asked. "It's far too elegant."

"Meals should be civilized events," Fletcher replied. "And it's just my small way of saying thank you for all the fun I had yesterday. I honestly think I would have made a superb detective."

"What brings you to this modest opinion?" Kerney asked, as he took a bite of the omelette. It was perfectly done.

"Because I believe—modestly, as you put it—that I have uncovered new information which may further our investigation."

"You have my full attention."

Fletcher beamed a smile at Kerney. "Good. My informant, Frank Bailey, owns a gallery on Canyon Road. He recently attended a social function where he overheard a woman named Amanda Talley complain about the lack of protection for the art collection in the governor's office. Bailey said that la Talley went on at some length about how easy it would be to steal it."

"That's excellent work, Fletcher. Just who is Amanda Talley?"

"Ms. Talley works at the fine arts museum. She supervised the selection of the art for the governor's offices."

Kerney swallowed another bite. "Maybe you *should* have been a detective. Did you get a description of the woman? Is she a blonde?"

Fletcher nodded. "Indeed, she is. Frank Bailey seems to know a good deal about her personal life."

"I'll have somebody talk to him."

The doorbell rang and Kerney took the opportunity to finish his meal while Fletcher went to answer it. Fletcher returned towing Sergeant Gilbert Martinez by the hand.

"Do you know this dear boy?" he asked Kerney. He guided Gilbert to a chair. "He's come looking for you."

"Yes, I do."

Martinez flushed slightly and sat.

"Well, I've known him all his life," Fletcher announced. "He grew up across the lane in that lovely two-story home. It broke my heart when his parents sold it and moved away. Such a delightful family."

Fletcher dipped into the chair next to Gilbert and patted his hand. "It's so good to see you. How do you know this Irish cop, Gilbert?" He waved Gilbert off before he could answer. "No, don't tell me. Let me guess. You must be the police chaplain. Although the fact that you're wearing a suit and tie raises some doubts in my mind."

"Chaplain?" Kerney asked.

Fletcher nodded. "Yes. The last time I saw Gilbert he was going off to a seminary in the Midwest to study for the priesthood. That was twenty years ago."

Gilbert smiled. "Well, I am a father. I have two daughters."

"Were you defrocked?" Fletcher asked. "Excommunicated? Tell me everything."

"Nothing that dramatic, Fletcher. I changed career paths. I'm a state police sergeant in criminal investigations."

"Unbelievable." Fletcher turned his gaze to Kerney. "He was the perfect altar boy. Angelic."

"Stop exaggerating," Gilbert said. "The old neighborhood doesn't look like it has changed too much."

"I try to keep the riffraff out."

"Who lives in my parents' old house?"

"It has changed hands five or six times since you moved away. The current owners are a New York couple. They use it as a vacation home. He's a book publisher and she's a literary agent. I've been thinking of approaching them with a proposal to write my memoirs."

"Maybe I should try to buy it back the next time it comes on the market."

"Would that you could."

"You don't think a sergeant's salary could swing it?"

"Perhaps you might want to wait until you get another promotion or two," Fletcher said.

Gilbert's laugh was bitter. "That, along with another full-time job, would probably get me a mortgage on the garage my father built." He turned to Kerney. "I'd like to bring you up to speed, Chief."

"What have you got, Sergeant?"

"My conversation with Roger Springer went basically nowhere, although I did get the names of two women he took on unofficial, late-night tours of the Roundhouse. He swears he wasn't there last week after hours, and the two women aren't blondes."

"What else?"

"A curator at the fine arts museum by the name of Amanda Talley—she's a blonde, by the way—picked out the art for the governor's office."

"I've already told Kevin about her," Fletcher announced.

Gilbert gave Kerney a perplexed look.

"Fletcher made a round of the galleries yesterday at my request," Kerney explained, "and Amanda Talley's name came up. It seems she did some public complaining about lax security for the art in the governor's office, and talked about how easy it would be to rip it off. What did you learn from her?"

"Nothing," Gilbert answered. "Talley started a vacation late last week. She's in Belize. She left a hotel number where she could be reached, and I called. She's on a three-day boat expedition, touring some wildlife sanctuaries off the coast. The boat's not due back until the day after tomorrow.

"One more thing, Chief," Gilbert added. "The three O'Keeffe paintings were due to be sent to the O'Keeffe Museum this week."

"Find out where Talley lives," Kerney ordered.

"She has an apartment on Yucca Road. I have the address. It's one of those big rental units."

"Have the apartment manager let you in. If you're questioned, treat it like a missing person case. See what you can turn up."

"Without a search warrant, whatever we find will be fruit from the poisoned tree. The courts won't admit it into evidence."

"Do a plain-view search only. Bring back a sample of any hairs you can find."

Gilbert nodded as Kerney stood. Fletcher held up a hand to keep Kerney from departing.

"Frank Bailey said that Amanda Talley was with Roger Springer and some other people the night she made her little speech," he said.

"That's very interesting," Kerney replied. "Did you get the names of the other people?"

"There was a local couple who dabble in collecting art, Bucky Watson, and a Spanish or Mexican gentleman. Frank wasn't sure which nationality he was."

"I need their names, Fletcher," Kerney said.

Fletcher made a dismissive gesture with his hand. "I have them written down somewhere."

Kerney nodded. "Give them to the sergeant." He switched his attention to Martinez. "I want deep background checks done on everybody who may have overheard what Talley said."

"You've got it, Chief."

"Allegedly, she was tipsy at the time," Fletcher added.

"Fletcher, tell Sergeant Martinez everything you learned from Frank Bailey."

"Of course."

"Meet with Bailey personally, Sergeant. Find out what else he knows and go over everything in detail with him."

"It's already on my list, Chief."

"Hook up with Chief Baca and fill him in."

"Will do."

"What's my next assignment?" Fletcher asked.

"Have you finished talking to gallery owners?" Kerney replied.

"The local ones are covered, but I need to start calling Albuquerque dealers."

"Do that, but pass any leads on to Sergeant Martinez. He'll assign men to do the follow-up interviews, if anything looks promising."

Fletcher's unhappiness showed on his face. "So, am I to be consigned to the back room with a telephone?"

Kerney stepped around the table and squeezed his old friend's shoulder. "Don't fuss, Fletcher. You're still my expert consultant on this case. I'd be lost without your help."

Kerney nodded at Gilbert and left the kitchen. Gilbert waited until Kerney's footsteps faded away before he asked the irresistible question that had formed in his mind.

"Tell me, Fletcher," he said in a low voice, "is Chief Kerney gay?"

Fletcher laughed deeply. "Not in this lifetime, I'm sorry to say," he answered.

AFTER burning the van, retrieving Amanda Talley's body at Emory Pass, and recrossing the border, Carlos dropped Facundo

and the body at the rancho in the desert DeLeon used as a landing field for drug shipments arriving from South America.
Facundo knew what to do with the body; he'd disposed of several in the past.

Carlos finished the long drive back to Santa Fe, parked the
Range Rover in the garage, and climbed the stairs with tired,
heavy feet, hoping DeLeon would be satisfied with his report.
One could never be sure how the *patrón* would react.

He found DeLeon at his desk in the library.

Enrique looked at Carlos kindly before smiling and gesturing
to an empty chair. "Sit down, Carlos, and relax. You look very
tired."

Only somewhat relieved by the *jefe*'s reaction, Carlos sat and
waited for DeLeon to question him.

"Did all go well?" DeLeon asked.

"Yes, *patrón*. All matters have been attended to. Nick is dead,
the woman's body has been disposed of, and the van has been
destroyed."

"I am pleased," Enrique said.

"Thank you, *patrón*."

"I have additional work for you after you have rested. You are
to assemble a complete dossier on Kevin Kerney. I want to know
where he lives, where his office is, and who his friends are. Full
particulars are essential. What is the arrangement of his living
quarters? His office? Is either place accessible? Does he maintain
a routine schedule? Does he travel the same route to and from
work? Is he seeing a woman? If so, would he be vulnerable when
he is with her?"

Carlos nodded. "I understand."

DeLeon pushed an envelope across the desk. "There is sufficient cash in the envelope to purchase a car which will not
attract attention. Buy it from a private party, so that you do not
have to register it immediately. Follow Kerney closely and take

exacting notes. Remember, he knows you. Do not expose your-self to him."

"I will be careful," Carlos replied, pushing his thumb against his upper plate.

DeLeon saw hate flash in Carlos's eyes. "You are to take no action against Kerney."

"As you wish, *patrón.*"

"Go now and get some sleep."

Carlos rose, picked up the envelope, and departed.

Enrique leaned back and thought about Kerney. His last attempt to have the policeman killed in Juárez failed when Ker-ney had been rescued by an undercover army investigator posing as a hunchback. That failure meant that Kerney had to be killed in just the right way to make everything balance out. Retaliation against an enemy was a normal part of doing business. But in this case, the reprisal would be all the more satisfying to achieve.

THE SNOWSTORM parked over the city stopped before it reached the Galisteo Basin. The escarpment that broke across the valley stood like a vast, ominous battlement looming over the rangeland.

For several years, while he recovered from the wounds that had forced him to retire from the Santa Fe PD, Kerney had lived and worked on a ranch in the basin with a view of the escarpment and the Ortiz Mountains in the far distance. He had never tired of the sweep of the land against the sky, and the ever-changing colors that painted the scenery new again each passing day.

Kerney made good time on a clear road. He arrived at the Torrance County courthouse in Estancia and went looking for Wesley Marshall, who wasn't in his office. He found Marshall, Bradley Pullings, and Gary Dalquist waiting for him in an empty jury room.

Pullings had brought in a co-counsel with impressive credentials. Dalquist specialized in capital murder cases. He was a short, older man with a deep, rumbling voice and a cherubic face. Criticized as a flamboyant showman, he had a strong track record of acquittals, dismissed cases, and reduced felony plea bargain agreements. Prosecutors hated to go up against him.

Marshall got up and walked to the door.

"Aren't you staying?" Kerney asked.

"Can't," Wesley replied. "I meet with the grand jury in ten minutes. You can handle it without me."

Kerney handed him a copy of Robert Cordova's statement.

"What's this?" Marshall asked in a surly tone as he stuffed the papers in a jacket pocket.

"Something you might want to read." He nodded in Dalquist's direction. "Looks like you have some serious opposition, Counselor."

Marshall grunted and walked away.

After a quick introduction, Kerney gave another copy of Robert's statement to Dalquist before the actual Q and A began. Dalquist read it, glanced at Kerney with a gleam in his eye, and passed the document to Pullings.

"Shall we get started?" Dalquist asked, his finger poised over the tape recorder.

"By all means," Kerney replied.

Dalquist was thorough in his questioning. He concentrated on the arrest procedure, Nita's mental state at the time both confessions were made, and the fact that Nita's first confession preceded Kerney's Miranda warning. He was looking for screwups he could use to have the confession thrown out.

Kerney's answers didn't please Dalquist.

Dalquist moved on to Nita and asked whether or not Kerney thought she knew what she was doing the night she shot Gillespie; Kerney declined the bait.

Finally, Dalquist turned to Robert's statement and grilled

Kerney about Cordova. Kerney obliged with the facts he had at hand.

"Do you think Mr. Cordova would make a competent witness?" Dalquist asked as he hit the stop button to the tape recorder.

"I'm not a psychiatrist," Kerney said. "But along that same line, has the psychological evaluation on Ms. Lassiter been completed?"

"The report will be in the judge's hands in the morning," Dalquist said. "I expect Ms. Lassiter to be released on bail by noon."

"That's good to know."

"Do you plan to force Robert Cordova to corroborate Ms. Lassiter's statement that he saw her leaving the murder scene?" Dalquist asked.

"I don't think I can force Robert to do anything," Kerney replied.

WESLEY MARSHALL waylaid Kerney on his way out of the building.

"Why the hell didn't you tell me you planned to interview Robert Cordova? The case fell under my jurisdiction when I signed off on the paperwork. You don't take this kind of action without my approval."

"Robert found me. I didn't go looking for him. Do you want all the facts, Counselor, or just those that will help you win the case?"

"I want them all, of course," Marshall said. "But you may have given Dalquist an early Christmas present."

"Wouldn't it be helpful to have Robert put Lassiter at the scene of the crime?"

"I'm not calling him as a witness. He's a mental case, for chrissake. Totally unreliable."

"Then impeach him on the witness stand, if Dalquist decides to use him for the defense."

"Don't do this again, Kerney. This is the second time you've messed with me."

"I think you're fairly new at the game, Mr. Marshall, so let me remind you of the drill. My responsibility to you consists of gathering all the facts, and that doesn't end until a decision is reached in a court of law."

"Whose side are you on?"

"This isn't about taking sides."

ANDY BACA was waiting for Kerney when he got back to the office. The clerical staff and most of the civilian workers were gone for the day and the building was quiet.

"You look wrecked," Andy said.

"I am." Kerney flopped on the couch and stretched his right leg. The throbbing in his reconstructed knee felt like sharp hammer blows.

"Bring me up to speed," Andy said as he sat with Kerney.

"What don't you know?"

"How did your meeting with the governor go?"

"I survived it," Kerney answered. "Springer is determined to keep any hint of staff sexual misconduct buried under the rug. Correction—buried under the carpet."

"He called and gave me the same marching orders."

"Did he sweeten the pot with money to pay for all the overtime we're burning?"

"He did. And he ordered me to reinstate Howell and the security detail to duty immediately."

Kerney grunted. "Then the only thing I can add is a warning: Vance Howell is in the governor's hip pocket. Only tell him things you want Springer to know."

"Is it that bad?"

"You bet," Kerney said.

"How did the Lassiter deposition go?"

"Aside from pissing off the ADA, it went well. I turned over a witness statement that the defense counsel loved and the ADA hated. He might call you up and bitch about me. Did Martinez stop by to brief you?"

"Yes. He dropped off some hair samples from Amanda Talley's apartment. The lab report came in an hour ago. They're a perfect match with the hairs found in the governor's office and the van. You should be pleased. It ties the two crimes together."

"It also means that Amanda Talley is probably dead," Kerney noted. "So who in the hell is using her name and vacationing in Belize?"

"Beats me. Let's get a search warrant and have Martinez take a closer look at Talley's apartment."

The supervisor of the fingerprint unit, a bookish-looking man carrying some papers in his hand, stepped tentatively into the office with a pleased expression on his face.

"Chief Baca. Chief Kerney. Got a minute?"

"What is it, Stan?" Andy asked.

"We got a hit back on a clean thumbprint from the van. The ID didn't come through normal channels. Army Intelligence made the guy. His name is Carlos Ruiz. He works for a Mexican national named Enrique DeLeon, who operates out of Juárez. Interpol says DeLeon is a major international smuggler; drugs, art, rare artifacts, anything with a big-ticket value. I've got Ruiz's mug shot and rap sheet."

"I'll be damned," Andy said.

Kerney had gone up against DeLeon and Ruiz once before, and Andy knew the case well. He had put a badge in Kerney's pocket when he was the Doña Ana County sheriff, on what appeared to be nothing more than a missing person case involving Kerney's godson. By the time the dust settled, Kerney had uncovered murders, a major smuggling scheme, and a rogue military intelligence agent in league with DeLeon.

"Bring it here," Kerney said. He took the photograph from the supervisor's hand and studied it. Carlos Ruiz's ugly, pock-marked face stared back at him. "Can you run the investigation without me for a day?" he asked.

"Where do you think you're going?" Andy asked.

"Juárez. The art theft is just DeLeon's kind of caper. Ruiz's involvement cinches it. I need to find out where DeLeon is and where the goodies are stashed. I'll need some money."

Andy bit his lip and thought about it. Kerney had tracked DeLeon down before using a paid Juárez informant, and he knew the lay of the land better than anyone else.

"Okay," he finally said. "We got some confiscated drug funds you can use. I'll have you flown to El Paso on our plane. But get some sleep before you cross the border, and for chrissake be careful. DeLeon will take you out if he has the chance. You hit him hard in the pocketbook on the White Sands case, and I don't think he's inclined to be forgiving."

"I'm leaving now," Kerney said. "Call the pilot."

7

After spending a night at an El Paso motel, Kerney got up early and took a taxi across the border to Juárez. He had the driver pull to a stop at Plaza Cervantine, a bohemian enclave for writers, artists, and community activists. Well away from the Juárez tourist strip, the plaza consisted of a mixture of apartment houses, cafes, artist studios, neighborhood businesses, and offices.

Kerney paid the driver and stepped out of the taxi. A street vendor was opening his food cart for business. The rich smell of tortillas, beans, and dark Mexican coffee filled the air. The business signs, posters, and murals that peppered the walls of the buildings were a riot of hot colors: bright yellow, brash pink, and screaming orange.

The only other person on the plaza aside from the vendor was a man walking a dog. Wearing a wool scarf thrown casually around his neck, a beret set at a cocky angle, and a V-neck sweater, the man hurried his pet into one of the doors of a walk-up apartment building.

Kerney followed a passageway through an office building to a courtyard cafe where several people sat smoking cigarettes and drinking coffee in the chilly early morning air. From the serving counter under the landing to the second story he could hear the clatter of dishes and the chatter of kitchen workers as they prepared for the breakfast rush. Upstairs, he found the office to the small weekly newspaper locked. He returned to the courtyard cafe, ordered coffee, and asked the server when Rose Moya usually arrived for work. He was told that she kept to no fixed schedule.

Rose had been a source of information for Kerney during the White Sands case, and put him on the trail to Enrique DeLeon. An investigative reporter, she had written a series of articles for her left-wing newspaper that exposed government collusion with the Juárez underworld.

While Kerney waited, the patio cafe filled with neighborhood locals, who flashed him inquisitive looks as they sipped coffee and talked. The man with the beret came into the courtyard without his dog, and joined a group of friends at a nearby table. A lively discussion sprang up on the political importance of street theater.

Rose Moya arrived and Kerney intercepted her at the foot of the stairs. She wore pleated brown cord slacks and a ribbed off-white wool sweater, and carried a canvas laptop computer case. An attractive woman with high cheekbones and full lips, Rose looked at Kerney with serious dark eyes.

"Señor Kerney," she said. "Surely you must know that Enrique DeLeon will try to kill you if he learns you are in Juárez."

"I will not be in Juárez long," Kerney said. "Please join me for a coffee."

Rose brushed her dark hair back from her forehead, searched Kerney's face, gave a quick glance at his table, and waited for more of an explanation. Behind Kerney the customers' chatter faded away.

"Is there a problem if you're seen talking to me?" Kerney asked.

Rose laughed sharply. "I do not have a death wish, Señor Kerney."

"Does my presence place you in danger?"

"Apparently Francisco Posada made it known that you reached him through me. I was questioned extensively after your visit by a high-ranking police official with ties to the *Mafiosios*. The meeting was cordial, but the threat was clear. It would be unwise for me to continue to cooperate with any *norteamericano* police officers or drug agents."

"Have the *Mafiosios* silenced your reporting?"

Rose forced a small smile. "Not completely, but I walk a fine line. They like to read about themselves. They expect to have their political assassinations reported—it reinforces the terror and fear they spread. And they enjoy articles about their wealth and influence as long as any account of government corruption is not too specific."

"Have you been instructed to report any contact by *norteamericano* agents or police?"

"Of course," Rose replied, looking over Kerney's shoulder at the cafe patrons. "And if I don't, someone else will."

"Give me a few minutes to tell you why I'm here. If you cannot help me, I'll understand. Disclose everything to the *Mafiosios*' police official when you make your report. Hold nothing back."

"What do you want, Señor Kerney?"

"Enrique DeLeon. And this time I plan to get him."

Rose's eyes widened with curiosity. "You make an appealing offer. Buy me a coffee, and I will listen to your story."

At the table, Rose drank coffee while Kerney filled her in on the art theft and the facts pointing to DeLeon's complicity.

"DeLeon enjoys stealing from *norteamericanos*," Rose said, touching the small mole under her right eye. "He delights in it, and has been very successful over the years. Not once has he been charged with any crime on either side of the border."

"I understand that."

"If you truly wish to put DeLeon out of business, you face much more difficult obstacles than before. He is virtually untouchable."

"Has he hired more bodyguards and goons?" Kerney asked.

Rose laughed. "Nothing quite so commonplace. In our last national election, several Juárez politicians won prominent government positions. They benefited from major *Mafiosios'* campaign financing. DeLeon donated several million dollars and was rewarded with a minor cultural affairs appointment and a diplomatic passport."

"That's unbelievable."

"I thought you were better acquainted with our country, Señor Kerney. You can buy anything in Mexico. We have a fugitive ex-president living in Dublin who has millions of stolen dollars in a Swiss account. He cannot be touched; we have no extradition treaty with Ireland. At one time, he was compared to your Jack Kennedy. He turned out to be nothing but a common thief."

"So what is DeLeon doing with his new diplomatic status?"

"Business as usual, only more so. I understand he is now investing in foreign real estate and buying into many *maquiladora* enterprises, businesses jointly owned by American and Mexican corporations."

"Is he going legitimate?"

"That, and diversifying."

"Do you have any specifics on his holdings?"

Rose shook her head. "I'm afraid not."

"Does he still use Juárez as his base of operations?"

"When he's here," Rose replied.

"Do you know where he is?"

"Traveling, I've heard, but I have no idea where. Allegedly he has houses in the United States, the Caribbean, Central America, and Spain. But he could be at his hacienda outside of Juárez, or at one of his ranches. He won't be easy to find. You aren't planning to go to the Little Turtle, are you?"

"No," Kerney answered. "Is Francisco Posada still alive?" Posada was the information broker who had set up Kerney's first and only face-to-face meeting with DeLeon.

Kerney had finessed Posada into connecting him with DeLeon by posing as a rogue ex-cop trying to smuggle valuable merchandise across the border. He had hooked Posada with some up-front money and the promise of a percentage from the proceeds.

"Barely. His niece now lives with him. She will inherit his estate. A private nurse cares for him. I don't think it would be wise for you to try to see him."

"I learned that firsthand a while back," Kerney said. "Does Juan Diaz still work for him?"

"The houseboy? No. He moved out and is now brokering for the *contrabandistas* in El Paso. He specializes in the low-end trade to avoid any conflicts with the drug *jefes*. He arranges buyers for smuggled cigarettes, liquor, cosmetics, and pharmaceuticals."

"Do you know where he lives?"

"He rents a cottage in a development near the Casa Grande Highway. He should be easy to find."

"*Gracias,*" Kerney said as he slid five one-hundred-dollar bills into Rose's hand.

"What's this?" she demanded warily.

"It's confiscated drug money taken from a Mexican smuggler," Kerney answered. "I read your article on homeless refugees. Use the money to help some of them."

Rose's hand closed over the bills. "Are you a policeman with a sense of poetic justice, Señor Kerney?"

"A character flaw, no doubt," Kerney replied.

"No doubt," Rose echoed, as she picked up the laptop computer case. "Move quickly, Señor Kerney. I have a telephone call I must make."

"Will you say that you told me how to find Juan?"

"I believe that would be in my best interest."

"IT IS GOOD to see you again, Señor Kerney," Juan said. "I owe you a great deal." He sat behind an expensive tubular-steel-and-glass desk, which held a computer and a laser printer. The rest of the home office furnishings consisted of a chair and love seat with plush cushions and bolsters, some sleek brushed-metal floor lamps, and a large Guatemalan folk art weaving on one wall.

Kerney sat in the chair across from the desk. "You owe me nothing, Juan," he said.

Juan's cottage was in a middle-class subdivision outside the Juárez city limits. The area had an Americanized look to it with neatly tended houses on small lots.

Juan no longer dressed like a domestic houseboy: His white linen costume had been replaced by a button-down broadcloth shirt and a pair of twill slacks. The change in attire was a striking contrast that heightened Juan's full-blooded Indian features. His long, thick black hair was pulled tight against his temples and tied with a band so that it draped down the back of his neck.

"But you're doing well, I take it," Kerney added.

"Very well. And I have you to thank, in part, señor. The customs agent you put me in touch with was able to get me a green card. I now have an apartment in El Paso and, in return for information I pass along now and then, I cross freely over the border. It has made doing business much less complicated."

"I'm glad to hear it."

"How can I help you, señor?"

"I need to locate Enrique DeLeon. I want to know exactly where he is."

Even before Kerney had finished speaking, Juan shook his head. "As much as I would like to, I cannot help you. DeLeon is out of the country. He travels often and does not announce his itinerary."

"Does he fly out of Juárez?"

"No. El Paso. It is much less suspicious to the *norteamericanos* for him to do so."

"I understand he owns houses in many countries. Can you get me exact locations?"

"Your friend at Customs asked for the same information, and as much as I tried, I was unable to supply it. It is my belief that whatever property DeLeon owns outside of Mexico is not in his name."

"You have no sources of information that you can tap into?" Kerney prodded. "There must be some information on his whereabouts floating around."

"Do you wish to have us killed, señor? DeLeon has bought more than diplomatic immunity from our government with his riches. He now has former federal intelligence agents on his payroll. Simply asking questions could make us both targets for assassination. And if the former *rurales* didn't murder us, either DeLeon's gangsters, the Juárez *policía,* or one of your corrupt Drug Enforcement Agency operatives surely would."

"That's not what I want to hear."

Juan raised his hands in an expression of helplessness.

Frustrated, Kerney changed the subject. "There may be a shipment of stolen art moving into Mexico sometime soon." Kerney handed Juan the inventory. "DeLeon is behind the theft. Will you keep your eyes and ears open?"

"That, I will gladly do," Juan replied.

Kerney extracted an envelope and laid out three thousand dollars.

Juan's long, dark eyelashes fluttered. "You pay me more than my normal fee," he said, "and I have given you very little in return."

"Use what you need to buy information, and consider the balance a retainer."

"As you wish, señor."

"You may be questioned about my visit."

"Do you have a cover story you wish me to use?"

"Tell them about the art theft, but try not to disclose that I'm looking for DeLeon."

"I will do my best to maintain the confidentiality of our conversation."

THE ROAD to the Rancho Caballo clubhouse where the O'Keeffe Museum fund-raiser had been held was barred by electronic security gates. Gilbert Martinez pulled to a stop next to the guard station. A young Hispanic male wearing a green sweater and khaki pants popped out of the small building, flashed Gilbert a big smile, and informed him that he needed a visitor's pass to get in.

Gilbert flashed his shield in response. After a few minutes of bickering with the kid over whether or not he had the right to proceed with police business on private property, Gilbert got testy. He made clear the implications of interfering with an officer in the performance of his duties, and the guard grudgingly opened the gate.

Gilbert drove a mile down a paved private road to the club-house and coasted to a stop, his mind disbelieving what he saw. The clubhouse had a two-story central core with single-story wings that stretched out on either side. At the front of the build-ing, stone walkways wandered through landscaped rock gardens to a wrought-iron bridge that spanned a man-made pond. A flag-stone driveway led to a portal reserved for valet parking.

Behind the clubhouse, the lush green of a fairway flowed up to piñon-studded hills. With a Spanish-tile pitched roof, the place had the feel of a Palm Springs resort. It was uncommonly glitzy looking, and the fact that Santa Fe had become just another trendy resort destination for the wealthy depressed Gilbert.

The sprinklers were on, pumping fine streams of water in arches over the golf course, and the grass glistened in the soft light from a hazy sun. As he parked and walked toward the entrance, Gilbert wondered what bureaucratic idiot had approved such a waste of water. Arid New Mexico survived on groundwater and snowpack runoff; it was not a commodity to be wasted on a rich man's playground.

Before he reached the entrance, the door opened and a styl-ish woman in her late forties stepped out to meet him. Her blond hair was carefully curled and tinted. She wore a long Santa Fe–style dress that accentuated her trim figure and a pair of snakeskin cowboy boots. She held a cellular telephone in her hand.

"I'm afraid we're closed today," she said, before Gilbert could introduce himself.

"I need to speak to the concierge," he replied.

"I'm the concierge," the woman replied with a casual glance at Gilbert's badge and ID. "I can't talk to you right now. I'm very busy."

"I'd like to ask you about the Georgia O'Keeffe Museum benefit event held here last month."

"What do you want to know?"

"Who attended the function?"

"I'm sorry, I can't help you."

"Don't you keep a guest list?"

"Of course we do. But this is a private club. We don't release any information without the permission of the board of directors."

"Your cooperation would be helpful," Gilbert replied. "Could you bend the rules this time?"

"Certainly not," the woman said. "If you want access to any information, you'll have to talk to our legal counsel. If your request is approved, I'll be glad to cooperate with you."

"And who is that?"

"Cobb, Owens, and Mackintosh."

"Is there anyone else besides your lawyers who might be able to help me?"

"The staff at the Museum of New Mexico Foundation co-sponsored the event and sent out invitations to their members. You might want to talk to them."

"Would they have a complete list of all the guests?"

"Only the museum foundation members, I would imagine," the woman said. "A blanket invitation went out to all Rancho Caballo residents through our monthly newsletter."

"I'm particularly interested in talking to a gentleman with a Hispanic surname. Supposedly, he owns a home here. He may be Spanish or Mexican." Gilbert consulted his notebook and read off the description Frank Bailey had provided him. "Do you know anyone like that?"

"As I said before, I'm afraid I can't help you."

Gilbert got the concierge's name, thanked her, and walked back to his car. Nothing about this case seemed to come easy. He checked the time. First, he would try the two women Roger Springer had admitted taking on late-night tours of the Round-house. He had been unable to reach either of them yesterday.

After that, he would stop at the county assessor's office and get a listing of who owned lots and homes in Rancho Caballo. He doubted that too many Hispanic surnames would pop up on the tax records for the subdivision.

GILBERT'S interviews with the women confirmed Roger Springer's account of impromptu, innocent after-hours tours of the governor's suite. But Gilbert came away with the sense that he'd heard a canned, rehearsed story from each woman. Neither had struck him as the type who would be thrilled by the opportunity to have just a private tour of the Roundhouse. He couldn't help but harbor the suspicion that Springer and the women might have had a completely different agenda for the late-night visits—like having sex on the floor in the governor's private office.

It wasn't all that kinky. Once, when investigating a report of fraud at a state agency, Gilbert had walked in on a manager who had forgotten to lock his office door while he was performing oral sex on his girlfriend.

He walked down the long wide hallway of the old county courthouse, a lovely WPA building two blocks from the plaza. The hand-carved beams, finely crafted corbels, delicate tin light fixtures, and the sweeping staircases had been retained, but the guts of the building had been ripped out and modernized after the district court and sheriff's department had moved to other locations.

As a child, Gilbert had occasionally accompanied his father to the courthouse when it still housed all the county services. Back then, his father knew most of the people who worked there on a first-name basis. Gilbert knew none of the workers he passed in the hallway, and it only deepened his feeling that he was a stranger in his hometown.

Maybe it had been a mistake to take the promotion to

sergeant and move back to Santa Fe. So far, it had been nothing but a painful, disconnected experience.

He found the assessor's office and asked for the Rancho Caballo subdivision property tax records. The printout he got wasn't helpful at all. No Hispanic-surnamed owners were listed, but a sizable number of the houses were owned by out-of-state corporations and foreign companies.

He compared the records with the names Fletcher Hartley and Frank Bailey had given him. None were listed as Rancho Caballo owners. But one local business, Kokopelli Design Studio, was carried on the books as a corporate owner of two homes.

Gilbert noted the address for the studio. It was one block off the plaza.

On his way out of the building, he stopped at the land-use planning office and asked to speak to the director. Gilbert had one question to ask, of purely personal interest.

"How MUCH water does the Rancho Caballo golf course use?" Gilbert asked, after introducing himself to the head of the planning office.

The director, a nearly bald, gray-faced older man, scowled at the question. "On the average, between three hundred thousand and four hundred thousand gallons a day."

"How did that kind of consumption get approved?"

"Rancho Caballo was initially approved to use only recycled gray water for the golf course," the man answered. "That was part of the original subdivision master plan."

"That's impossible," Gilbert said. "There isn't enough development in the area to supply that volume of gray water."

"Rancho Caballo bought additional water rights from an adjoining landowner last year. They can legally pump hundreds of acre-feet of groundwater from now until the wells run dry."

"Who sold the rights?"

The man chuckled sourly. "You don't follow local politics much, I take it. Sherman Cobb sold the water rights to the corporation. He owns a couple of sections of land that butt up against the subdivision. It caused quite a stink in the press, and the environmentalists raised hell about the depletion of the underground aquifer. But it got approved anyway."

"I see," Gilbert replied, thinking maybe not much had changed in the 150 years since the end of the Mexican-American War, when the Stars and Stripes were first raised over Santa Fe.

AT THE museum foundation offices, just behind the fine arts museum, Gilbert was directed by a receptionist to the publicist's office on the second floor. He climbed the stairs and found Fletcher Hartley sitting at a cluttered table in a small staff lounge near the stairwell, poring over photographs.

"What are you doing here?" Gilbert asked.

Fletcher waved off the implied censure. "I'm doing research. The publicity director is an old friend. She was more than willing to share the guest list for the O'Keeffe benefit, as well as photographs she took at the gala."

"Aren't you supposed to be calling art dealers?"

"I've done that, to no avail. Now I'm gazing at candid snapshots of smug art patrons. Care to join me? From the look of it, there are untold numbers of potential suspects. So far, I have ten shots taken of Amanda Talley with distinctly different groups of people. She appears to be quite the social butterfly."

"Hand me a stack," Gilbert said as he sat down at the table.

They sorted through the pictures and assembled two piles of photos. One accumulation featured Amanda Talley in every shot, while a larger stack included everyone else who had been photographed at the gathering.

With the help of the publicist, they whittled down the number of unidentified people in the photographs to slightly under twenty.

"What's next?" Fletcher asked.

"Do you know who owns a company called Kokopelli Design Studio?" Gilbert asked. He stretched to ease the stiffness in his shoulders, and started stuffing the two sets of pictures into envelopes.

"Bucky Watson owns it. Buckley is his given name. He's unscrupulous. Once he made me an absurd offer to buy my inventory of completed works. I threw him out of my studio."

Gilbert picked through the Amanda Talley photographs until he found one with Watson, Roger Springer, and Frank Bailey standing in front of the clubhouse bar with two unidentified men. He studied the picture.

"Watson's design studio owns two houses in Rancho Caballo," Gilbert said. "Both in the million-dollar range."

"My, my, Bucky's doing quite well for himself."

"Can a design studio generate that kind of cash flow?"

"Bucky is really a small conglomerate. He owns the design studio, a gallery on Canyon Road, and an art crating company. And he also dabbles quite a bit in commercial real estate."

"So, he's got big bucks. I get the feeling you don't like him," Gilbert said.

"I do not," Fletcher replied, as he reached for his topcoat. "Besides being greedy, he has no aesthetic sense and a shallow charm that wears thin."

"Why do people like Watson come here?" Gilbert asked.

"I see we share the same resentments about the new pioneers," Fletcher noted. "While Santa Fe still has appeal, it is not the place we once loved."

Outside, in the lateness of the day, Gilbert said good-bye to Fletcher, who waved his umbrella in response, and jaywalked to the plaza.

Gilbert smiled as he watched. He remembered the image of Fletcher sitting in the deep shade under the portal of his house on summer evenings, sipping his single malt scotch, and entertaining the endless stream of friends who dropped by.

Gilbert's family had a standing invitation to Fletcher's informal soirees, and the gatherings sparkled with eccentrics, bohemians, artists, writers, and the intelligentsia. Fletcher's friends were men and women of every imaginable persuasion and inclination who loved the city with a passion that made them a vital part of the community.

For Gilbert, going to Fletcher's house had been like opening a window on the world. He smiled at the memory of Fletcher and his pals leading everybody off on a walk to the plaza for band concerts and other festivities. Those were magical evenings when Gilbert was young.

What did Fletcher call the people who had recently migrated to Santa Fe? New pioneers—that was it. The city was glutted with affluent colonists busy discarding identities, leaving relationships, abandoning careers, forging new lifestyles, pursuing New Age aspirations, and picking through the Santa Fe scene like shoppers at an outlet mall. There were probably more psychic healers, spirit guides, psychotherapists, and self-help gurus per square foot in Santa Fe than anywhere else in the country.

Stolen art and stolen culture, Gilbert thought. He pushed back the sour feeling. It was close to the end of the business day. Maybe Bucky Watson would still be at his design studio on Water Street.

"I FELT like I was the target of an investigation," Bucky Watson said. He'd been bitching from the minute he'd arrived in Roger Springer's office to discuss his meeting with Sergeant Martinez.

"Stop worrying," Springer said. He sat across from Bucky, who drummed his fingers against the arm of the chair and shifted nervously. "I told you on the telephone the state police would be asking questions," he added.

"About the O'Keeffe fund-raiser," Bucky shot back. "Not my property holdings."

"It's no big deal. I talked to Vance Howell at the governor's office. They've got no leads, so the cops are taking a scattergun approach to the case, hoping something will turn up."

"I still don't like it." Bucky ran a hand through his hair. "Is Amanda really a suspect?"

"Howell says the working assumption is that her loose talk may have planted the idea for the robbery."

"Can't she straighten this thing out?"

"She's on vacation in Belize."

"Do the cops know about you and Amanda?" Bucky asked.

Roger laughed. "Amanda likes to keep her trysts secret."

"And I like to keep my business affairs private," Bucky snapped.

"Relax. I can ask the governor to flex a little political muscle, if need be. Given the size of your contribution to his reelection campaign, I'm sure he'd oblige."

"That would help," Bucky said.

"I'm always glad to be of service to a friend."

Bucky changed the subject. "I need to move more money into Rancho Caballo. What's the status on the equestrian center plans?"

Springer got up and went to the desk. "It's ready to go. All I need is a signature and a check." He picked up a document and walked back to Bucky. "Now that we've attracted the wealthy golfers, it's time to bring in the rich horsy set."

"How much?" Bucky asked, taking the papers.

"Nine million, to cover design, planning, and land acquisition. Can you swing it? The corporation is cash poor until we finish selling the remaining lots. We went overbudget on the clubhouse and golf course."

Bucky scanned the papers for the bottom line. "Cobb stands

to make a hell of a profit on the land sale to the corporation," he remarked.

"Stop complaining, Bucky. You get what you need out of the arrangement."

Bucky scrawled his signature and handed the papers back to Springer. "When do you want the check?"

"Anytime this week will do."

NEIL ORDWAY fumed as he slugged back the double shot of whiskey. He wanted to grind the shot glass into the face of the owner of the Cottonwood Bar, who stood behind the counter smirking. His scuffle with Kerney had been reported to the town council, and instead of accepting his resignation, the council had fired him instead. His chances of getting another law enforcement job were now less than zero.

It had taken all of thirty minutes for the news to spread throughout the village.

After turning in his equipment, the keys to the office and patrol car, and his badge and commission card, Ordway had walked from the town hall to the bar brooding over ways he could get back at Kerney.

He glared at the proprietor, a chunky man who always dressed Western and prided himself on looking like Kenny Rogers, the country singer. Ordway was sure the man dyed his carefully trimmed white beard and razor-cut long hair to intensify the similarity.

He pointed at his empty glass. The owner filled it quickly and moved away.

It was dinnertime and Ordway was the lone customer in the bar. The Cottonwood, a sleazy joint that smelled of sweat, stale liquor, cigarettes, and cheap perfume, catered to hard-core boozers. The crappy, dingy atmosphere suited Ordway's shitty mood perfectly.

He downed his drink, ordered one more for the road, drank it quickly, bought a fifth to carry home, and stepped out into a cold night wind. There was no one in sight, and the main drag was virtually empty except for a few cars parked across the street in front of the Laundromat.

Ordway buttoned up against the cold and started walking. A car passed by and he stiffened with embarrassment as the glare of the headlights caught him. Even though his rented house trailer behind the Shaffer Hotel was just a few minutes' walk away, Ordway felt humiliated at the thought of being seen hoofing it home. He hurried across the main drag before another car cruised by, and ducked down a side street.

At the corner where Pop Shaffer's old, long-deserted motor lodge cabins stood, Ordway stopped and looked down the sidewalk toward the hotel. He smiled wickedly at the sight of Robert Cordova parading up and down in front of the weird concrete fence next to the hotel.

Half drunk, Ordway remembered getting a message earlier in the day that the county jail had released Cordova from protective custody. He stuffed the paper bag with the whiskey bottle inside his jacket, walked to Cordova, reached out, and yanked Robert's hands away from his ears.

"Hey, Robert," he said pleasantly.

Robert opened his eyes. "Fuck you," he snarled, trying to pull away.

"Be nice. I got something for you."

"You ain't got nothing I want," Robert said, still struggling to free himself from Ordway's grip.

"It's from Kerney. He sent you a present, a carton of smokes. Asked me to make sure you got them."

Cordova relaxed and Ordway released his hold.

"Where are they?" Robert asked.

"In my police car around the corner. Come on. Let's go get

them." He patted Cordova on the shoulder and walked him away from the hotel lights.

When they reached the darkness of the motor lodge, Ordway pushed Cordova into the small courtyard that separated the stone cabins and slammed his fist into Robert's mouth. He heard Cordova's rotten teeth crack. He hit him again and felt some teeth break free.

Robert sank to his knees, blood bubbling out of his lips.

"How do you like your present, you crazy little mother-fucker?" Ordway asked as he brought his knee up to Cordova's chin.

Robert collapsed on his side and Ordway started kicking him with his steel-toed boots.

8

Carlos Ruiz found planes nerve shattering. During the flight, he stayed glued to his seat while the three men with him oiled weapons, loaded ammunition clips, and chatted with one another. He tensed up when DeLeon's pilot announced through the open cockpit door that they would touch down at the Santa Fe Airport ten minutes behind Kerney. Takeoffs and landings bothered Carlos most of all.

After Carlos had followed Kerney to the airport the night before, DeLeon had ordered him to continue the surveillance, no matter where the gringo went. Fortunately, it didn't take long to round up DeLeon's pilot and tail Kerney to El Paso. Once Carlos was back on the ground, shadowing the gringo had been easy. Kerney had no idea he had been followed.

Carlos had stayed in contact with the *patrón* by telephone, advising him of Kerney's movements. As soon as Kerney crossed into Juárez, DeLeon ordered Carlos to find out what the gringo was up to. That too proved to be a simple task. First, Kerney spoke with Rose Moya, and then immediately moved on to meet with Francisco Posada's former houseboy, Juan Diaz. After Kerney left, Carlos put another man on Kerney while he paid a visit to Juan.

Experience had taught Carlos that men feared the loss of physical capacity. If you threatened to cripple a man, blind him, or cut off his cock, most became cooperative within a very short time. Juan proved to be no exception. Carlos didn't need to rough up Juan to learn that Kerney was investigating the Santa Fe art theft. But when Juan hesitated to say more, Carlos loosened his tongue by smashing the bones in his right hand. It alarmed Carlos to discover that Kerney suspected DeLeon.

He reported Juan's disclosures to the *patrón*. Don Enrique seemed unsurprised, which probably meant Carlos had simply confirmed information already at DeLeon's disposal. The *jefe* ordered continued surveillance.

Kerney spent the rest of the day meeting with *norteamericano* law enforcement officials in El Paso. As luck would have it, Kerney spoke with a DEA agent on DeLeon's payroll. Carlos talked to the agent after Kerney and learned that fingerprint evidence from the burned van had led the gringo to suspect DeLeon's organization. That was all the agent knew. Carlos passed on the news to DeLeon, who once again seemed unperturbed.

Carlos ran over the torching of the van in his mind. He thought he had destroyed the vehicle sufficiently to erase all the evidence. Would DeLeon hold him responsible for the oversight?

He would find out soon enough, and although the thought of facing DeLeon's anger chilled him, he knew better than to try to run or hide.

Carlos switched his attention to the three men in the plane. He wondered what plans the *patrón* had for them. Hopefully, they were coming to Santa Fe only to kill Kerney. But DeLeon could also use them to mete out punishment. Carlos needed to remain mindful of that possibility.

The wheels thudded over the runway, and for the first time during the flight Carlos looked out the window. The bright lights of the small control tower were a welcome sight. He let go of the armrests and grunted in relief only when the plane touched down and the pilot applied the brakes.

NITA LASSITER stood at the railing on the second floor of the state police headquarters and watched Kerney walk slowly up the stairs. With his head lowered, he didn't see her. She had noticed Kerney's limp previously, but now it seemed much more pronounced; he was almost dragging his right leg up each step. He saw her, masked a small smile, and picked up his pace.

"I see you made bail," Kerney said as he reached the top of the landing.

"Yesterday," Nita replied. Dressed in blue jeans, a blue cotton shirt, and work boots, Nita held a brown leather bomber jacket in her hand. Her arm was no longer in a sling.

"What can I do for you, Ms. Lassiter?" Kerney asked, concentrating on her worried expression. Even in casual attire Nita looked feminine and elegant.

"I'm here about Robert," Nita replied. "He's been severely beaten. He wants you to visit him at the hospital."

"What happened?"

"He won't talk about it. He has a fractured arm, a broken rib, and he lost some front teeth."

"Who found him?"

"A deputy sheriff."

"Where?"

"Near the Shaffer Hotel in Mountainair. He was lying in the courtyard of the old motor lodge."

"What hospital is he in?"

"The university hospital in Albuquerque."

"How did you find out about it?"

"Robert carries my business card in his wallet. The hospital called to see if I was his next of kin."

"No wonder Robert thinks of you as his sister."

"He really has no one else," Nita answered with a slight shrug and small smile. "Will you go and see him?"

"Of course I will. As soon as I finish up here."

"Thank you." Nita dropped her gaze as Kerney's blue eyes studied her. "I wish you wouldn't look at me like that."

"Like what?"

"If you have another question, just ask it."

"You don't seem to like my questions," Kerney replied.

"I'm not going to apologize for being upset when you came to take me to jail."

"Why should you? I've watched hard cases break down and cry when the jail door slammed shut behind them. You held up very well."

"Is that a compliment?"

"You bet it is."

"Why do I get the feeling you don't think of me as a criminal?" Nita asked.

"Extenuating circumstances make some people less guilty than others."

"Your compassion surprises me."

Kerney grimaced at the sarcasm.

"I sound like I'm spoiling for a fight, don't I?" Nita said.

"You're angry."

"Mostly with myself. That doesn't mean I have to take it out on you."

Kerney extended his hand. "I hope things work out for you."

"So do I." Nita slipped her hand into Kerney's and didn't let go. "You're a rare breed, Mr. Kerney. Under different circumstances, I think I would enjoy knowing you."

"I share the feeling," Kerney replied. "Take care of yourself."

Nita smiled and let go of Kerney's hand. "I plan to. Addie is about to have her baby. She went into labor an hour ago. I'm on my way to Socorro."

"Will you tell her the truth about Paul Gillespie?"

Nita shook her head. "There's no need. She's agreed to put the baby up for adoption."

She walked down the stairs with her back straight and her head up, and Kerney fought off the unpleasant image of Nita dressed in prison garb, locked in a cell. He wondered if there was anything he could do to help her.

"How DID it go?" Andy asked from behind his desk as Kerney entered his office.

"Nobody seems to know where DeLeon is, but I did learn that he now has a diplomatic passport and he's buying into legitimate businesses along the border."

Kerney sat, gave Andy the details, and finished up. "I've got an informant in Juárez trying to scour up some more facts."

"By the name of Juan Diaz," Andy noted. "He called looking for you."

"Did he leave a message?"

"It's not one you're going to like to hear. Carlos Ruiz laid some heavy muscle on him after your visit. Ruiz roughed Diaz up and forced him to snitch you off."

"How the hell did Carlos get on to me?"

"You were probably tailed as soon as you crossed the border," Andy ventured. "I never should have let you go down there."

"If DeLeon knows I'm looking for him, it might force him out into the open."

"What an optimist you are. DeLeon has any number of resources he can use to kill you, without exposing himself."

"Should I go into hiding?" Kerney asked sharply.

"Don't get testy on me," Andy answered gruffly. "But until the dust settles I've put Fletcher's house under a close patrol, and Sergeant Martinez will be your partner. Where you go, he goes."

Kerney opened his mouth to protest and Andy cut him off. "No arguments, Kerney."

Kerney clamped his mouth shut and nodded. "Has Gilbert made any progress while I was gone?"

"He's got his team working hard on the Amanda Talley connection, and he's searching records on the companies that own Rancho Caballo property to see what might be lurking behind the corporate veil."

"No breakthroughs," Kerney summarized.

"We're running with one foot nailed to the floor," Andy groused in agreement. He pointed to the open door to the conference room. "But if it will make you feel any better, there are a shitload of inconclusive field reports you need to read through."

Kerney pulled himself out of his chair with a rueful look on his face.

"In the morning," Andy ordered, holding up a hand.

Kerney nodded. "Yeah. In my current state, I'd just have to read them all over again anyway."

"Go home. Better yet, get a home."

"Fletcher would be heartbroken to know that you don't approve of my living arrangements."

"Fletcher may not want you staying in his guest quarters for the next couple of years."

"I doubt the investigation will last that long."

"I didn't make you my chief deputy to work one case. As

soon as we get through this mess, I'm going to fill your plate. There's a hell of a lot of work we need to do in this department."

"Don't try to shanghai me for the long haul, Andy."

"You're in for the duration."

"We'll just have to see about that," Kerney noted as he left the office.

CARLOS found DeLeon in the living room, sitting in his favorite chair, reading some papers. The *patrón* was dressed to go out. He wore a lightweight camel hair jacket, a silk shirt buttoned easily at the collar, and a pair of charcoal trousers.

Carlos hesitated before entering. The preserved head of a fighting bull, famous for its performance in the Plaza de Toros in Mexico City, looked over the room from above the fireplace. It glared at Carlos forebodingly with its glass eyes. He composed himself and walked toward DeLeon.

Enrique waited for Carlos to draw near.

"*A sus órdenes,* Don Enrique," Carlos said.

"*Inglés,*" Enrique snapped. "Speak English."

"I am sorry, *patrón,*" Carlos said, lowering his head slightly. "I am at your service."

"That's much better. Are the men in the guest quarters?"

"They are. With orders to stay out of sight until instructed otherwise."

"Very good."

"Do you have orders for them?" Carlos asked.

"Not yet. Why do you look so troubled, Carlos?"

"Because I failed to completely destroy the van, Don Enrique."

DeLeon flashed a reassuring smile. "No blame attaches to you. Palazzi's stupidity created the circumstance. You did all that I asked to correct the situation."

"But now you are exposed to Kerney," Carlos replied.

"It is Kerney who is at risk. You must complete the dossier on him. I want to know where he is the most vulnerable."

"Do you wish to kill him yourself?"

"I may allow you that privilege."

"I am glad that you still retain confidence in me, *patrón*."

"As always, Carlos. Go now. You have work to do."

Carlos departed with the feeling that he might soon be a dead man lifted from his shoulders.

FLETCHER'S reputation as an artist who sold his work at high prices had given him sufficient cachet to arrange a late dinner meeting at the clubhouse with the exclusive broker who worked for Rancho Caballo. The broker had a visitor's pass waiting for him at the security gate.

He met her in the lobby. She was a cheery, perfectly dressed young woman with a big hairdo that framed her glossy face and cascaded down to her décolletage. She oozed with the desire to find the perfect Rancho Caballo home to meet his every need.

Over dinner, the woman patted his hand and talked about the host of contractors who could build a house exactly to his specifications if there was nothing available that he liked.

The food and service were excellent and the large number of dinner guests surprised Fletcher. He had expected far fewer people. He knew not a soul, nor did he want to. But it was clear that the rich had made Rancho Caballo a haven from the rigors of the outside world.

The dining room had a California decor, with two walls of windows that looked out over the golf course, where the lights along the golf cart paths cast a glow over the fairways. A fireplace crackled with cedar and piñon logs, and a series of wrought-iron chandeliers were suspended from the ceiling. The paintings on the wall were mundane pastel watercolors that Fletcher's trained eye had immediately dismissed as bogus hackwork.

"Do you plan to sell your home in town?" Heather Griffin asked as she dabbed at the corner of her mouth with a linen napkin. Fletcher could see the wheels turning as she contemplated the possibility of two fat commissions.

"Oh, I suppose my accountant will insist on it, if I decide to buy in Rancho Caballo," he replied.

"Rancho Caballo is blessed with many talented people," Heather crooned. She named two prominent entertainers who owned vacation homes. "You would fit right in."

"An elite community in every way, I'm sure," Fletcher said, eyeing a tableful of richly dressed young matrons wearing squash blossom necklaces, concho belts, and turquoise earrings. "The ambiance must draw them here."

"Exactly," Heather replied gaily.

"I suppose it would be best to have one broker handle the sale of my house and the purchase of a new one."

"That's the most efficient way," Heather agreed as she leaned forward to give Fletcher her pitch.

Half-listening, Fletcher nodded and smiled every so often to keep her talking. His visit to Rancho Caballo, which Kerney would most certainly reproach him for, had yielded nothing. He had hoped to come away with something useful. He eyed the young woman across the table and thought what a nice warm blaze it would make if all Santa Fe realtors were burned at the stake, the fires fueled by the catalogs, brochures, and marketing material they spewed out to attract potential buyers. Next summer's annual city fiesta would be the perfect time to do it.

After dinner, Fletcher made his excuses and said good night. He arrived in the lobby just as Bucky Watson entered with a male companion—one of the unidentified guests in the O'Keeffe benefit photographs.

He approached Watson with a smile, hand outstretched. "My dear Bucky, how are you? It's been so very long since I've seen you."

"I'm fine, Fletcher," Bucky answered, shaking Hartley's hand, a little perplexed by the cordiality. He knew the old queer didn't like him.

"Who is your friend?" Fletcher asked, turning to look squarely at the man for the first time. He was definitely Hispanic, perhaps in his mid to late thirties, with a fair complexion, blue eyes, and curly light brown hair.

"Vicente Fuentes, meet Fletcher Hartley," Bucky replied. "Fletcher is one of our living treasures."

"Ah," DeLeon said. "I have heard of this custom. Your city honors elders who have contributed their talents to the community. It is an admirable idea."

"I've enjoyed the distinction," Fletcher said. "Have you been with us long in Santa Fe, Señor Fuentes?"

"I am only an occasional visitor," DeLeon answered.

"I believe you've met a friend of mine, Frank Bailey. At the O'Keeffe benefit last month."

"I don't recall the name," DeLeon said. "I've met so many people since I arrived, it is hard to keep everyone sorted in my mind."

"Of course. Perhaps I am mistaken," Fletcher said.

"Perhaps," DeLeon replied. He touched Watson's back in a signal to move on. "Good night, Mr. Hartley."

"Good night, Señor Fuentes."

Fletcher drove home in great anticipation of his next conversation with Kerney. He would reveal a tidbit that, he hoped, would be new and helpful information.

AT A CORNER table in the clubhouse bar, Bucky Watson waited for DeLeon to speak. DeLeon expected to be treated with deference, and while Bucky privately resented the attitude, he knew better than to confront it. He took a sip of his drink and remained silent.

Aside from the hostess behind the bar and an older couple about to leave, the room was empty. DeLeon watched the man hold the woman's coat as she slipped her arms into the sleeves. When they walked out the door, he glanced over at Bucky.

Bucky looked like an athlete, with wide shoulders, narrow hips, and a trim waist, but his petulant face spoiled the image.

After the hostess left to deliver drinks in the dining room, DeLeon finally spoke. "How much inventory do you have on hand?"

Bucky did a quick calculation in his head. "A six-week supply of cocaine," he answered. "Maybe a little less than that in heroin. Smack has been moving well lately."

"Send everything to Chicago immediately."

"That's a lot of product to put on the road at one time."

DeLeon answered with an icy look.

"I'll have it shipped out by morning," Bucky said, recovering quickly. It would mean calling in the crew to build special containers at the crating shop, packing the drugs in with some cheap art, forging lading bills, and putting two large trucks on the road. It was an all-night job.

"When will I be resupplied?" Bucky asked.

"You won't be, for a time."

"I've got people who expect product waiting out there."

"They can wait," DeLeon said, thinking how tiresome Bucky could be.

"They may start moving to other suppliers."

"Or they'll cut back on bulk sales and raise their prices. When can more of my funds be moved into Rancho Caballo?"

"We can wash an additional nine million right away," Bucky answered.

"Do Springer and Cobb continue to believe it is your money they are using?"

Bucky snickered. "Yeah. They don't seem to care where it comes from, as long as they get their slice."

"Excellent. There is a shopping mall south of the city that is about to come on the market. When it does, offer the asking price and secure the largest mortgage possible. I'll transfer funds to cover the down payment and closing costs."

Bucky masked his surprise. If DeLeon was right about the mall, no one else in the city knew anything about it. "I'll take care of it."

"Have the police returned to question you further about the art theft?"

"No," Bucky replied. "Roger Springer will ask the governor to intervene if the cops get too nosey."

"Since you had nothing to do with the theft, you should have no worries."

"I'd love to know who pulled it off. It was a slick piece of work."

"So it seems," Enrique said. "What have you learned about it?"

"The police are operating on the assumption that Amanda Talley was somehow involved in the heist. I introduced you to her at the O'Keeffe benefit. The cops think she may have been murdered."

"How interesting. Is this information reliable?"

"It comes right from the governor's chief of security, a state police captain."

"Police make such excellent informants. The gentleman you introduced me to in the lobby. Tell me about him."

"Fletcher? He's local color. He's a very successful artist, collected on a national level."

"Does he own property in Rancho Caballo?"

"Not as far as I know. He lives near the Roundhouse, in one

of the older neighborhoods. He was probably someone's dinner guest."

"I did not like the degree of interest he showed in me. Who are his friends?"

Bucky chuckled. "Every queen, queer, transvestite, and transsexual in Santa Fe. The latest Fletcher story I heard is that he has a gay cop living with him."

"Really?"

"I don't know who it is. But knowing Fletcher, he's probably young and good-looking."

"He sounds harmless," DeLeon noted, glancing at his wrist-watch.

Bucky took the cue, stood up, and smiled at his boss. "I'll stay in touch," he said.

"Make sure that you do."

Bucky left the bar feeling miffed. Working for DeLeon had made him a rich man, but he didn't have to like the son of a bitch's condescending attitude.

AFTER learning a bit more about Amanda Talley, Gilbert Martinez believed his hunch about Roger Springer and his after-hours trysts with women at the governor's office deserved to be tested. Although it was fairly late, lights burned inside Roger Springer's house. Gilbert was pleased; he had timed the visit to catch Springer away from the office and off guard, if possible.

He stopped his unit next to a BMW in the driveway, and exterior floodlights controlled by motion sensors immediately switched on.

Average in size by neighborhood standards, the house was situated off Gonzales Road in the foothills, with Santa Fe aglow below it, spreading haphazardly across the valley floor.

A round structure low to the ground, the home seemed

anchored to the hillside. The curved walls had large windows and doors separated by buttresses, and all the rooms appeared to open onto a semicircular patio. Gilbert found his way to double glass doors that allowed him to see into a sunken living room. A fireplace glowed in the center of the room, and a wine bottle and two glasses were on a coffee table in front of a couch.

No one was in sight, so he knocked and waited, his attention drawn back to the cityscape below. He could remember a time when except for the highway strip into town, Santa Fe stopped at the private college on St. Michaels Drive. Now the profusion of city lights ran for miles past the college and washed out the night sky.

He looked through the double glass doors just as Roger Springer yanked one open. Wearing a terry-cloth robe and a waspish expression, Springer ran a hand through his rumpled hair and gave Gilbert an irritated look.

"What is it, Sergeant?"

"I have a few questions, Mr. Springer. May I come in?"

"At this hour?"

"Only for a minute."

Springer nodded brusquely and stood aside. Gilbert stepped into a wide arched foyer that opened onto the living room. Recessed lights along the back wall of the living room accentuated an arrangement of paintings and lithographs above a stereo sound system on a low, built-in bookcase.

"What questions do you have?" Springer asked as he closed the door. He made no gesture for Gilbert to move into the living room.

"I understand you're a friend of Amanda Talley."

"I know Amanda."

"You were with her at the O'Keeffe benefit, I believe."

"I was hardly with her, Sergeant."

"But you saw her there," Gilbert countered.

"We had a drink together with several other people."

"Was Bucky Watson one of them?"

"I believe so."

"There was another man with the group. He may have been Hispanic or Mexican. Do you remember meeting him?"

"I can't say that I do."

Gilbert held out a photograph. "Please look at the man at the extreme left of the picture with his head partially turned away, and tell me if you know him."

Roger leaned forward and looked. "I don't know him."

"He may own a house in Rancho Caballo."

"I wouldn't know."

Gilbert put the photograph away. "I understand that some time back you lost a key to the governor's private elevator and had to have it replaced. Did you ever find the key?"

"No."

"You didn't loan the key to anyone?"

"No."

"Did you ever date Amanda Talley?"

"Yes, we dated for a while, two years ago, soon after she came to town."

"But not recently?"

"I said it was two years ago."

"I'm a little confused about your answer. Last month you were seen in the governor's suite after hours with Amanda Talley."

"I may have run into Amanda at my uncle's office one evening, Sergeant, but that's all there was to it."

"Why would Ms. Talley be in the governor's office after hours?"

"Do you suspect Amanda, Sergeant?"

"What was your business there that night?"

"I believe I left a legal brief for the governor's chief of staff to review."

"You didn't rendezvous with Amanda at the governor's office that evening?"

"Are you suggesting a romantic interlude of a sexual nature? Isn't that how you referred to it in my office? I did not. As I told you, our relationship has been over for a long time."

"Several of Ms. Talley's closest friends suggest otherwise. They report that you and Amanda continue to meet privately upon occasion."

Springer blinked. "If you've spoken with Amanda, I'm sure you know that's simply not true."

"We haven't been able to reach her yet. She's out of the country."

"Isn't it premature to make accusations you can't substantiate?"

"We found some pubic hairs on the carpet in the governor's office. Right in front of his desk."

"Did you?"

Gilbert reached out, plucked a loose hair off the collar of Springer's bathrobe, and inspected it. "From two different individuals," he lied.

Springer paled considerably as he watched Gilbert place the hair between the pages of his notebook and close the cover.

"You just violated my constitutional rights," Springer said. "You have no authority to collect physical evidence without a search warrant."

"Physical evidence?" Gilbert replied innocently. "You're not a suspect, Mr. Springer. Didn't I make that clear? I don't think you have any reason to be concerned."

"It's time for you to leave, Sergeant."

Outside, Gilbert took a deep breath. A piece of the puzzle had fallen into place, although it probably didn't matter much, since he couldn't actually prove Roger Springer had jumped Amanda Talley's bones on the governor's carpet.

The whole thing had been a bluff, and the ploy could cost

him, big time. Gilbert was sure the brass would hear about it in the morning, and the thought that he might get bounced off the investigation and stuck in some cubbyhole, sorting evidence inventories for the rest of his career, didn't sit well.

Gilbert doubted he would get much sleep when he got home.

THE DOCTORS had given Robert painkillers. He woke up to Kerney's gentle shaking with a small groan. His beard had been shaved off, and there were bruises on his mouth and chin. His lip was split and two upper front teeth were missing.

Without the beard, Robert's face had an unused quality to it, except for his eyes, which looked very old. His left arm was suspended in a cast, and his torso had been wrapped to immobilize a broken rib.

He looked at Kerney and said nothing. It made Kerney wonder if Robert was hearing voices in his head. Finally, Robert licked his lower lip and coughed.

"How are you, Robert?" Kerney asked.

"*Un poco de agua, por favor,*" Robert said.

With great care, Kerney tilted Robert's head off the pillow and placed the straw protruding from the plastic water jug between Robert's lips.

Robert took several small sips and then pulled the straw from his lips. "It hurts to use my mouth," he said.

"You don't have to talk now, if you don't want to."

"You understand Spanish, Kerney," Robert said.

"Who did this to you?"

"*El Malo.*"

Kerney knew the term. It meant "the evil one," a colloquialism for the devil.

"How did he do this to you?"

Robert blinked and looked confused. "My head feels better."

"I hope it stays that way."

"*El Malo* never stays with me. He's just *un hatajo de mentiras.*"

"He lies to you?"

Robert smirked. "He says I'm not crazy."

"That must be good to hear."

"It's a lie." Robert paused for a moment. "Once I dreamed I was Jesus Christ. You know what I did in the dream?"

"What did you do?"

"I killed myself." Robert giggled. "Isn't that funny?"

"That was some dream."

"*El Malo* makes me dream shit like that. It's bad luck to dream you're Jesus."

"Who beat you up, Robert?"

"I was *naguitas,* Kerney. A real sissy. I didn't even throw one punch. Not one."

"Maybe you didn't have the chance."

"You're supposed to fight back. That's the rule."

"Even *tofe botos* like you can get tricked," Kerney ventured.

Robert considered Kerney's statement. "You got fucked up pretty bad, shot and everything. Isn't that right?"

"That's right."

"Were you scared when it happened?"

"Terrified. Who beat you up, Robert?"

"That fucker Ordway said you sent him some smokes to give to me."

"Ordway did this?"

"Yeah."

Kerney stayed with Robert until he closed his eyes and fell asleep.

ON THE drive back to Santa Fe, Kerney made contact with the state cop who lived in Mountainair, and asked about Ordway's whereabouts. The officer reported Ordway had cleaned out his trailer, loaded up a small U-Haul, and left town.

Tired to the bone, Kerney turned down the squawk box volume and popped a Wynton Marsalis tape into the cassette deck. Some deep-down, throaty blues would carry him home. Or not exactly home, as Andy had so correctly pointed out.

He would love to put his cowboy boots on the coffee table at Harper Springer's ranch and call the place his own, but that was a pipe dream. If he stayed in Santa Fe, reality would be a furnished box apartment with all the charm of a minimum-security federal prison. That just wouldn't do.

He was approaching the off-ramp to St. Francis Drive when the realization hit him that he wasn't thinking clearly. He switched his attention to the rearview mirror. The headlights of three cars behind him flickered in the mirror. He slowed to let them close, clicked on the turn signal, and continued past the exit. Two of the cars turned off while the third stayed behind him.

He didn't know if he was being followed or not, but it was time to start playing it safe. He moved into the left lane, swung the car off the pavement onto a dirt crossover that connected the divided highway, and merged with the southbound traffic. The northbound car continued on without slowing.

From now on, he would take alternate routes to and from work and vary his routine. With an eye on the rearview mirror, he got off the interstate, and took side streets to Fletcher's house.

At the house, he scanned the grounds for anything out of the ordinary before going inside. Everything looked perfectly peaceful.

9

Kerney turned on the table lamp in Fletcher's bedroom and found him curled up in a ball under an old hand-stitched, floral-wreath quilt. The bed, a massive nineteenth-century four-poster, was angled to provide a view of a walled garden at the rear of the house. *Nichos* carved in the adobe walls displayed an assortment of folk art animal figures that included Acoma Pueblo owls, Cochiti storyteller bears, and mythical Mexican beasts. On the floor in the four corners of the room stood carefully grouped menageries of hand-carved, painted animals. Pigs, skunks, donkeys, lions, and chickens of various sizes were arranged facing the bed.

"Wake up, Fletcher," Kerney said.

Fletcher pulled a pillow over his head. "It's much too early to wake up," he muttered.

"It's time for our run."

Kerney removed the pillow and Fletcher opened his eyes. Dressed to go running, Kerney wore a fanny pack around his waist.

"Why are you wearing that ridiculous thing?" Fletcher asked as he sat up.

The pouch, designed with a special sleeve for a quick draw, held Kerney's loaded semiautomatic and a spare clip, but Fletcher didn't need to know that.

"Dress," Kerney said, ignoring the question and tossing Fletcher's sweats on the foot of the bed. "I'll wait for you outside."

When Fletcher joined him, Kerney took a different route for their morning run, half-expecting Fletcher to complain. But as Kerney led the way out of the neighborhood and up a narrow street that gave them a view of the mountains, Fletcher said nothing.

The first full light of morning streaked speckled carmine on the flat underbelly of some stratus clouds, brushed the Sangre de Cristo Mountains, and flickered against the peak of Sun Mountain. Sunlight tipped the mountaintops as though it were a hazy rivulet of gold spreading across the high summits.

"Why do you look so pleased with yourself?" Kerney asked as they jogged past an open field that gave them a better view of the mountains.

"No particular reason," Fletcher replied. "Unless you might have some small interest in learning the identity of the mysterious man who was with Bucky Watson at the O'Keeffe benefit."

Kerney slowed to a trot. "What have you been up to, Fletcher?"

"I happened to run into Bucky and his friend at the Rancho Caballo clubhouse. The man's name is Vicente Fuentes. He's

Hispanic, with classic Castilian features—quite good-looking. A Mexican from his accent, I would say. Gilbert has a picture of him."

"What were you doing at Rancho Caballo?"

"Having dinner. The food was excellent."

"Did you learn anything more about Fuentes?"

"Only that he's an occasional visitor to Santa Fe. He looks to be quite wealthy."

"I want you to be careful, Fletcher."

"Careful about what?"

"The men we're looking for can be very dangerous."

"Have you identified the crooks?"

"We've got a line on them. Don't let any strangers into the house, and if you see anyone suspicious in the neighborhood, I want you to call me right away."

"Have you been sending patrol officers to check on my house?"

Kerney nodded. "Andy has. It's just a precaution. Do you have to go anywhere during the next few days?"

"A trip to the grocery store. I need to fill my larder. That's all."

"Do that, but otherwise stay home, and keep the doors and windows locked."

"You're scaring me a bit, Kerney. Whatever is the matter?"

"Just do as you're told," Kerney said. "And no more playing Hercule Poirot. This isn't one of those cozy mystery novels you love to read."

The hurt look on Fletcher's face made Kerney stop. "I don't want anything bad to happen to you."

Fletcher smiled wanly. "I'll do as you've asked. But I must say you have a rather fierce way of showing your concern."

• • •

BUCKY WATSON's art crating business was housed in a two-story Victorian, on a side street in the Guadalupe District of Santa Fe. A red brick structure with a wide front porch and a gabled roof, it had a loading dock at the back of the building that led to an alley. Two other Victorians were on either side, one used as a dance studio, and the other rented by a high-end furniture maker.

Across the street stood an upscale nightclub and restaurant. It was one of the few buildings on the street Bucky's company, Milagro Properties—Spanish for "miracle"—didn't own.

The Guadalupe District, within walking distance of the plaza, had once been a blend of homes and family-owned businesses. As the tourist industry expanded, and all the buildings on the plaza were fully leased to serve the growing market, the new galleries, boutiques, and specialty shops began spreading into the Guadalupe area. Using DeLeon's money, Bucky had started buying before other investors jumped on the bandwagon.

He stood on the loading dock and watched the trucks start off on the long haul to Chicago. His breath cut a ribbon through the frigid air of early morning. It had taken all night to put the shipment together. Moving nearly a half ton of cocaine and an equal amount of smack was no easy proposition. It had to be hidden in specially constructed crates and loaded precisely in the trucks to avoid raising suspicion.

Bucky turned off the overhead lights and walked to the back of the crating room to the large tool closet. The drivers had been the last employees to leave, and the building was empty. He flipped on the closet light and swung open a floor-to-ceiling shelf that led to a secret basement. Six wetbacks supplied by DeLeon had built the hidden passageway and fashioned a cellar under the crawl space. All the excavation work had been done at night; dirt had been hauled up in buckets by hand, loaded into trucks, and carted away before daybreak.

Bucky walked down the stairs and checked his inventory. He'd deliberately held back some product so he could fill two upcoming shipments, one for Colorado and one for Kansas. He saw no reason not to make the deliveries just because DeLeon wanted to bolster the Chicago market. The drugs would be gone within a couple of days, and because the well would be dry for a while, Bucky planned to bump up the price of a kilo and skim the difference, with no one the wiser.

He turned off the light, locked up, went to his office, and logged on at the computer. Except for Kansas and Colorado, it was time to let the network know that the pipeline would be shut down until further notice.

GILBERT MARTINEZ got to work early and found a memorandum tacked to the office door. The memo, signed by the vehicle maintenance supervisor, directed Gilbert to produce his unit for servicing immediately. It cited departmental policy, and noted that failure to comply could result in disciplinary action.

It was the second memo Gilbert had received in a week, and while he didn't expect to be reprimanded, the car badly needed a tune-up. He unlocked the office, dumped his briefcase on the desk, and walked down the hall to a back suite that looked out on the maintenance building. The overhead doors were open and the lights were on. Maybe if he got the unit in immediately, he could have it back in a couple of hours.

He drove to the shop, parked by an open bay, found the vehicle supervisor in his office, dropped the car keys on the desk, and asked when he could pick up the unit.

"End of the day," the man said gruffly. "I'm gonna have to fit you in where I can."

"I need another car," Gilbert said.

"Don't have one," the man replied. "You'll have to borrow

from somebody who isn't using their vehicle, or catch rides with one of the uniforms."

"That won't work," Gilbert said.

The man shrugged. "You caused the problem, Sergeant, not me. I had you scheduled for maintenance last week. Next time, get your car in when you're supposed to and I'll have a loaner for you."

Back in his office, Gilbert discovered two manila envelopes on the seat of his desk chair containing information on Rancho Caballo sent over by the Environment Department and the Santa Fe county clerk.

He thumbed through the paperwork. One set was compliance documents for the effluent discharge and gray water system at the clubhouse. He set it aside.

The Santa Fe county clerk's packet contained release of mortgage documents, warranty deeds, and copies of the mortgages held on Rancho Caballo. Gilbert read the material carefully. Twelve liens against Rancho Caballo had been released by a company called Milagro Properties, based in Santa Fe. The total amount paid off to Milagro exceeded a hundred million dollars. Milagro held another hundred million in paper against the corporation.

Gilbert checked the due dates on the release documents. Each were ten-year notes that had been paid off way ahead of schedule.

Gilbert wasn't a financial expert, but paying off so much debt so quickly seemed unusual to him, especially for a real estate project with land and houses still unsold. He went through the forms again, this time scanning the signature blocks. Sherman Cobb, Roger Springer, and Bucky Watson had signed off on each of them, Cobb for Rancho Caballo, Springer as corporate counsel, and Watson for Milagro Properties.

It's such a small world, Gilbert thought, as he heard footsteps in the hallway. He looked up, expecting to see Chief Kerney appear in the doorway, ready to ream him out for his late-night visit to Roger Springer. He relaxed when the footsteps receded.

Gilbert leafed through the papers again. Milagro Properties was taking a hard hit on interest earnings because of the accelerated payback on the notes. And while everything appeared legal, he wondered why Watson would keep financing a project that yielded such low returns. He needed some expert advice.

The official workday had begun, which meant that Joe Valdez should be in his office. Valdez, a senior investigator and a certified public accountant, specialized in white-collar and corporate crime. Gilbert picked up the paperwork and went looking for Valdez. He found him anchored behind his desk, reading glasses perched on his wide nose, punching the keys of a desk calculator.

Valdez had a full chin and big ears with thick lobes. He wore his hair short with no part. He looked more like a prizefighter than a cop or a CPA.

"Hey, Sergeant," Joe said as Gilbert walked in. "What's up?"

"Doing the monthly family budget?" Gilbert asked.

"There is no family budget," Joe grumbled, pushing the calculator aside. "A budget assumes that I can actually plan for expenditures. That's impossible to do with two teenage daughters in high school."

"Marry them off," Gilbert suggested, sliding into a chair.

"Too young," Valdez replied with a shake of his head. "Plus, they both want to go to college before they get married. As it is, I'm running a tax service out of the house in my spare time, trying to put some money aside for tuition. It costs a bundle to send kids to college. Now that the wife is working, we just might be able to swing it."

"The rewards of police work come from the satisfaction of the job, not money."

"Don't give me that crap."

"You'll have both girls in college at the same time?"

"One right after the other, starting in two years."

"I'm looking forward to the same experience with my girls later down the line."

"You'll love it," Joe predicted sourly. "What have you got?"

"Take a look at these and tell me what you think." Gilbert handed Valdez the documents and waited for a reaction.

"I don't like what I'm seeing," Valdez finally said, flipping back and forth from document to document. "These kind of real estate development projects usually attract more than one financing source, especially at this level. Two hundred million is a hell of a lot of money for one company to invest in this state, unless it's a banking institution."

"What about the accelerated loan payoffs?"

"That, too," Joe replied. He rubbed the bald spot on the back of his head. "There's a lot of cash moving back and forth here over a short period of time."

"Between the same group of people."

"Exactly. I'd be looking hard at Milagro Properties, if I were you. Scope out the assets of the corporation."

"That's the place to start?"

Joe nodded. "You bet. Track down the source of that money. What kind of income is generating that level of investment capital? If it looks clean, then jump over to Rancho Caballo. The corporate earnings to debt ratio might prove interesting, once you know what amounts from the loan proceeds were actually plowed into the development."

Valdez held out the paperwork for Gilbert to take back.

Gilbert didn't move. "Would you do it? I don't know the first thing about all this crap."

Valdez dropped the papers on the desk. "Have I just been suckered into something here?"

Gilbert grinned. "Only if you think it's worth your time."

Joe scratched his chin. "It may be. I'll make some calls. If I learn anything interesting, I'll let you know."

"Fair enough," Gilbert said. "Are you using your unit today? If not, I'd like to borrow it. I'm stranded without a vehicle."

"No way," Joe answered with a snort. "I only do one favor a day for newly anointed sergeants."

CARLOS couldn't remember a time in the past when he had been invited to join the *patrón* for a cup of coffee. He sat at the dining room table holding the delicate cup carefully in his hands while the maid cleared away the breakfast dishes. DeLeon gazed out the window at the snowcapped mountains and didn't speak until the woman departed.

"So Kerney has no girlfriend? No private life outside of his job?" DeLeon asked, shifting his gaze to Carlos.

"No, *patrón*. He works and goes home. That is all."

"What did he do in Albuquerque last night?"

"According to a nurse at the hospital, he visited a patient, a man who had been found beaten in a small village called Mountainair."

"What prompted Kerney to visit this man?"

"I do not know, *patrón*. But he identified himself as a police officer to the nurse in charge of the unit."

"Where is this village?"

"South of Albuquerque, east of the mountains."

"Tell me about Kerney's workplace."

"The buildings are fenced, isolated from the highway, and on a small hill. There are many police around, including students and officers who stay at the police training academy. Those who work there must either pass through a reception area or use security cards to enter the exterior doors. Cards must also be used after hours to open the security gate."

"Could Kerney be killed from a distance as he leaves?"

"Yes, but at some risk," Carlos replied. "The highway is very busy and there are nearby businesses along the strip that attract customers."

"What is the best vantage point?"

"There is a new car lot directly across the highway. From there I can see who comes and goes, but only if I use binoculars. I have been able to follow Kerney by identifying his vehicle. He parks in the same reserved space every day."

"Using a sniper won't work."

Carlos nodded. "We would have better success where Kerney lives. He resides in the guest quarters of a house near the state capitol. It is on a private lane at the end of a street, shared by only one other residence. The house is situated in a hollow, almost hidden from sight. From the lane, you can see only the roofline and part of the driveway. There are many places that can be used for concealment."

"Who is Kerney's host?"

Carlos pulled a scrap of paper from his shirt pocket. "His name is Fletcher Hartley."

DeLeon's eyes closed. Fletcher Hartley was the man at the Rancho Caballo clubhouse who had forced Bucky to make an introduction. Had Hartley been acting on Kerney's behalf?

"Can the house be entered easily?" Enrique asked.

"Yes, *jefe*. There is one door at the front, a patio door at a rear garden, and a separate entrance to the attached guest quarters. There are no alarm or security devices to contend with. Under cover of darkness, with three men to assist me, there should be no problem."

Enrique nodded, pleased with Ruiz's thoroughness. He now had a clear picture of what needed to be done.

"Is the information sufficient?" Carlos asked.

"You've done well," DeLeon replied as he refilled his coffee cup. "Go to the house tonight. After Kerney arrives, send the men in. One through each entrance. Have them kill Kerney and his host. When it is done, rendezvous with me at the airport."

"Are we returning home, *patrón?*"

"For a time."

GILBERT dug through the sheaf of National Crime Information Center reports on the people who had been interviewed and questioned since the investigation began. There were no hits for arrests or convictions until he reached Bucky Watson. In the early seventies, Bucky had served eighteen months in a California state prison for drug dealing.

Gilbert reached for the telephone just as Chief Kerney appeared in the doorway. "Chief," he said, pulling his hand away from the receiver.

"Sergeant," Kerney replied with a smile. "I understand you've been assigned as my partner."

"I'll try not to cramp your style," Gilbert said, smiling back.

"Do you have anything new on Carlos Ruiz?"

"Nada. We don't even know where he is."

"What about Enrique DeLeon?"

"Nothing."

"Fletcher met a man last night named Vicente Fuentes. He's pretty sure Fuentes is a Mexican national. He said you have a snapshot of him that was taken at the O'Keeffe Museum benefit."

"Has Fletcher been playing detective again?" Gilbert asked, handing the photograph to Kerney.

"It would seem so." Kerney looked at the photograph and froze.

"What is it?"

"Enrique DeLeon," he said, tossing the picture on the desktop. "Have this photo enlarged and cropped. Give it to every officer in the district. I want DeLeon located ASAP. Hit Rancho Caballo hard. Put an entire team on it."

Gilbert slid the NCIC hit on Bucky across the desk.

Kerney scanned it. "What else do you have on Watson?"

"He's been funneling millions into Rancho Caballo through a company called Milagro Properties, and getting it back in accelerated repayments."

"Put somebody on it to do a full probe," Kerney said. "We need to know if Watson is linked to DeLeon."

"Sherman Cobb and Roger Springer are officers in Rancho Caballo."

"Dig into it," Kerney said.

"Is that all?" Gilbert asked as Kerney stood in the doorway.

Kerney grinned. "Try not to piss off Roger Springer again for a while."

"Don't make me wait for the other shoe to drop, Chief," Gilbert said. "Give me the full skinny."

"I've been ordered to reprimand you."

Gilbert sighed. "What should I expect?"

"Nothing. I refused to comply. What did you do to Springer, anyhow?"

Gilbert laid out the specifics. "Springer's reaction sealed it," he concluded. "If he wasn't screwing Amanda Talley on his uncle's office carpet, I'll eat my hat."

"Very slick, Sergeant," Kerney said. "Slightly over the edge, but slick nonetheless."

Gilbert smiled at the compliment. "I won't do it again, promise. Any word from Belize on the Amanda Talley double?"

"Yes, indeed," Kerney replied. "The Belize authorities reported that Amanda Talley fell overboard from an excursion vessel and has presumably drowned. The body hasn't been recovered."

"This could turn into a very interesting day."

"It already has."

"Chief, can I borrow your unit, if you're not using it? Mine's in the shop."

Kerney tossed him the keys. "While you're out, check in on Fletcher occasionally, will you?"

"Sure thing," Gilbert said. "Thanks for going to bat for me."

"What got into you with Springer?"

"It's a long story."

"Maybe you can tell me about it over a beer when the case is wrapped up."

"I'd like that," Gilbert said.

KERNEY returned to the conference room and found a telephone message from Addie Randall, asking him to come to the Socorro hospital maternity ward to talk with her. He was about to call her back when Andy walked in looking very unhappy. He sat down, scratched his cheek, and scowled.

"Well, do you have to fire me?" Kerney asked.

"If the governor's chief of staff had his way, you'd be out the door on your ass for refusing to reprimand Sergeant Martinez."

"Did you get raked over the coals?"

"Big time. It's not nice to upset the governor's nephew. I told the chief of staff to put the request to terminate you and transfer Martinez in writing over Harper Springer's signature. I also told him if I was ordered to do it, he could have my shield."

"You put it on the line, didn't you?" Kerney said.

Andy grunted. "It didn't win me any popularity contests at the Roundhouse."

"But the troops will love it when the word gets out," Kerney predicted. He looked at the message in his hand. "Can I use the helicopter for a quick trip to Socorro? I've got one last interview to conduct in the Gillespie murder case."

"Do it. Get out of my sight. Today, you'd be nothing but an albatross around my neck."

"You get so irritable when your butt gets chewed."

"I know it," Andy said. "Don't waste time in Socorro. I want these cases cleared before we both get the boot."

"Is that likely?" Kerney asked.

"Politics is the art of the possible."

THE STATE police helicopters and all the fixed wing aircraft were tied up on assignments until mid-morning. When he finally boarded a chopper, Kerney expected to reach Socorro in under an hour. Instead, he found himself stranded at the Los Lunas Airport, fifty miles north of his destination. A winter squall had moved across the central plateau, bringing sleet, freezing rain, and wind gusts of fifty knots an hour.

By radio, Kerney asked for ground transportation, but all available units were out handling fender benders on the interstate.

The morning passed as he waited in the chopper with the pilot and listened to the sleet and rain pelt against the metal skin of the aircraft. There were no public facilities at the airport, and nowhere to go; Santa Fe and Albuquerque were socked in under heavy fog.

Every ten minutes the pilot checked by radio on weather updates. A young man with an easy, laid-back attitude, the kid had plucked two stranded hunters out of a remote canyon near the Colorado border before flying down to pick Kerney up for the trip to Socorro.

The pilot cracked chewing gum, hummed to himself, and kept looking for a break in the cloud cover.

"If the wind lets up and I see a hole, we can slip right through, Chief," he promised.

During his tour in Vietnam—maybe about the time this kid was born, if he stretched it a bit—Kerney had decided that chopper pilots were a totally insane breed of adrenaline junkies. Over the years, his opinion hadn't changed.

"You think so?" Kerney asked.

The pilot nodded emphatically and rubbed his nose. "No sweat. A little less wind, a little more sky, and we can cut right through the squall. Most of these low-level disturbances come in pulses. I can usually find a window to get through. But I've got to get airborne to see it."

Kerney knew that seasoned chopper pilots, aside from being crazy, were highly competent. They had to be to survive in such unforgiving flying machines.

"How long have you been a pilot?" he asked.

"Six years. Three in the army and three with the state police."

Kerney latched his seat belt. "Find your window and get me to Socorro," he said.

"You got it, Chief," the kid replied as he hit the starter switch.

AFTER three abortive attempts and two hours in the air, Kerney arrived at the Socorro Airport a little green around the gills, where an obliging city cop waited to drive him to the hospital.

At the hospital, he almost ran over Nita Lassiter on his way to the maternity ward. She looked tired and her eyes were red from crying.

"What are you doing here?" she demanded.

"Did Addie have her baby?"

"A girl, early this morning. The adoption agency has guardianship. Addie signed the papers." She searched Kerney's face with her eyes. "Now, answer my question."

"Addie wants to see me."

"No," Nita snapped. "I don't want you to see her."

"It's her decision."

"Please don't do this."

Kerney looked down at her. "Addie can help you, Nita. Why don't you let her?"

"I don't want her damaged any more than she has been."

"Did you tell Addie that you're her mother?"

Nita bit her lip and nodded.

"How did she take it?"

"She cried a lot. We both did. Then she got angry with me."

"Is she still angry?"

"Drained. I've been forgiven. On a gut level, I think she already knew. I think she's glad to have the truth finally come out."

"Only part of the truth has come out," Kerney noted. "Addie is young and resilient. Don't force her to live under another cloud."

"Let it be, Mr. Kerney. Please."

"In ten or twenty years, if the parole board ever releases you from prison, your chance to help Addie make a life for herself will be long gone. Are you willing to throw that away?"

The thought hit Nita full force and her body stiffened. "You make it so hard," she finally said, forcing a pinched smile.

"It is hard," Kerney replied. "But I think you're up to it."

Nita searched Kerney's face with a probing look. His eyes were sympathetic, his expression concerned. "Why do you care?"

He smiled. "You make it hard not to."

"It makes my stomach hurt."

"You'll do it?"

"Yes."

"Good for you."

"Only if you come with me for moral support."

"Of course," Kerney said.

In the hospital room Verdie Mae sat on the edge of the bed holding Addie's hand. Her eyes flickered from Kerney to Nita as they entered, and she squeezed Addie's hand before rising.

Addie looked pale and drained. The ruffled high-collared nightgown gave her face a touch of innocence that Kerney could only hope the girl retained.

Verdie Mae walked to Nita and touched her cheek. "Is everything all right?" she asked Nita with a quick glance in Kerney's direction.

"Everything's fine," Nita said, looking past Verdie Mae at Addie. "Give us a minute with Addie."

Verdie Mae held Nita's gaze with an unspoken question in her eyes.

Nita smiled tightly and nodded once.

Verdie smiled back, relief showing on her face, and patted Nita reassuringly on the arm. "I'll wait outside."

She left the room, closing the door behind her.

"Hello, Addie," Kerney said.

"Hello," Addie replied. "I wasn't sure if you would come."

"I got here as soon as I could," Kerney said.

"When we talked before, you said you wanted to help me."

"I did say that," Kerney replied, "and I meant it."

"Would it help Nita?" She switched her gaze to Nita. "I mean, would it help my mother?"

"You know what your mother might be facing, don't you?"

"Maybe going to prison for a long time. You know what I think, Mr. Kerney?"

"What's that, Addie?"

"I think rapists should be killed or castrated. Every one of them."

"The world would be a much better place without rapists," Kerney said. "Did Paul Gillespie rape you?"

"Yes."

Kerney held up a hand to stop Addie from continuing. "Before you say more, your mother has something to tell you."

Hesitantly, Nita approached Addie and sat on the edge of the bed.

"What is it?" Addie asked.

"A long time ago, Paul Gillespie raped me. I got pregnant and had a baby," Nita said. "Do you know what that means?"

Addie's expression turned to stunned repulsion. "Oh God, no."

"Yes," Nita said. "It's true." She pulled her daughter into her arms and held her tightly.

Kerney slipped out of the room. Fifteen minutes passed before Nita opened the door and gestured for him to come in. Both Nita and Addie were red faced and teary eyed.

"You don't have to talk to me now," Kerney said.

"I want to," Addie answered flatly.

He turned on the tape recorder and started the session. Addie answered Kerney's questions in a lifeless voice.

After it was over, Kerney left feeling as deadened as Addie had sounded during the interview.

A FOUR-FOOT wall enclosed the front yard of the two-story house across from Fletcher's residence. Mature pine trees fanned thick branches over the wall into the lane. Where the lane ended stood a six-foot cedar fence. An old garage sat perpendicular to the house, close to the property line. There were no lights on inside the two-story house.

Carlos knew no one was home. Using his cellular phone, he'd called the residence every five minutes since arriving at the stakeout and putting the team in place.

He stood shivering in a dark recess between the fence and

the garage. From his vantage point he could see the locations of two of his men. One was crouched behind the wall under a tree directly across from Fletcher Hartley's house. The other was in a prone position behind some large landscape boulders near the guest quarters. The third member of the team was at the back of the house, ready to climb the garden wall and storm the patio door as soon as Carlos gave the signal.

Each member of the team wore a radio headset with an attached microphone, a black hood, and a black police-style tactical duty outfit.

Headlights came into view on the street and slowed to enter the entrance to the narrow lane. He watched through binoculars as the car turned into Fletcher's driveway, and read the license plate. It was Kerney's police car.

"He has arrived," he whispered in Spanish into his headset. "Wait for my command."

"THIS IS the third time today you've checked up on me, Gilbert," Fletcher said. "I'm starting to feel that I'm under house arrest."

"Has everything been quiet?" Gilbert asked, following Fletcher into the kitchen.

"I'm completely bored." Fletcher stood at the counter and poured coffee into two cups. "There have been no strangers at the door, no mysterious phone calls, and the only traffic in the lane has been police cars driving back and forth every hour or so." He carried the cups to the table and joined Gilbert. "This is all rather silly."

"Probably," Gilbert said.

"Then why all the fuss?"

"Just a precaution," Gilbert answered.

"Piffle," Fletcher said.

"Piffle? Do you think you're Nero Wolfe?"

Before Fletcher could answer, the sound of shattering glass from the back of the house brought Gilbert to his feet. He heard wood splintering at the front door. He pulled Fletcher out of his chair, put the cordless kitchen phone in Fletcher's hand, and pointed to the garage passageway.

"Go," he ordered. "Crawl under your car and hide. Call 911, give them the address, and say a crime is in progress and an officer needs assistance. Do it now."

He pushed a panicked Fletcher toward the passageway, doused the kitchen lights, and drew his weapon. Another cracking sound against the front door shattered the silence. He dropped into a low crouch, crept into the dining room, and killed the lights. He could feel cold air coursing along the floor from the front hallway.

Gilbert figured there were two, maybe three people inside, converging on him. The only possible escape would be through the garage, if it wasn't covered by somebody on the outside.

He retreated to the kitchen, removed the cups, and quietly dropped the massive table on its side. He rotated it until the top could be used as a shield, and pulled it by the legs as he inched backward to the passageway.

He crouched down, took a quick glance above the barricade, and saw the hallway lights go out. He counted five seconds and took another look. He could see the shapes of two men in the dining room, one with his back pressed against the wall, the other bent low.

Gilbert's options were limited. He could either make a stand or back off. Risking a break could put Fletcher in danger. He pulled his spare clip from the magazine holder. If he could take these two out, maybe he could protect Fletcher until help arrived.

He fixed the position of the two men in his mind's eye and stretched out on his back with his head up and the nine-millimeter clutched in both hands between his legs. He took one deep breath and kicked hard at the table to upend it. The shooters opened up on full automatic, rounds tearing into the wall and pantry inches above Gilbert's head. He double-fired repeatedly at the two targets until his clip emptied.

He ejected the spent magazine and loaded the spare. As he readied to pull off more rounds, he realized the shooting had stopped. He looked at the target zones; there were two downed bodies. He fanned his weapon back and forth, ready to fire again if either moved. Nothing happened. He slithered around, keeping the targets in sight. Then he flipped quickly onto his stomach, belly-crawled to the bodies, and checked them. Both were dead.

He hurried into the garage and found Fletcher hiding under his car, shaking like a leaf. "Did you call?" he whispered.

"Yes."

"Stay put. Where's the remote for the garage door opener?"

"On the visor in my car."

"Where are your car keys?"

"In the house."

"Dammit."

"What are you going to do?"

"There may be more people outside." Gilbert climbed on the hood of Fletcher's car, popped off the light cover to the opener, and unscrewed the bulb. "Crawl to the front of the car and hide behind the tire. Make yourself as small as possible."

"What can I do to help?"

"Do you have a gun in your glove box?" Gilbert asked as he jumped off the hood of the car.

"No, I don't own a gun."

"Too bad." In a crouch, he worked his way around the vehicle, opened both car doors, grabbed the remote door opener, and turned off the interior light.

"What are you doing?" Fletcher hissed.

"Trying to buy us some time." From the driver's side with the doors open, Gilbert had a clear shot if someone stormed through the passageway door, and a good field of fire into the driveway once he opened the overhead door.

He hoped to God only one shooter was left. He didn't have enough ammunition to take one man out and keep up a running gun battle with another.

He steadied himself and waited.

RAMON slipped into the dining room and checked the bodies. "Javier and Raul are dead," he whispered into his headset. "The house is empty."

"Are the targets down?" Carlos demanded.

"No."

"Where are they?"

"In the garage."

"Do you have an advantage?" Carlos asked.

"No."

"Can you see into the garage?"

"No. The door is closed."

Carlos moved down the driveway. The exterior garage door had a row of shoulder-high small windows. "When I tell you, put heavy fire into the garage through the door. I will do the same from outside."

"We haven't much time," Ramon said.

"Then we must do it quickly," Carlos replied. He stopped near the garage, pulled a night-vision viewer from the pouch at his waist, and scanned through the windows. The device could not magnify, but it did show a man's outline behind an open car door.

"I have him," Carlos said into his headset. He kept the viewer fixed on Kerney and braced the assault rifle against his shoulder.

"Move down the passageway. Aim high and to the right. Tell me when you're in position."

"I'm there," Ramon whispered.

"Fire now," Carlos said as he squeezed the trigger.

OFFICER Yvonne Rasmussen heard automatic-weapons fire as she rolled into the lane with the unit headlights off and the window open. She ground to a stop, hit the quick-release button to the racked shotgun, grabbed the weapon, and tumbled out of her unit. She keyed her handheld radio as she ran down the lane.

"Shots fired," she said. "Officer needs assistance." She gave her location and asked for backup.

The automatic-weapons fire continued to come from the direction of Fletcher Hartley's house. She cut across the property at an angle and stopped before she broke cover at the driveway. A man in tactical garb wearing a headset stood spraying the garage door with an AK-47.

She chambered a round into the shotgun and dropped to a kneeling position. The distance was too great to be effective, but maybe she could draw fire away from Sergeant Martinez. She pulled off a round, and the shooter wheeled and fired back. She felt something slam into her thigh, lost her balance, and fell. She looked down at her leg in stunned surprise. Her uniform trousers had a bloody hole in them. It was a brand-new pair. When she looked up, the man was gone.

"Get out, now," Carlos said into the headset as he ran to the back of the house. "The police are here."

"Did we get them?" Ramon asked.

"It's done," Carlos replied. "Meet me at the car."

Rasmussen limped across the driveway and down the path to the front door. She could feel blood dripping down her leg. The front door was smashed and almost off the hinges. She got on her belly, cradled the shotgun in her arms, and started crawling down the dark hallway. The numbness in her leg was gone, replaced by a hot pain that made her clench her teeth to keep from groaning aloud.

A silhouette entered the hallway from a side room.

Rasmussen stopped crawling and aimed the shotgun. "Don't move."

The figure turned toward her and the barrel of a weapon swung around. She fired once and the blast caught the man full force in the chest.

She keyed her handheld radio. "Officer down," she mumbled. From outside she could hear sirens in the distance. She crawled to the body and checked it. The man was dead. She moved over the body into a dining room and switched on her flashlight. The beam caught two more bodies under the kitchen archway. She checked them both before moving into the kitchen. An overturned table, thick legs peppered with bullet holes, blocked a short passageway. At the end of the hall, a door had been virtually blown apart by heavy fire.

Yvonne switched off the flashlight and pulled herself down the passageway. "Police officer," she called out.

"In here," Fletcher said.

"Identify yourself."

"Fletcher Hartley."

"Are you alone?"

"No. Gilbert Martinez is with me. He's been shot."

"Are you all right?"

"I think so."

"Are you armed?"

"No."

"Stay where you are. I'm coming in."

She pulled her handgun, hobbled to the garage, and fumbled for the light switch. She searched low and saw Fletcher Hartley huddled at the front tire of a bullet-riddled car. The arm of a man holding a nine-millimeter was draped over Hartley's back. She approached cautiously. The man was lying on his side with his face blown away.

As shock from her wound kicked in, Officer Rasmussen realized the faceless dead man was Sergeant Martinez.

10

Carlos finished briefing DeLeon just as the *jefe*'s airplane reached cruising altitude. The takeoff, which he hated as much as landings, had distracted Carlos and sweat trickled down his armpits. He jiggled his false teeth with a thumb and tried to remember if he'd forgotten anything in his report.

DeLeon sat at the desk in the private compartment of his airplane examining the statue of Our Lady of Guadalupe. He seemed more interested in the statue than he did in the details of the firefight. Carlos waited for a reaction from DeLeon as he turned the *bulto* in his hands and carefully inspected it. All the other stolen items had been left locked in the wine cellar of the Santa Fe house.

Finally, DeLeon spoke. "I did not think Kerney would be so easy to kill."

"I could not determine if the old man is dead," Carlos said. "The police arrived too quickly. Ramon may also be alive."

"Ramon is dead and Fletcher Hartley is alive," DeLeon said as he concentrated on the intricate elements of the statue.

The statement came as no surprise to Carlos. The *jefe* frequently had important information at his disposal within a very short period of time.

"You are not dismayed?" Carlos asked.

DeLeon placed the *bulto* on the desktop. "The most important goal of killing Kerney was accomplished. The loss of the team is of no consequence. None of them can be traced to me. They were men without identities. Did you enjoy your assignment?"

"It gave me great pleasure, *patrón*."

"I am glad." DeLeon waved a hand in the direction of the compartment door. "You are sweating heavily, Carlos. This fear you have of flying makes your smell intolerable. Go have a drink, relax, and ask Our Lady of Guadalupe to carry you safely home."

Carlos nodded apologetically and left.

Enrique turned his attention back to the wooden statue. It was beautifully fashioned and wore an elaborate blue-colored robe. A gesso over the wood smoothed out the figure, and tempera paints created a creamy flesh tone to the face and hands. The wood-carver had added arched eyebrows and wide, staring eyes. The circular base contained a filigree of delicate flowers and stems.

The unknown New Mexico artist had followed the Spanish tradition of crafting an *esplendor*—a rayed nimbus of gold prongs—around her head, which made the statue exceedingly rare.

DeLeon estimated the piece to be three hundred years old. A treasure, he thought. It would add much to the chapel at his hacienda.

. . .

FLETCHER'S studio was the only room in the house not overflowing with cops, medical examiners, and crime scene technicians. He sat in a paint-splattered armchair in front of an easel
that held an unfinished painting of fluttering magpies alighting
on a tree branch. He had a thousand-yard stare in his eyes and a
drained, empty expression.

Kerney stood by quietly.

"Did you see Gilbert?" Fletcher finally said.

"Yes."

"His face is gone." Fletcher shuttered slightly at the thought.

"Yes."

"Who will tell his parents?"

"It will be taken care of."

"He has a wife. Do you know her?"

"No," Kerney answered. "I don't."

"And children. Two girls."

"I know."

"I have his blood all over me. Why did this happen, Kevin?"

"Because of my stupidity."

A plainclothes officer holding a notebook knocked at the studio door and stepped inside.

"What is it?" Kerney asked.

"The police chaplain wants to know if Mr. Hartley would
like to see him." He smiled sympathetically in Fletcher's direction.

Fletcher shook his head.

"Send him away," Kerney said.

"I need to take Mr. Hartley's statement," the officer added.

"Do it tomorrow," Kerney replied.

The officer nodded, turned on his heel, and retreated.

"I can't stay here tonight," Fletcher said.

"We'll find you a place."

"No need. I'll make arrangements with friends. Someone

will take me in. Why do you blame yourself for Gilbert's death?"

"Because the men who came here wanted to kill me, not Gilbert."

"I don't understand."

"I'll tell you about it later. Let's get you ready to go. You need to clean up and change your clothes."

Fletcher nodded sluggishly, got to his feet, and tried to pull himself together. An expression of self-loathing crossed his face. He looked at Kerney and shook his head as color rose on his cheeks.

"What's wrong?"

"I started worrying about the mess that needed to be cleaned up. Isn't that crass of me?"

"Not at all."

"I think it is."

Kerney stayed with Fletcher until the body in the hallway had been removed, and Fletcher could get to his bedroom without distraction. Fletcher made telephone arrangements to stay with a friend, picked out some fresh clothes from the closet, placed them under his arm, and walked toward the bathroom. He paused at the door.

"I may stay away for a while," he said.

"There will be officers posted here round-the-clock, while you are gone and after you return."

"Thank you."

IN THE hallway, near a pool of blood on the floor under the shattered frames of the Peter Hurd lithographs hanging on the wall that had been damaged by Rasmussen's shotgun blast, Kerney corralled an officer. He asked the uniform to keep Fletcher sequestered and get him quietly out of the house without fanfare.

"Wait until the reporters are gone," he added.

Crime scene tape blocked Kerney's passage into the dining room. A technician working near the bodies by the kitchen archway bagged and tagged spent shell casings and empty ammunition clips. Blood stained the carpet and walls near the bodies. A photographer took pictures of the corpses.

Kerney could see into the kitchen. Bullet holes riddled the pantry next to the passageway, and the garage door had taken sustained heavy fire. Outgunned and outnumbered, Gilbert had put up one hell of a fight.

Outside, the driveway had been cordoned off and the garage door was open. Portable gas-operated klieg lights washed away the night. Officers and technicians swept the grounds, searching for additional evidence.

Inside the garage, Fletcher's car looked as though it had been attacked by a heavy-weapons squad. The windows were shattered and dozens of bullet holes pierced the vehicle. A storage shelf had been strafed, and paint and solvent from demolished cans dripped onto the bloodstain on the concrete pad.

Gilbert's body had been moved to an ambulance. Kerney looked inside the open doors. The body bag was zipped shut. Without thinking, Kerney reached in and gently touched Gilbert's leg. He pushed away the thought that he was the one who needed some consolation, not Gilbert.

At the entrance to the lane, television crews stood in a semicircle around Andy, their camera-mounted lights raw beacons in the night. Kerney checked by radio with the hospital on Officer Rasmussen's condition while he waited for Andy to finish with the media. An ER nurse reported that Rasmussen required surgery, but a full recovery was expected. It was the only bright spot in an otherwise terrible night.

The camera lights went dark and Kerney spotted Andy coming down the lane toward the house. He met him halfway.

"Thank God, that's over," Andy said.

"Do you want me to notify Gilbert's wife?" Kerney asked.

Andy paused momentarily. "I'll do it. Do you know what pisses me off, Kerney?"

"What's that?"

"I don't even know her name. What does that tell you?"

"I don't know her name, either."

"That makes us both shitheads. Will you be able to tie the hit men to DeLeon?"

"I don't think DeLeon is that sloppy. But I'll find a way to get to him."

"Squeeze Bucky Watson," Andy said.

"I plan to, just as soon as I get all my ducks lined up."

AGENT Joe Valdez sat in the conference room and watched Kerney read through the file on Milagro Properties. Kerney had called Joe at home and pulled him back to the office without explanation. He had heard about Gilbert's murder from the radio traffic on his drive to headquarters, and the news had stunned him into an angry silence.

His silence didn't matter; Chief Kerney wasn't asking any questions or talking. He had his elbows on the table, fingers at his temples, head lowered, and his eyes focused on Joe's paperwork. His mouth was a hard, thin line. He finished reading, closed the file, and looked up.

"What else have you got?" he asked tersely.

Valdez consulted his notebook. "Milagro Properties owns some thirty commercial buildings in the city. Mostly high-end or historic buildings on the plaza, Canyon Road, and in the Guadalupe District. The company leases space to galleries, restaurants, retail shops, and various professionals. It owns two major apartment complexes on St. Francis Drive."

"What's Watson's ballpark net worth?"

"I'm still digging to get those numbers. But it appears Milagro has had sufficient cash assets to lend big bucks to Rancho Caballo. If Milagro controls any subsidiary companies, Watson's total net worth could jump considerably."

"Is Watson carrying a heavy debt on his businesses?"

"If he is, I haven't found it yet."

"Is that unusual?"

"I'd say so. I've talked to all the commercial lenders in the area who offer jumbo mortgages. None of them are doing business with Milagro. But he may be using out-of-state financing."

"What do you think?" Kerney asked.

"Money laundering would be a good guess."

"How can you get a handle on it?"

"If Milagro is a holding company, it might have one master casualty-and-loss policy with an insurance underwriter for all its properties, including subsidiaries."

Joe reached for the file, tapped the papers into a neat pile, and stood up. "Once I know exactly what the corporate structure is, I'll start looking at how the money gets moved around."

"Keep me informed."

"I'll start calling insurance agents right away."

"Do we have a list of local security companies?" Kerney asked.

"I've got one in my office."

"Get it for me, would you?"

"Sure thing, Chief." Joe hesitated. "I'd like to start a collection for Gilbert's family. They're going to have a lot of expenses."

Kerney dug for his wallet, extracted all the currency, and put the bills in Joe's hand.

•   •   •

RETIRED city police officer Toby Apodaca watched the unmarked police cruiser stop in front of his Cerrillos Road office. He unlocked the door and held it open as Kerney got out of the car and approached.

"There aren't too many people who can get me out of a warm bed in the middle of the night," Toby said after Kerney stepped inside the Guardsafe Security office. "How are you, Kerney?"

"Fine, Toby," Kerney answered. "And yourself?"

"I'm doing okay," Toby said, brushing an errant eyebrow hair back into place. His bushy eyebrows flared wildly in every direction. He scratched the thick stubble on his chin and ushered Kerney around a counter, past a bullpen for security guards that was shielded by portable partitions, and into a back office.

"I heard you were back in harness," Toby said. "Do you like it?"

"I can't seem to avoid it," Kerney answered as he studied Apodaca. Toby had spent his last ten years as a cop on the Santa Fe Plaza, chasing purse snatchers and giving directions to disoriented tourists. He'd retired a few years before Kerney's shootout with a drug dealer.

"And carrying a deputy chief's shield," Toby noted. "That's pretty impressive."

"We'll see how long it lasts."

Toby had aged well, Kerney decided. In his late fifties, he carried about a 150 pounds on a five-six frame. He had a full head of hair, and light brown eyes accentuated by wire-rim glasses.

Toby chuckled. "I hear you. The thing I hated most about the job was the chickenshit politics. I don't miss being a cop at all. Now I've got my own company, with regular hours, weekends off, and a personal life again. Well, most of the time, anyway."

"Sounds sweet."

"It is. So what's up with Milagro Properties?"

"The owner may be a target of an investigation," Kerney said.

"That doesn't tell me jackshit," Toby said with a smile.

"Deputy chiefs don't pull peace-loving private citizens out of bed after midnight to talk about the possibility that a rich guy like Bucky Watson may have done something illegal."

"We think Bucky may be connected to a Mexican drug lord."

"Connected how?"

"I'm not sure. But if he is, it means he's working with a man who just had one of my officers assassinated."

"You lost an officer?"

"Several hours ago. Gunned down at a south capitol residence. I can't tell you more than that right now."

"What a damn shame." Toby shook his head.

"Tell me about your contract with Milagro."

"It brings in a good third of my gross annual billings. I've had the contract for five years."

"Does the contract cover all his properties?"

"Just about. He lives in Rancho Caballo, and the subdivision provides security, so we don't cover his home."

"How many separate buildings do you patrol?"

"Forty-six, but it's more than just patrol work. At the apartment complexes I provide twenty-four-hour security. And I staff the larger retail outlets with round-the-clock personnel."

"How many properties does Watson own?"

"A bunch of them," Toby said. "I've got two contracts with Watson, one for his Milagro Properties and one for his Magia Corporation."

"What do you cover for Magia?"

"Shopping malls, mini-malls, strip malls, discount malls, warehouses, self-storage units—that sort of stuff."

"Is there anything you don't cover?"

"Well, not really."

"Meaning?"

"Bucky owns an art crating business in an old Victorian house. He said it didn't need any security."

"He told you about it?"

"No, I asked him. We patrol a nightclub and restaurant across the street for another company. My night man who works that sector saw Bucky at the house a couple of times and told me about it. I asked Watson if he wanted to add the building to the contract, and he said no. But I have my man keep an eye on the place, anyway."

"Have you gotten any reports of unusual activity at the shop?"

"Nope."

"How long has your man worked for you?"

"Over four years. He's an ex–correctional officer from the state pen."

"Reliable?"

"Absolutely."

"Is he on duty now?"

"He sure is."

"What's his name?"

"Max Olguin."

"Can you have him meet me outside the nightclub?"

"Can do." Toby wrote down the address and gave it to Kerney. "I'll have him there in ten minutes."

MAX OLGUIN opened the passenger door to Kerney's unit and got in. The bench seat sagged under his bulk. An overweight man somewhere in his late thirties, with a chubby face and a crew cut, Olguin shook Kerney's outstretched hand.

"I'm Kevin Kerney."

"I know," Max said. "I used to see you at the pen when you were still with the city police."

"It wasn't my favorite place to visit."

"Or work at," Max added. "They ought to send the staff home, seal the perimeter, give each convict a loaded assault rifle, and let them have at it. Those sons of bitches would be killing

each other within minutes. That would solve prison overcrowd-
ing, big time."

"Until the courts filled them up again," Kerney noted.

Max grunted in agreement. "But still, it would give us a
break from the scumbags for a while. Toby said you needed to
talk to me."

"I understand you keep an eye on the art crating business."

"Yeah. It's not official or anything. I check it when I patrol
the nightclub. Just a visual from my car."

"Have you noticed anything suspicious or unusual?"

"Not really. A couple of times I got a little concerned."

"About what?"

"Trucks in the alley late at night."

"Was there any activity around the trucks?"

"Yeah. Guys loading and unloading crates. Watson's car was
always there, so I figured everything was cool."

"You know Watson's car?"

"Sure do. I give it special attention, so it doesn't get broken
into or stolen. The boss says it doesn't hurt to keep the clients
happy with a little extra service."

"Describe the trucks to me."

"One time they unloaded a panel truck and a minivan, and
another time they were loading a ten-ton Ford."

"Did you ever get a look at the cargo?"

"Nope. I just saw them carrying crates. All different sizes."

"Have you seen Watson at the crating shop recently?"

"Last night I saw his car parked outside on the street."

"Did you see Watson?"

"No, just his car and two other vehicles parked in front of
the building. The inside lights were on, so I figured Watson was
there and had some of his people working."

"What other kind of vehicles were parked there?"

"A pickup and a subcompact. I've seen both before."

"No large trucks?"

"Nope. But trucks could have come and gone before I came back on my next round."

"Thanks, Max."

"Sure thing," Max said, easing his bulk out of the unit.

Kerney sat in the unit mulling over what Max had told him. He had a strong hunch Bucky wasn't shipping only fine art. He needed to find a way to prove it without conducting an illegal search.

He waited until Olguin drove away, got a flashlight from the glove box, walked across the street, and stood in front of the Victorian house. It had a deep porch supported by white-painted columns with two large windows flanking the front entrance. He walked around the building. A concrete loading dock jutted out from the rear entrance with steps on one side and a ramp on the other. A power line ran from a pole to an electric meter mounted on the corner of the building. The junction box below the meter caught Kerney's attention. A circuit had been added to the house, and a conduit ran from the box into the ground. Kerney wondered if the building had a basement.

At the front, he inspected the latticework grill that bordered the porch. A side section was hinged to provide access. He crawled under the porch and found a wooden insert covering a hole cut in the rock foundation, wide enough for a man to crawl through.

He pulled the insert loose, set it aside, and swept the darkness with the beam of the flashlight. About a quarter of the crawl space was sectioned off by walls that disappeared below grade. The electrical conduit at the back of the house ran straight into it.

Kerney crawled in for a better look. A three-sided stud-and-plywood enclosure butted up against the foundation. It was sloppy, substandard construction, and Kerney had no doubt it had been built without a permit.

Outside, Kerney dusted himself off. He wanted to know what was in the basement. If his hunch about the permit was right, it might be possible to find out without risking an illegal break-in.

ALEX CASTILLO, a customs narcotics agent called up from Albuquerque, held a Vietnamese potbellied pig in his arms and eyed the state cop.

"What's the pig's name?" Kerney asked.

"Mabel."

"Does she have a good sense of smell?"

Castillo grimaced. It was four o'clock in the morning and he wasn't in a mood for pig jokes. Every cop who met Mabel for the first time turned into a stand-up comic.

"If the narcotics are there, Mabel will tell me," Castillo replied. He scratched the pig behind the ears. Mabel snorted.

"Can she detect drug residue?"

"Mabel has a great nose, Chief. Bury it, bag it, sweep it up—it doesn't matter to Mabel. She'll sniff it out. Where do you want her?"

"Under the porch in the crawl space to the house."

"Do you have a search warrant?" Castillo asked.

"I have reason to believe there are controlled substances stored inside."

Castillo shook his head in disagreement. "Anything we find will be considered an illegal search and seizure."

"I plan to find the stash legally," Kerney said.

"How are you going to do that?"

"Whatever I do won't involve you or Mabel."

"That's what I wanted to hear," Castillo said as he dropped to his knees. "Give me your flashlight, Chief."

Kerney handed it over, and Castillo tugged gently at Mabel's leash before disappearing under the porch. The pig lowered her snout and waddled willingly along.

Kerney spent an anxious five minutes waiting for Castillo to reappear. Mabel came out first. She snorted once and gave herself a good shake.

"Bingo," Castillo said as he crawled out. He stood up, reached into a pocket, and fed Mabel a treat. "Mabel tells me you've got a lot of product in there."

"She told you that?"

"She gets real excited when she sniffs out a big stash."

"That's not possible. You and Mabel were never here," Kerney said with a smile.

"I like your style, Chief," Alex said. "Good luck catching the bad guys."

AT THE office, Kerney called the city building code supervisor, woke him up, and asked to meet him in person as soon as possible. Morris Wadley grudgingly agreed, and Kerney drove the predawn empty streets to a small residential subdivision that bordered Cerrillos Road. Built soon after World War II, it was a respectable middle-class neighborhood of pueblo-style, flat-roofed houses on good-size lots. Like most post-war developments, many of the homes had been expanded with second stories and additions as the baby boom swept the country.

Wadley opened the door dressed in a robe and slippers. A pale, short fellow with baby-fine blond hair, he had sleep-filled eyes and a prominent vein in his forehead that caught Kerney's attention.

In a dining area off the living room, Kerney joined Wadley at the table.

"You said on the phone that you needed some information immediately," Wadley said through a yawn.

"And perhaps your help," Kerney added. "I want to take a look inside a building without violating anybody's constitutional rights."

"Is the building under construction or being renovated?"

"No, but I believe a basement has been added without benefit of a permit. Does your office accept anonymous complaints from citizens?"

"All the time. Most neighbors don't like to get in squabbles with each other. Let's say some guy is building a carport without a permit. We'll get a call and go check it out."

"What about commercial remodeling and renovation?"

"We inspect every commercial project in the city."

"Do you have unrestricted access to the site?"

"You bet we do. The city ordinance gives code enforcement inspectors the authority to enter any structure for the purposes of determining compliance with building standards. It's part of the health, safety, and welfare laws."

"What if you're denied entry?"

"That happens a couple of times a year," Wadley replied. "I usually refer the problem to the city attorney and let the lawyers fight it out. In the end, we always get inside."

"Have you ever asked for police assistance to enter a property?"

"Once, I had to. State statutes allow it. Any structure under construction or being remodeled must pass an inspection. Police officers can be called upon to render assistance."

"What if the construction or remodeling was completed sometime in the past?"

Wadley smiled for the first time. "That doesn't matter. We can still inspect, if it's brought to our attention."

"What kind of inspection do you do?" Kerney probed.

"We go through the skin, down to the studs, into the footings if we have to—you name it. We can check the composition of the concrete pour, the wiring, plumbing, heating, the rafters—whatever. We can even order a structure to be demolished if it's deemed unsafe for occupation. That's especially important in times of a natural disaster or catastrophe."

"Would you be willing to use a state police officer to assist in gaining entry to a building?"

"You want to take a look around, do you?"

"That's the idea."

"I don't see why we can't use your people. What building do you want to take a look at?"

Kerney filled Wadley in on the building's location.

Wadley nodded. "That structure is in the Guadalupe Historic District. I know exactly where it is. I don't remember any review hearing for a building permit."

"You'd remember?"

"You bet I would. The code is strict when it comes to historic preservation. We're constantly battling owners who want the rules bent for old structures. We stay on top of those projects. Have to."

"I believe the passageway to the basement may be concealed."

"That sounds interesting," Wadley said with a smile. "I may do this inspection myself. If it's there, I'll find it. You still haven't told me what you're looking for."

"Faulty wiring," Kerney answered with a grin.

Wadley laughed. "When do you want to meet?"

"The business opens at nine o'clock. I'll have a patrol officer standing by to assist you. He'll be fully briefed."

"I'll be there with bells on."

KERNEY checked with his personnel before going to talk to Andy. Two agents were keeping tabs on Bucky Watson. As soon as Watson had settled into his Rancho Caballo house for the night, one agent had taken up a position at the gated entrance road, while the second kept close surveillance on Watson's house with night-vision goggles. Watson hadn't moved.

At the art crating shop, a patrol officer watched the premises from a discreet distance. Everything was quiet.

Kerney briefed Andy on the scheme.

"How many men do you want to use?" Andy asked.

"Just three," Kerney replied. "Two agents stationed out of sight, and a uniformed officer to accompany Wadley into the premises."

"Narcotics agents?" Andy asked.

"No. I don't want the slightest hint to crop up that we expected to find drugs."

"This Wadley guy; he's willing to say the complaint was anonymous?"

"If everything goes right, he won't have to say anything."

"But if he's called as a witness in court, we can kiss the case against Watson good-bye."

"Do you have a better way to squeeze Bucky?"

"What about the money laundering angle?"

"Joe Valdez is working on it, but it could take time."

"What if all you find in the basement is some drug residue?"

"My friend Mabel the pig assures me there's more than residue inside. I'll set up a meeting with Watson, tell him I need to ask him about Amanda Talley, and time it to coincide with the building inspection at the shop. If all goes well, I'll arrest him as soon as the drugs are uncovered."

"You have a lot of faith in Mabel."

"She's got a great nose."

Joe Valdez, looking decidedly rumpled and glassy-eyed from his all-night stint at work, appeared in the doorway. "Got a minute?" he asked.

"Sure, Joe," Andy said. "What have you got?"

"I've located the insurance agent who handles Bucky Watson's commercial accounts. He's faxing me a list of all the Milagro holdings insured by his company."

"Good work," Kerney said.

Joe nodded his thanks. "This agent also insures Bucky's Rancho Caballo homes. Just as a matter of interest, I asked him if he insured any other Rancho Caballo homeowners. He carries one other policy in the subdivision, for a client Bucky referred to him. It's a Mexican corporation called Tortuga International."

"Tortuga?" Kerney said. The word meant "turtle" in Spanish, and DeLeon's Juárez casino was called the Little Turtle.

"That's right," Joe replied. "Anyway, I asked a buddy who works at the corporation commission to go in early and do a search on Tortuga. It's a real estate holding company with an office in the southern part of the state. The CEO's name is Vicente Fuentes, aka Enrique DeLeon."

"Do you have an address for the property?" Kerney asked.

"I wrote everything down," Valdez said, handling Kerney a piece of paper.

"That's damn good work, Joe," Kerney said.

"I just asked the right question, Chief. By the way, Watson controls two corporations: Milagro and Magia. I'd like to follow up to see if there's any connection to Tortuga. It may take me a while."

"Hit it as hard as you can," Andy said, "and keep Chief Kerney informed."

"Okay," Joe said as he cracked a tired smile and left the room.

Andy got out of his chair, walked to the front of the desk, and perched against it. "I'm assuming you have everyone briefed and ready to go."

"They're on station," Kerney answered, unwinding from his chair. His knee felt stiff and cranky. He stretched it out to ease the muscles.

"Well, then, have at it," Andy said as he plucked the piece of paper with DeLeon's Rancho Caballo address from Kerney's hand. "I'll put a surveillance team on DeLeon's house."

"Remember, DeLeon's got diplomatic immunity."

"Yeah, but Vicente Fuentes doesn't. I'll think of a way to get us inside."

"That would be nice."

"Cut the sarcasm, Kerney."

SENIOR Patrol Officer Clyde Piatt knew exactly who was inside the art crating shop. Using the onboard computer in his unit, he'd run a record check on the vehicles as soon as each of the two men drove up, parked, and went into the house.

It was amazing what could be learned from a license plate number these days. The registered owners were Skip Cornell and Kiko Segura, and his screen even displayed driver's license photos, which allowed Piatt to confirm their identities.

There were no wants, warrants, or rap sheets on either man, but that didn't mean shit.

A seventeen-year veteran of the force, Piatt had come to appreciate the new technology. It sometimes made it possible to know in advance whom you would be dealing with. Clyde thought that was fucking marvelous. The more you knew, the less the danger, if you stayed prepared for the unexpected.

He released the thumb snap to his holster as he followed Morris Wadley up the stairs of the loading dock. From inside, Piatt could hear the harsh whine of a table saw.

Wadley went in first, carrying a clipboard. As soon as Skip and Kiko saw Piatt, they shut down the saw.

Interior walls in the back of the house had been removed to create an open workspace. Floor-to-ceiling racks along one wall held lumber, and there were various drills and machine tools on stands near the saw. A small office and an adjacent walk-in storage locker ran along another wall.

Piatt noticed a lot of hand tools on tables and workbenches. Each could be used as a weapon.

"What's up, Officer?" Skip asked as he pulled off his ear protectors.

Clyde smiled and shrugged nonchalantly. "Nothing to worry about."

He closed in slowly, visually scanning the men for hidden weapons. Both wore blue jeans and T-shirts with no obvious bulges. Exactly as he'd been told to do, Wadley stepped off to one side and waited. Piatt stopped walking when he reached the angle he wanted between the two men. He glanced at the hammer on a table within Kiko's reach and stayed well out of striking range.

"We just need a few minutes of your time," Clyde said.

"What for?" Skip demanded.

Kiko looked ready to bolt for the front door. Piatt put his hand on his holster and Kiko froze. It was time to move Kiko and Skip outside.

"Let's go outside," Piatt suggested. "I'm allergic to sawdust."

"What in the fuck is this all about?" Skip asked.

"Building inspection," Piatt answered. "Do you have a problem with that, Skippy?"

Piatt's use of his diminutive nickname, which he hated, made Skip's face turn red. "You know me?"

"I sure do. I know your friend Kiko, too. Now, let's go outside." Clyde smiled broadly at Kiko. "Don't even think of reaching for that hammer."

Outside, Piatt stood them with their backs against the loading dock. Skip wanted to smoke a cigarette and Clyde suggested he could do without. Kiko kept shifting his weight from one foot to the other. Every time he moved, Clyde clamped a hand on his pistol grip and Kiko froze.

Finally, Wadley appeared on the dock with a flushed, excited look on his face and looked down at Piatt.

"This place is a building code disaster," he said. "The first floor has been ruined."

"That's a shame," Piatt replied, staying focused on the two men in front of him.

"There's something I think you should see, Officer," he said. "I'm no expert, but it looks like drugs to me. A lot of drugs in a hidden basement."

"Don't touch anything." Clyde took his handheld radio out of the belt case and called for assistance. "Turn around, boys," he ordered, after he ended the transmission.

He cuffed and frisked them while he read them their rights, and sat them both on the ground.

"Are there really drugs inside, Skippy?" Clyde asked as he stepped back.

"I don't know nothing about that shit," Skip replied, his face turning red.

"How about you, Kiko? Do you know anything about drugs?"

"I just build shipping crates. That's all."

"Well, you're both going to have to answer a lot of questions."

"I want a lawyer," Skip said.

"Me too," echoed Kiko.

"Fair enough," Clyde said. "But first you get a ride in a shiny new police car."

Piatt turned the men over to an arriving patrol officer and waited for the agents to appear. As the arresting officer, Clyde needed to confirm the presence of narcotics in the building. He went in with the agents, and Wadley led them to the storage locker and a built-in shelf that swung open to reveal steps to the secret basement. Bundles of crack cocaine and heroin were stacked on pallets. It was a hell of a lot of dope, enough to fill the trunk of a full-size car.

The agents did a quick test of the drugs and pegged the street value at a million plus.

"What charges do you want on Kiko and Skip?" Piatt asked.

"Start with trafficking," an agent said, "and then be creative."

11

Like most of the shops along Canyon Road, Bucky Watson's gallery had once been a private residence. The interior of the building had neoclassical features accentuated by antique furniture and expensive art in ornate frames. Watson's office continued the theme. Behind the Shaker table that served as a desk, logs burned in a fireplace bordered by a gilt-edge Georgian surround. An old Mexican grain chest sat on sturdy legs under a window that looked out on the narrow street. On a high shelf over the window was an impressive array of Apache Indian baskets. Paintings by early twentieth-century Santa Fe artists and a bookshelf of art reference publications completed the decor.

Kerney sat across the table from Bucky. Watson's eyebrows

had started twitching the moment he arrived. He smirked at Kerney's questions, toyed with a ring, and answered impatiently.

"Is all this rehashing necessary?" Watson said.

"Sometimes it can jog a recollection or two," Kerney replied genially.

"Go ahead and finish asking your questions."

"You said Amanda attended the benefit alone. Did you see her arrive unescorted?"

"No. That's just the impression I had. She didn't act like she was with anybody."

"Why do you say that?"

"Because she was milling around, mixing, chatting people up."

"Did any of the men at the benefit seem interested in Amanda?"

"Every straight man who meets Amanda is interested in her."

"What about Vicente Fuentes? Was he interested?"

Bucky flinched slightly. "I don't know if he was or not."

"Is Fuentes straight or gay?"

"I don't know."

"Can you put me in touch with Fuentes? I'd like to talk to him."

"I don't know how to do that. I've only met the man a couple of times." Bucky ran his finger under the collar of his teal blue linen shirt.

"Doesn't he own a home in Rancho Caballo?"

"He's a member at the club, so I suppose he does."

"I had the impression you knew him fairly well."

"You're mistaken."

"I understand Fuentes is wealthy. How did he make his money?"

"I have no idea." The phone rang and Bucky grabbed the receiver. He listened momentarily and handed the instrument to Kerney. "It's for you."

Kerney took the call, and listened as the agent reported that over a million dollars in black tar heroin and crack cocaine had been found in the secret basement. Suppressing a smile, he expressed his thanks and handed the receiver to Bucky.

"Are we finished?" Bucky asked as he dropped the phone in the cradle and stood up.

"I'm afraid you have a problem, Mr. Watson."

"What kind of problem?"

"With the city. It appears a citation has been issued."

"What for?"

"Building code violations."

"Which building?"

"The Victorian house where you have your art crating shop. Supposedly, you gutted the inside without a permit."

"Those jerks at the city are always trying to screw with me. I'll have my lawyer handle it."

"There's one more problem, Mr. Watson," Kerney said, reaching for his handcuffs. "A large quantity of heroin and cocaine was found in the basement of the building."

"I don't know what the fuck you're talking about."

"Call it the luck of the draw," Kerney said as he stepped to Bucky, spun him around, and cuffed him.

BUCKY'S refusal to talk without his lawyer present came as no surprise to Kerney. After the lawyer arrived at headquarters, Kerney assigned four agents working in pairs to interrogate Watson. The teams switched every hour to keep the pressure on, while search warrants were executed. Officers were at the art crating shop, the gallery, the design studio, and Bucky's residence, looking for anything that could be added to the list of charges against Watson.

Kerney hoped to overwhelm Bucky with hard evidence and

force him to cooperate. Watson's two employees, Skip Cornell and Kiko Segura, were undergoing separate interrogations and being pressured to cut a deal and testify against Bucky. The chances looked good; fingerprints from both men had been lifted from the drug parcels, and the sheer volume of the stash guaranteed a felony-one fall, unless they rolled over on Watson.

Joe Valdez, armed with a special search warrant, had seized Watson's electronic mail and computer files. He had several technical specialists running programs to break Bucky's privacy codes and locate any off-site network terminals. Valdez was digging into Watson's hard copies, looking for the money trail and the drug distribution network.

If all went well, Kerney planned to be Bucky's final interrogator of the day. He wanted to have the pleasure of cracking Bucky open.

Noontime passed before he could get away from the office. A contractor's truck was parked in Fletcher's driveway. He found the man inspecting the damaged front door, while the patrol officer assigned to watch over Fletcher's house looked on. Kerney introduced himself and showed the contractor around.

When the inspection concluded, the man consulted his clipboard notes, did some quick calculations, and stuck a pencil behind an ear. He had dark curly hair, a skinny neck, and a large Adam's apple.

"It must have been one hell of a gunfight," the man said. "The newspaper said four people were killed. I thought shit like that only happened in the movies."

Kerney had no desire to chitchat about the shoot out. "I want everything put back in its original condition."

The contractor caught the tone in Kerney's voice and changed the subject. "Will insurance pay for it?"

"Probably."

"Is it a full-replacement policy?"

"I don't know."

"The front door alone is going to cost plenty to reproduce. It was hand-carved from old oak. I'll have to subcontract it out."

"That's fine," Kerney said. "When can you start?"

"In the morning."

"How long will it take?"

"A week, but I can't guarantee you'll have the new front door by then. What's the deductible on the insurance policy?"

"I don't know."

"Isn't this your house?"

"No, I'm acting on the owner's behalf," Kerney said as he wrote out a check that dug a hole in his savings and gave it to the man. "This should get you started. If it doesn't, let me know."

The man looked at the amount, smiled, and nodded. "I've got some scrap plywood in my truck. I'll board everything up and be back tomorrow with my crew."

"I'll let the owner know you'll be here," Kerney said. He shook the man's hand and left.

He hoped that arranging to have the house restored would ease some of Fletcher's pain. The way Kerney saw it, he'd been the houseguest from hell.

GARY DALQUIST's law office was in an old brick cottage across the street from the county judicial building. The front room served as a reception and waiting area. It had a tongue-and-groove oak floor, and a hand-stenciled fruit-and-floral motif that ran at the top of the walls next to the high plaster ceiling. Dalquist was leaning over a desk at the back of the room, talking to a secretary, when Kerney walked in.

He looked up and stepped across the room. "I thought I might be hearing from you," he said. "Nita told me you took a statement from Addie."

Kerney held out the transcript. "I did. Here's your copy."

"It's not often an arresting officer in a murder case is so helpful to the defense."

"You're not the only lawyer who's made that observation recently," Kerney said. "But Wesley Marshall didn't put it quite so nicely."

Dalquist chuckled. "I'm sure he didn't. I have a message for you. Robert is being discharged from the hospital today. He'll be staying with Nita for a while. She wanted to make sure that you knew where he would be."

"Is he well enough to be discharged?"

Dalquist shrugged. "He's a welfare case. Hospitals push indigent people out the door as quickly as possible."

"I hope Ms. Lassiter knows what she's doing. Robert isn't easy to manage."

"I said about the same thing to her, but she wouldn't be swayed. It may work out; Robert is back on his medications and seems fairly stable."

"He's acting okay?"

"He seems to be, according to Nita."

"When will you go to trial?" Kerney asked.

"Not soon, that's for sure," Dalquist replied. "But when we do, I plan to mount a defense that won't leave a dry eye in the courtroom." Dalquist tapped the papers in his hand. "Thanks for dropping Addie's statement by."

"You're welcome."

Outside, Kerney watched two deputies march shackled prisoners out the back door of the courthouse and into a waiting sheriff's van. The new officer uniforms, off-blue and gray in color, had been selected by the county sheriff in an attempt to professionalize the appearance of his deputies. To Kerney's eye, it made the cops look like valet parking attendants with sidearms.

He called Andy from his unit and said he was on his way back to the office.

"I'll meet you in the parking lot," Andy replied.

"What's up?"

"We're going to take a tour of DeLeon's Rancho Caballo house."

"Okay, I'll bite: How did you arrange it?"

"By using the prestige of my high office."

"Will DeLeon be there to give us a tour?"

"Unfortunately, no. He left last night."

"How do you know that?"

"He informed Rancho Caballo security that he was leaving."

ANDY had the key to DeLeon's house and the access code to the security gate that barred the road.

"Amazing," Kerney said in mock wonderment as Andy punched in the numbers on the keypad and the gate swung open. "How did you get the code?"

"Rancho Caballo keeps all the access codes on file, so they can shut off systems when there's a false alarm and the owners are away."

"Park off the road so we can approach the house on foot," Kerney suggested.

"I don't need a lesson in tactics," Andy said as he coasted to a stop.

They scrambled up the hill, Kerney taking the front while Andy looped around the back. He finished his sweep just as Andy joined him on the veranda.

"Looks quiet," Kerney said.

"Same in the back," Andy said, positioning himself at the side of the front door with his .357 in his hand. "Some place," he added.

"Do you like it?" Kerney asked as he took his station on the side of the door, the nine-millimeter in the ready position.

Andy put the key in the lock. "Not really." He turned the key slowly. "Don't get me shot. Connie wouldn't like it."

"Should I call for backup?"

"You are my backup," Andy said as he pushed the door open.

The burglar alarm went off and they waited a few beats before entering. They cleared the house room by room with the alarm bleating in their ears. They finished up in the garage and went back to a locked door in the lower hallway. It was protected by a keypad system.

"Well," Kerney said, "aren't you going to open it?"

Andy hit some numbers on the keypad and the alarm shut off. He punched in more numbers and smiled at Kerney. "Try it."

The doorknob turned freely. Kerney swung the door open and turned on the lights. The stolen paintings were stacked neatly along the walls away from the wine racks, and the antique and pottery pieces were on a tasting table in the center of the room.

"Sweet Jesus," Andy said, his face cracking into a grin.

"I didn't know you were a religious man."

"I am now," Andy replied as he patted Kerney's shoulder and stepped into the room. "Let's get some techs and people from the museum over here pronto."

BUCKY WATSON broke off his conversation with his lawyer when the door to the interrogation room opened and Kerney walked in. He leaned back in his chair and sneered at the cop.

"Sorry to keep you waiting, gentlemen," Kerney said.

"Are you the arresting officer?" Earl Buffett asked.

"I am." Kerney smiled in Watson's direction and dragged a

chair across the floor to the table. Bucky's sneer remained intact.

"I want this interrogation ended," Buffett said. "It has gone on much too long."

"Mr. Watson is under arrest," Kerney noted. "We can keep him here for quite a while." He sat down and carefully stretched out his right leg. "How are you holding up, Bucky?"

"Better than you," Bucky answered sarcastically, studying Kerney's drawn, exhausted face.

Kerney switched his gaze to Buffett. The man had very little space between the tip of his nose and his upper lip, and a pinched jaw that pulled his lower lip down at the edges.

"Aside from the drugs found in the basement, what other evidence do you have against Mr. Watson?" Buffett asked.

"Have patience, Mr. Buffett," Kerney counseled. "Gathering evidence takes time."

"You've had most of the day to search the shop," Buffett replied. "Surely it doesn't take that long."

"Bucky's shop is only one of the places we've searched today."

"I assume you had search warrants?"

"Certainly."

"Where else have you been?"

"So far? His house, gallery, and the design studio," Kerney answered. "Are you ready to do some hard time, Bucky?"

"That's not going to happen," Bucky said.

Buffett shot Bucky a glance to shut him up. "You have presented us with no proof that my client had knowledge of the drugs stored in the basement."

"Weren't you told?" Kerney asked, feigning surprise.

"Told what?"

"Bucky's fingerprints are all over the kilos of smack and cocaine."

Watson snickered.

"Does that amuse you?" Kerney asked.

"You can plant as much evidence against me as you want," Bucky replied. "It doesn't mean anything."

Buffett held up a hand to cut Watson off. "Please, Bucky. We can deal with the evidence issue later. What else?"

"Skip and Kiko have agreed to testify against your client. From what they've told us so far, both have made a number of drug deliveries. We'll be adding additional charges against you, Bucky."

"Is that the extent of your investigation?" Buffett demanded.

"No. I'm sorry if you haven't been given all the facts," Kerney replied apologetically.

"What facts?" Bucky snapped.

"We were able to access your computer files. That's quite a nice little distribution network you've got going. We have your shipment records with all the details. It's the next best thing to a confession. Have you told your lawyer about Enrique DeLeon?"

Bucky flinched.

"Who?" Buffett said.

"You need to be more forthcoming, Bucky," Kerney chided. "Mr. Buffett can't help you if you withhold information from him."

"Back up," Buffett said.

"Forget it," Bucky growled, cutting Buffett off.

"DeLeon is a Mexican drug lord," Kerney explained. "Probably the biggest smuggler on the border. A very nasty man. Are you sure you don't want to talk to your lawyer about him, Bucky?"

Watson glared and clamped his mouth shut.

"Then on to other matters," Kerney said, switching his attention to Buffett. "We're asking the United States Attorney to prosecute your client under the federal drug trafficking statute."

"That carries an automatic death penalty upon conviction," Buffett said.

"That's why we thought it would be a good idea. How does that sit with you, Bucky? Will a death penalty be enough of an object lesson for you?"

"Fuck you."

"I'd be angry, too," Kerney said with a shrug. "You're between a rock and a hard place. If DeLeon doesn't kill you, eventually the government will. It's not a pretty picture."

Buffett leaned over and whispered in Bucky's ear.

Bucky gulped, nodded, and whispered something back.

"Can we deal?" Buffett asked, when he broke away.

"Nothing happens without a full confession," Kerney said.

"That's hardly accommodating to my client. What, exactly, do you want?"

"Full disclosure on DeLeon's money laundering scheme and his drug distribution network."

"Forget it," Bucky said. He would rather make a seven-figure cash bond and disappear with his considerable nest egg as soon as the judge released him.

"DeLeon knows you've been skimming money from him," Kerney said.

"Get real," Bucky said.

"I faxed the information to him myself." Kerney had taken no such action, and had no proof that his accusation was true, but the thought of DeLeon's retaliation might make Watson reconsider his position.

Bucky reacted by rubbing his nose, putting both elbows on the table, and crossing his legs—sure signs of stress and guilt.

"I know DeLeon, Bucky. And I guarantee that he'll have you killed before you can leave town. Tell me I'm wrong."

"If you know DeLeon so well, how did you contact him?" Bucky asked.

"The information went to his hacienda and to the Little Turtle Casino in Juárez. You're going to need to be someplace safe for a while. DeLeon has a long reach."

The smug look on Bucky's face vanished and he swallowed hard. "Just where the fuck is that?"

"I can get you into a special federal prison under a new identity. I understand it's quite a nice place, as prisons go. We can hold you there until your trial."

"Would you be willing to have my client tried in state court?" Buffett asked. A state court trial would keep Bucky off death row, if he was convicted.

"That might be arranged."

"I want more than that," Bucky said. "If I talk, some important people in this state are going to fall hard."

"First you talk and then we deal," Kerney countered. "But the DA might be willing to reduce the charges. It would mean less hard time. A lot less, perhaps."

Bucky thought about his options, and decided he had none. Everything he'd built up was crashing down around his ears. "Okay," he said weakly.

"I'll send the team back in," Kerney said. "Give them your statement." He looked at the lawyer. "Don't let your client change his mind, Mr. Buffett. This is a onetime offer."

Buffett made no response.

"By the way, Bucky, did you know that DeLeon masterminded the art theft and killed Amanda Talley?"

"That's absurd," Bucky said.

"Did Amanda leave with DeLeon after the O'Keeffe benefit?"

Bucky's eyes widened. "They both left about the same time."

KERNEY caught a night's sleep at a Cerrillos Road budget motel. In the morning, he found the construction crew working on Fletcher's house. A laborer scrubbed away at the bloodstains in the garage. The ruined dining room carpet had been pulled up and dumped on the porch, where a workman was hanging a temporary front door.

The man nodded and stepped aside to let Kerney pass. He

found Fletcher on his knees cleaning out the kitchen pantry. Many of the cans, bottles, and containers had been raked by gunfire, resulting in a gummy mess.

Fletcher dumped a gooey container in a wastebasket, wiped his sticky hands on his trousers, and got to his feet.

"You came back," Kerney said.

"Better to face what happened than hide from it," Fletcher said.

"I'm glad you feel that way."

"I didn't expect to find my home already under repair. Thank you for arranging it."

"It was the least I could do."

"You gave the contractor a sizable deposit. I want to reimburse you."

"We can talk about that later."

"Let me show you something," Fletcher said. He went to the kitchen counter, where the Peter Hurd lithographs, removed from their shattered frames, were laid out.

Kerney stepped over and looked. The lithographs were heavily damaged, peppered with holes from Rasmussen's shotgun blast. They appeared unsalvageable.

"Can they be repaired?" Kerney asked.

"I don't think so, but that's not the point," Fletcher said. "Once, I valued these inordinately. Art can enlarge life, but it can't replace it. I'm just happy to be alive. The loss of the lithographs pales in comparison. I must find a way to thank that young officer for saving my life."

"I'm sure you'll think of something unique."

"Have you gone to visit her?"

"Not yet, but she's going to be fine."

He scrutinized Kerney carefully. "You have a dangerous look about you, Kevin."

"I'm not in a very good mood."

252 • MICHAEL MCGARRITY

"There's more to it than that," Fletcher said.

Kerney nodded his head in the direction of the pantry. "I guess we each have our messes to clean up."

"Let me write you a check and pay you back for the deposit. My insurance is going to cover everything."

"No, Fletcher, I don't want the money. Use it, if you like, to replace one of the Hurd lithographs."

"As you wish," Fletcher said. "The door to the guest quarters has been replaced. I'll expect you back after work. We'll have a nice dinner together."

"I'd like that."

"I need the company," Fletcher added. "I still can't stop thinking about Gilbert."

"I can't either," Kerney said.

THE GOVERNOR'S receptionist announced Andy's arrival, and Vance Howell came out of the inner sanctum to escort him to Springer's office. Other than a greeting, Howell had nothing more to say. In the hallway, workers on ladders strung wires for a new closed-circuit television security system.

Another example of locking the barn door after the horses got out, Andy thought glumly.

Howell left, and Andy knocked and entered to find Harper Springer at his desk conferring with his chief of staff. The man glanced at Andy, gave him a tight smile, whispered something to Springer, and retired through the side door to his office.

New paintings had been hung on the walls, and the glass display cases on either side of Springer's desk held Indian pots and some small cowboy sculptures. Fewer pieces of lesser value had been used to redecorate the office.

The governor rose and gestured at the couch as he came around his desk. "Have a seat, Chief Baca."

Andy's antenna went up; Springer was usually much less formal with his senior staff.

"We haven't talked in a while," Harper said as he sank into a chair and crossed his legs. "I know you've been busy."

"That's true, Governor."

"Finding the stolen art was good work. Real good work. But the museum people aren't happy that the Lady of Guadalupe *bulto* wasn't recovered."

"I know that."

"Any chances of getting it back?"

"We'll do our best," Andy answered.

Springer nodded. "I visited with your officer at the hospital. That's one brave young lady. I think she deserves a citation, don't you?"

"It's in the works, Governor. Would you be available to present it?"

"Set it up with my press secretary. And I want to attend Sergeant Martinez's funeral service."

"I've given that information to your administrative assistant."

"Good. I'm still waiting for arrests, Chief Baca. We can't let these cop killers get away."

"I agree."

"I want closure, Chief."

"We'll push a little harder, Governor."

"I know you will. Get something out to the media on it. Let them know the manhunt is continuing. Now, tell me about these charges against Bucky Watson. How solid are they?"

"They're very substantial."

"Do your people have their facts straight?"

"Yes, they do."

"He was a heavy contributor to my reelection campaign."

Andy chose not to respond.

"Will Watson's arrest affect anyone else?"

"Watson has implicated your nephew and Sherman Cobb in a money laundering scheme."

No surprise registered on Springer's face. It was clear that Vance Howell had kept the governor well informed.

"I find that hard to believe, Chief Baca."

"It does create an uncomfortable situation," Andy noted.

"How are we going to handle it?" Springer asked.

"I plan to keep working the case, Governor."

"Let's think this through. I don't want any political fallout to occur because a member of my family may be accused of a crime."

"The situation will get the public's attention," Andy said.

"That's why we need a flexible strategy here. I think the investigation has to be completely separated from my administration. What if I asked the attorney general to step in?"

"I'm not sure such an abrupt change in the investigation would be wise," Andy said.

"I understand that. But the attorney general is a Democrat who holds an elective office completely removed from my administration. If he agreed to appoint a special independent prosecutor for the case, that would erase any doubts of political interference on my part."

"I'd rather not see the investigation slowed down."

"I'm sure the attorney general can act quickly," Springer said.

Andy gave up arguing and got to his feet. Springer was telling him what was going to happen, not asking. "I'll give the attorney general my full cooperation."

Springer flashed a winning smile. "That's the kind of talk I like to hear, Andy."

"This must be hard on you, Governor."

"It cuts deep, Andy. But we'll get through it. I've been talking to the legislative leadership about that budget expansion request you want for new equipment. If you can cut costs a little bit more, I'm sure we can get you that appropriation."

"I'll work up some new figures."

"Good." Springer stood, pumped Andy's hand, and showed him to the door. "Hold up any further action on this Watson mess until we've got the attorney general in the loop."

On his way back to the office, Andy stewed over his meeting with Governor Springer. It made no sense, except as political face-saving bullshit. Springer wanted him to catch cop killers, yet he had just pulled the plug on the only investigation that could possibly lead to an arrest and conviction of the murderers. And when Springer pledged his support for new money for the department, it made Andy feel like a co-conspirator in a cover-up. He didn't like the taste of it at all.

Two officers had given their lives and a third had been wounded. Turning over the case to the attorney general would be a slap in the department's face. The case belonged to the department and nowhere else.

He swung the car out of traffic, parked at a small diner, and went in for a cup of coffee. He had some heavy thinking to do.

NEIL ORDWAY had left no forwarding address with the Mountainair town clerk, and there was nothing in his police officer certification file that yielded information on his current whereabouts. Kerney phoned the agency that administered the police pension fund and got lucky; Ordway had made a request to withdraw his retirement contributions. He had asked that the check be mailed to a street address in the town of Bernalillo, just north of Albuquerque.

Kerney stopped by Andy's office and found it empty. He decided not to wait for Andy to return from the governor's office before taking off. It shouldn't take more than an hour or two to round up Ordway.

He paid a quick visit to Joe Valdez, who had his head buried in a stack of papers. Kerney cleared his throat and Valdez looked up. He had a gleam in his eye and a smile on his face.

"I was going to call you in a few minutes, Chief."

"To tell me what?"

"Do you want the technical or the bonehead explanation?"

"Keep it simple, Joe. I have trouble balancing my checkbook."

"It's a round-robin scam. Bucky's companies are nothing but conduits for DeLeon's money. He pumps it through Tortuga, which lends cash to Milagro, Magia, or some other front, and then it's funneled into projects like Rancho Caballo. Everything comes back to Tortuga nice and clean."

"Does it all come back as cash?"

"No way," Joe said. "Shopping malls, raw land, apartments, subdivisions, commercial and industrial developments—take your pick. DeLeon has too much cash; his quandary is finding ways to convert the money that keeps pouring in."

"How did you get to it so quickly?"

"It's a high-tech world, Chief. Even drug lords use computers nowadays. Bucky's computer was linked to the one at Tortuga International. When our computer specialist found the link, I asked him to search the data fields in the Tortuga computer system. It's been a damn gold mine."

"Have you seized the Tortuga computers and any hard-copy corporate records?"

Joe looked at his watch. "Agents from the Las Cruces office should be at Tortuga right now. It took a while to do the paperwork and get a court order signed."

"Have you been here all night?"

"Yeah. Again."

"Have you got any steam left?"

"I'm good for a few more hours."

"Where do we stand with Sherman Cobb and Roger Springer?"

"Both Bucky and DeLeon kept track of their payments to

Rancho Caballo by computer. Plus, I've got Springer and Cobb signing off on loan applications, countersigning checks, authorizing payments, approving contracts, and accelerating repayments. Put the hard-copy evidence together with Watson's confession and we've got more than enough probable cause."

"Arrest Cobb and Springer," Kerney said. "Take a couple of agents with you."

"Now, won't that be fun," Joe said with a grin.

ANDY pulled into his parking space just as Joe Valdez and two other agents hurried out the door. Valdez spotted Andy's car and walked to it. Andy opened the window and waited.

"Chief, I left a note on your desk."

"What does it say?"

"Chief Kerney went down to Bernalillo. You can reach him by radio if needed."

"Where are you off to?"

"To arrest Springer and Cobb."

"Tell me what you've got," Andy said.

Valdez ran down the facts while the two agents waited inside their units.

After hearing Joe out, and asking a few questions, Andy smiled. Over coffee at the diner, he'd decided to have Cobb and Springer picked up. Kerney had beaten him to it.

"Chief?" Valdez said.

Andy laughed and shook his head. "Do it."

He watched Valdez and the agents drive off, and the tight feeling in his gut started to evaporate.

In his office, he started making calls to the State Department, FBI, the Department of Justice, Customs, and the CIA. He talked to people he knew, several of whom owed him favors. He wanted to blow a bigger hole in DeLeon's operation, if possible. He hung up with promises from the feds to move quickly.

DeLeon was known throughout the criminal justice and intelligence systems, and every agency was eager to cooperate.

He had his secretary fax key documents to federal officials in Washington, Virginia, Albuquerque, and El Paso, and told his public affairs officer to set up a press conference.

To stay on the job in the face of his insubordination, Andy would have to play politics. Once word of his disloyalty reached the Roundhouse, Springer's people would come after him, and he wasn't about to make it easy for the governor to fire him.

ONCE A farming settlement along the banks of the Rio Grande, the town of Bernalillo was somewhat protected from the suburban sprawl of Albuquerque by an Indian pueblo that buffered the two cities. But the cushion of open land that cut a swath east from the river to the mountains couldn't hold back the development that filled the west mesa. A gently rising plateau with eroded cones of extinct volcanoes, sandy arroyos, black lava rock, and bunchgrass, the mesa had been transformed into a series of bedroom communities that filled the skyline.

It vanished from sight when Kerney got off the interstate and dipped into the shallow river valley that sheltered the town. He drove the four-lane main street to city hall, where he stopped and asked for directions.

Ordway lived one block off the main drag in an old two-story adobe farmhouse that had been carved into small apartments. Under the porch were two entry doors, and on either side of the building staircases led to second-story living units. There were lace curtains in the front window of a first-floor apartment, along with a picture of the Virgin Mary that had been taped to a glass pane. The name Abeyta was stenciled on the mailbox next to the door.

Kerney knocked on the door and a heavyset, elderly Hispanic woman wearing a drab gray dress opened it partway.

"Señora Abeyta," Kerney said, speaking in Spanish. "I hope I am not disturbing you." In the background he heard the loud chatter of a television talk show.

"Not at all, but I have no vacancies," Mrs. Abeyta replied in English. "All my apartments are rented."

"I'm looking for a friend of mine," he explained. "Neil Ordway."

"Oh yes, he just moved in, but he is not here now."

"Do you know how I can reach him?"

"He said that he had a job working for a carpet installer."

"Do you know which one?"

Mrs. Abeyta shook her head. "No, but I think he might be working in Rio Rancho, putting carpets in all those new houses they are building up there."

"He told you that?"

"Yes, when he rented the apartment."

"Gracias, señora."

"You're welcome, señor."

Kerney stopped at a cafe on the main street, and used a pay phone and directory to whittle down an interminable number of carpet installers until he located Ordway's new employer. Mrs. Abeyta had heard Ordway correctly; the company was doing subcontract installations for a builder in the Rio Rancho area. Kerney got the address where Ordway was working.

He left Bernalillo and drove up the mesa. The view east toward the mountains showed a sweep of pale hills that climbed from the *bosque*. The Rio Grande ran brown and languid around fingerlike sandbars Kerney glimpsed through the breaks in the thick cottonwood stands. But the drive into Rio Rancho took him into a different world altogether. High privacy walls bordered the wide thoroughfare, masking all but the second story of houses squeezed together on tiny lots. At major intersections, strip malls, convenience stores, and gas stations abounded. The stark, beautiful New Mexico landscape had been transformed into a place no different from the oozing Los Angeles megalopolis.

West of the main road, behind an established residential tract, was a checkerboard development of empty lots and high-density housing units under construction. Along the newly paved streets, stick houses and apartment buildings were going up in assembly-line fashion. While cement crews poured footings and pads at freshly prepped building sites, down the line carpenters framed walls and hung roof joists. The pattern repeated itself until Kerney rolled to a stop in front of three model homes in the final stages of completion. Little flagpoles with triangular pennants stood in front of the houses, and large signs planted in the yards blazoned the name of each model. A panel truck with rolls of carpet sticking out of the open rear doors was parked in a driveway.

Kerney called for backup before walking through the garage, past a laundry alcove, and into the kitchen. In the adjacent dining nook two men were unrolling a carpet pad. Both froze when they saw Kerney with his semiautomatic in one hand and his shield in the other.

"Ordway?" Kerney asked softly.

"Back bedroom, on the left," one of the men replied.

Kerney stepped into the room. "Wait outside," he ordered in a whisper.

The men scurried past him into the garage.

He found Ordway in the bedroom on his hands and knees with his back to the door, trimming carpet. Ordway heard him coming, rose to a kneeling position, and turned. He had a knife in his hand.

Kerney moved quickly before Ordway could react; he slammed the barrel of his gun against Ordway's cheek and kicked at Ordway's knife hand with his good leg. The blade went flying.

Neil came off the floor in a rush, diving for Kerney's midsection. Kerney sidestepped and used Ordway's momentum to drive him, face first, into a wall.

"Hands to the small of your back," Kerney ordered as he leaned hard against the man to keep him secure, and kicked his feet apart.

Ordway grunted and complied.

After cuffing Ordway, Kerney patted him down and spun him around. "Hello, Neil," he said affably. Ordway's nose looked broken.

Ordway seemed dazed. Blood flowed from his nose, dripping on the tan carpet. He swallowed hard and spat at Kerney. "Fuck you, Kerney."

Kerney wiped the spit off his face. "You're under arrest for aggravated battery. Beating up Robert was a stupid idea."

"I'll be out on bail in twenty-four hours," Ordway said.

"But unemployed once again, I would imagine," Kerney replied. "Let me read you your rights."

A state police officer arrived as Kerney brought Ordway out of the house. He explained the charges to the officer, who agreed to drive Ordway to Torrance County, book him into jail, and deliver Kerney's criminal complaint to the district attorney.

Kerney watched the patrol car drive away. Busting Ordway felt good, but it didn't relieve the anger that gnawed at him about Gilbert Martinez's murder. He wondered if he would get a chance to even things up with Enrique DeLeon and Carlos Ruiz.

12

Antonio Vallaverde turned off the main highway south of Juárez onto a blacktop road that cut through the saddle of two hills along the Rio Grande. He stopped at the security gate and announced himself. A high-ranking official in the Mexican Ministry of Justice, Vallaverde coordinated all cooperative borderland investigations with North American law enforcement agencies, including the New Mexico State Police.

Two miles in from the highway, a sprawling hacienda sat at the base of a hill with a lovely view of the *bosque* and the low-lying west Texas mountains across the river. The old rancho had been restored to its original splendor. The main hacienda, a private chapel, rock stables, a stone granary, and several other outbuildings had been rebuilt from the ground up. Old stone fences divided the grazing and farm land that bordered the *bosque,* and some of the melting adobe walls of the original peasant quarters still remained visible in the distance.

During the Mexican Revolution, the site had served as a government jail and execution grounds before being sacked and burned by Pancho Villa's troops.

A houseboy in white linen stood outside the arched hacienda doorway. Antonio parked in the circular cobblestone driveway and followed the servant into the courtyard, with its charming brick lattice balustrade and central fountain. They passed through the vast living room and into the billiard parlor. DeLeon had a guest: A young woman bent over the billiard table with a cue stick in her hands. She had strawberry blond hair that fell against creamy white shoulders, long legs, and a small waist. The woman made her shot as Enrique looked on.

Antonio had spent a number of pleasant evenings in the parlor with Enrique and various industrialists, senior military officers, and prominent politicians who were DeLeon's friends. It was a long room with a high ceiling and an arrangement of comfortable chairs in front of a fireplace at one end, where a well-stocked liquor cabinet stood close at hand. Above the fireplace hung an antique cavalry officer's sword in a scabbard.

In the center of the room, chairs for spectators and players lined the walls facing the billiard table. A door along the back wall provided passage to Enrique's richly appointed library, where key arrangements in the last national election had been brokered.

Antonio coughed and DeLeon looked in his direction.

"Go now," DeLeon said to the woman, taking the cue stick from her hand.

The woman left without saying a word, passing by Antonio with a look and a smile. She had a soft, sensual step, a long elegant neck, and lustrous green eyes. Antonio could smell her scent in the air.

"I hope I find you well, Enrique," Vallaverde said.

"Indeed, I am," Enrique replied. Antonio was one of the few paid informants he truly liked. "You have something to tell me, Antonio?"

"Not good news, I'm afraid. The New Mexico State Police have seized a large quantity of drugs in Santa Fe and arrested a man named Watson, who has confessed to being one of your distributors."

"Where is Watson now?" Enrique asked.

"In jail."

"How much merchandise was confiscated?"

"The street value is reported to be over a million dollars."

DeLeon knew immediately that Bucky had held back some product from the Chicago shipment. He would deal with him harshly. "Such things happen occasionally," he said. "It is the cost of doing business."

"There is more, Enrique. Records of Tortuga International were seized in Las Cruces by the New Mexico State Police this morning. A United States judge has been asked to freeze all your North American corporate assets."

"What else do you know?"

"Stolen art worth many millions has been recovered from your Santa Fe house. The authorities believe you are behind the theft. They are seeking your whereabouts in Mexico. Of course, I have suggested that they look for you in all the wrong places."

"You give the Americans such wise counsel," DeLeon said with a smile.

"I can do no less in light of your past generosities," Antonio replied. "May I offer some advice, Enrique?"

"By all means."

"A request has been made to the State Department to declare

you persona non grata, which would bar you from any future visits to the United States. It will be favorably acted upon. Additionally, the Americans are prepared to ask our government to strip you of your diplomatic status and extradite you for prosecution. I have been told on highest authority that we will be sensitive to their demands. It is a difficult time for trying to sweep such issues with the Americans under the rug."

"These political manipulations can be dealt with."

"In time," Antonio said. "But if the Americans fail to get what they want, they may come after you on their own. The new drug laws passed by their Congress give their federal agents that prerogative."

"What do you suggest?"

"Perhaps a trip abroad is in order, until matters settle. I would not wait long to decide, Enrique. The American ambassador plans to discuss your diplomatic status at the highest level of our government before day's end."

"Thank you, Antonio. You have been most kind to bring these matters to my attention. Do one small favor for me. Find out the identities of the persons overseeing the state police investigation. Perhaps they would not be unresponsive to an offer to become rich men, if an arrangement can be made."

"I'll get back to you," Antonio said.

Vallaverde departed and DeLeon went to the library. Antonio's report was troubling. The loss of the Tortuga assets would sting, but hardly ruin him. He doubted the complexities of the company could be easily unraveled by the police in a short period of time. If he moved quickly, millions of dollars could be saved.

He rang for Carlos, who answered promptly.

"I want arrangements made to have Bucky Watson killed immediately," Enrique said. "He is in the Santa Fe County jail. I do not want him to live to see another day. Report to me when your plans are complete."

"Sí, patrón."

DeLeon disconnected and dialed a different number.

Several hours passed before he put the telephone in the cradle. The time had been well spent; Tortuga's remaining cash assets had been transferred out of the United States through a series of complex banking transactions.

The phone rang almost immediately. He punched the speaker button. "What is it?"

"It is Antonio, Enrique. The man responsible for the police investigation in Santa Fe is Kevin Kerney, the deputy state police chief. Several related arrests have been made by his investigators; a nephew of the governor and a prominent attorney have been charged with money laundering."

"Continue."

"One of his detectives was killed in a shoot-out at a Santa Fe residence. I do not think Kerney can be bought."

"Do you have a dossier on Kerney and his investigations?"

"A slim one, yes."

"Please send it by courier to the hacienda."

"I will do so immediately," Antonio replied.

"Thank you, Antonio."

"But, *patrón*, he could not have survived so many bullets."

DeLeon patted the file folder on the top of his desk. "You killed a state police sergeant named Martinez."

"But it was Kerney's car." Carlos caught himself. There was no point making excuses. He lowered his head submissively. "I am sorry, Don Enrique. What are your orders?"

"Delfino and Felix will meet you at the airport in an hour. You will assist them in locating Kerney. Both he and Watson must be killed. What progress have you made on Watson?"

"He is in a seclusion cell at the jail. A court hearing has been scheduled for late this afternoon."

"Will he be heavily guarded during the court hearing?"

"Only one officer has been assigned to transport him."

"Excellent."

"What other orders do you have for me, *patrón?*"

DeLeon held out the file. "None. Felix and Delfino will instruct you in all matters. Do not keep them waiting."

Carlos took the file, risked a glance at the icy stare in DeLeon's eyes, lowered his gaze, and quickly left the room, wondering if there was any way the *patrón* would let him live.

OFFICER Yvonne Rasmussen gave Kerney a pleased smile when he came into her hospital room.

"I'm sorry it took so long for me to come and see you," Kerney said as he shook the young woman's hand. "I hear you're healing up nicely."

"I get to go home tomorrow," Rasmussen replied. "The doctor said I start light duty in a week."

"That's good news. You kept an old friend of mine from getting killed. I want to thank you for that."

Rasmussen's gray eyes clouded over. "I didn't do enough, Chief. If I had responded sooner, Sergeant Martinez might still be alive."

"Don't beat up on yourself. You did all that you could."

"That's not the way I feel," Rasmussen said.

"Would you like to talk about it?"

Rasmussen hesitated and shook her head slowly. "Not yet."

"I need to ask you a few questions. When you were patrolling Fletcher's house, before the gunfight, did you notice anything unusual?"

"Nothing."

"Did you run license plate checks on the vehicles parked in the immediate area?"

"Yes. All but one of the cars were registered to neighborhood residents. The one that wasn't belonged to an elderly Hispanic-surnamed male with a south-side address. I ran him through NCIC and there were no wants or warrants. It didn't seem suspicious."

"Where did you see the car?"

"On the street behind the lane to Fletcher's house."

"When?"

"Around dusk."

"Was anyone in it or nearby?"

"No."

"Did you see the vehicle again?"

"No. When I got the 911 call, I came in from a different direction."

"Did you log the information on the car?"

"Dispatch has the record. Do you think the car was used by the killers?"

"It's possible. I'll check it out. Take care of yourself."

"Chief Kerney."

Kerney stopped at the door. "What is it?"

Rasmussen flashed him a small smile. "Thanks for not treating me like a kid sister. Everybody else has. I really appreciate it."

"You don't strike me as an officer who needs to be coddled," Kerney replied.

"I'm not."

WITH PARTICULARS in hand on the car Rasmussen had spotted near Fletcher's house, Kerney drove down Airport Road. Ruben Contreras, age sixty-eight, owned an older-model full-size Buick, and lived in a trailer park behind a strip mall and a car wash. Most of the trailers were shabby-looking. Gravel lanes bisected the rows of trailers, and in the center of the park stood a cement-block building that housed a coin-operated laundry. A loose dog sniffed around an overflowing trash can at the front of the laundry.

Kerney found Contreras's trailer. Contreras answered the knock at the door and squinted at Kerney through thick glasses. A tube ran from his nose to a portable oxygen tank on wheels. The smell of beans cooking filled the air.

"Mr. Contreras?" Kerney asked with his badge case open.

"Yes?" Contreras wheezed as he spoke.

"Do you own a Buick?" Kerney described the car.

"I sold it. The doctors say I can't drive anymore. My granddaughter gives me rides. I don't like not having my car."

Kerney held up Carlos Ruiz's mug shot. "Did this man buy it from you?"

Contreras nodded. "He paid me cash. He said he would change the registration." A worried look spread across the old man's face. "If he had an accident, it's not my fault. I cancelled my insurance."

"There's been no accident, Mr. Contreras," Kerney said. "I just needed to identify the buyer."

"That's him."

"You're sure?"

Contreras nodded once more. Kerney left while the old man stood waiting for another question.

JESUS WANTED Robert to leave Nita's house. With his cracked rib and broken arm in a cast, Robert couldn't get both thumbs in his ears to fight off the voice inside his head.

He'd been awake all night in the guest bedroom with the door locked and the window open, smoking cigarettes. Robert had tried to obey Nita's ban on smoking in the house, but he couldn't do it. He took a deep drag on the cigarette and an ash fell on the new shirt Nita had given him. She had bought him a whole new set of clothes, including a winter coat. The smell of something burning made Robert look down at his chest; he spit on his finger and rubbed it on the burn hole in the shirt to make sure it was out.

Robert's legs felt nervous and itchy. Walking back and forth all night in the bedroom didn't make the feeling go away. He had stopped pacing when Nita came to the door and asked if he was awake. He didn't answer and soon heard the sound of her truck leaving the driveway.

He stayed in the bedroom for a long time. When he finally went out, the living room with the long row of windows that looked out on the road and the rangeland beyond made him nervous. Somebody could be out there watching, spying on him.

He went into Nita's bedroom, where the curtains were drawn, and searched through a chest of drawers until he found her panties and underwear. He took each piece out of the drawer, smelled it, and dropped it on the floor. Nita's panties had no scent, but Robert liked the feel of them in his hands.

The telephone rang and he ignored it until it stopped. He went into the bathroom with a pair of panties, sat on the toilet, and masturbated. He wiped himself with the panties and dropped them in the toilet. He felt better: Jesus had stopped talking to him. But his legs were still jittery and itchy. He needed to walk.

Robert dressed to go out. He took the laces out of the shoes—they were some kind of insulated boots—and slipped his bare feet into them. He draped the coat over his shoulders because the sleeve was too small for the cast on his arm.

At the front door, he stopped, unsure of where he should go. Maybe if he talked to Kerney, he could go back to jail. He liked jails with bare walls, small cells, and no windows. Jails helped him relax. Robert dug through all his pockets until he found his wallet with Kerney's phone number in it. He called, but Kerney wasn't there. A woman asked him to leave a message.

"Tell him I'm going away," Robert said.

"May I have your name, sir?" the woman asked.

"Satan," Robert said.

Outside, heavy clouds hid the sun and a cold wind blew in his face. He put the hood of the coat up, lowered his head against the wind, and started walking.

THE TWO men traveling with Carlos said nothing to him or each other. Carlos knew he was way out of his league; both men were former Mexican intelligence agents who had been trained by the U.S. Army Special Forces, the CIA, and the FBI. Each had carried out a number of high-profile political assassinations under contract with the *Mafiosios*.

Relegated to the role of driver, Carlos cruised past the county jail on Airport Road and then up to the courthouse, near the downtown plaza. Felix, the older of the two men, sat in the front seat, while Delfino rode in the back.

Carlos circled the courthouse. At the rear of the building warning signs restricted parking to police vehicles only, and a single security door was the only access to the inside. Parked against the curb was a television transmission truck with a satellite dish mounted on the roof.

"Go around again," Felix said. "Slowly."

Carlos drove past the church on the corner before turning down a narrow street of old brick houses used as offices. An elementary school stood at the end of the block, catty-corner to the courthouse. A row of small casitas and an apartment building faced the rear of the courthouse. A rental sign was posted on the porch to one of the casitas.

"Drive past the school and let me out at the traffic light," Felix ordered. "Park in front of the post office, and wait for me there."

Ten minutes later Felix returned. "A cottage across from the courthouse is vacant," he said to Delfino. "I can enter through a back door without difficulty."

"Unseen?" Delfino inquired.

"Yes. A wall behind the alley blocks the view." Felix handed Carlos a pair of binoculars. "You are my spotter. Make certain, this time, you identify the correct man. Park across from the school facing the courthouse. It provides the best view of vehicles approaching from any direction."

He gave Delfino a radio transmitter and stuck a receiver with an earplug in his coat pocket. "I'll need no more than ten seconds after your signal to make the kill. As soon as you see Watson fall, have Carlos drive slowly to the alley. I'll be waiting."

"And if the police should return fire?" Delfino asked.

"Only Watson dies, unless something goes wrong," Felix replied as he grabbed his briefcase and opened the car door. "But if necessary, we will kill them all."

He turned back to Carlos. "Do you understand what you are to do?"

"I will follow your orders," Carlos replied.

They had to wait an hour before Felix could put his plan into action.

NITA LET the telephone ring repeatedly before hanging up in frustration. She'd been calling home between appointments and Robert hadn't answered. She was worried about him, but couldn't break away from the office. After her arrest and all the press coverage that came with it, she'd expected business to fall off, but exactly the opposite had occurred. Not only were most of her regular clients sticking by her, a flood of new appointments had come in from area residents she had never seen in the clinic before. They came with their household pets, wanting annual shots, deworming, or examinations.

She knew damn well they were there for the gossip value the visit would generate, but she took the cases anyway. And while none of them dared to raise questions about her status as an accused murderer, she felt their intense curiosity when they brought their perfectly healthy dogs, cats, and gerbils into the examining room. Being in the presence of an indicted cop killer obviously had high entertainment value.

Nita finished her last case for the day and called home again, with no luck. She drove west at high speed into a setting sun shrouded by clouds, worried sick about Robert. Maybe she'd made a mistake in bringing him home. But he'd seemed so coherent in the hospital, and so pleased with the idea of staying with her.

She ground the truck to a stop in front of her house and hurried inside. Robert was nowhere to be found. In her bedroom, all her underwear had been scattered on the floor. In the guest bedroom, even with the open window, the smell of cigarette smoke lingered. The bed hadn't been slept in. In the bathroom, she found a pair of her panties floating in the commode.

She had to find Robert, and she needed help to do it. Calling the county sheriff wasn't an option. She doubted any of the deputies would be willing to assist a confessed cop killer. Her only course of action was to call Kevin Kerney. He was unavailable when she tried to reach him, so she left her name, and a message reporting Robert's disappearance.

Light snow had begun to fall and the temperature had dropped by the time she got in her truck. There were hundreds of miles of back roads that crisscrossed the rolling plains between the two state highways that cut south to Mountainair. Robert could be on any one of them, or so far away that it would be impossible to find him.

If bringing Robert home resulted in his death, she would feel like a murderer twice over.

•   •   •

BUCKY WATSON lay facedown on the pavement with his hands cuffed to the small of his back and his skull blown apart. Brain matter and blood splatter fanned out in an arc that spurted up the stairs and flecked the glass courthouse door.

Both the parking lot and the house across the street had been roped off, portable lights had been set up, and crime scene technicians were working the area. A state police agent and a city detective were talking to the officer who had brought Bucky to the courthouse.

Kerney stayed outside the police line and waited until they finished before calling the officer over.

The man came toward him shaking his head. Dried blood covered the front of his uniform shirt. "I don't know what to tell you, Chief. It happened so damn fast, I didn't see it coming."

"You weren't supposed to see it," Kerney replied. Although he had a good idea what the answer would be, he asked his next question. "Did you hear the shot fired?"

"I didn't hear a damn thing. The back of Watson's head just exploded. I hit the ground, rolled in front of my unit for cover, and drew my weapon. But there was nobody there."

"Did you see any traffic on the street?"

"I heard a car, but didn't see it. I took a quick look, but it was gone. From the sound it made, it wasn't speeding, or anything like that."

"Were you alone in the parking lot?"

"Just me and Watson."

"Are the investigators finished with you?"

"Yeah, except for the paperwork I need to do."

"Write your report at the office, then pack it in for the night and go home."

"Thanks." The man smiled and tugged at the front of his

shirt. He wore gold piping and two stripes, denoting his rank as a senior patrol officer. "You know what my wife is going to say when she sees this mess?"

"Probably something about a career change."

"You got it," the officer said as he walked off.

The radio in Kerney's unit squawked and he went to answer it. He had two messages; one from Robert saying he was Satan and he was going away, and a confirming report from Nita Lassiter that Cordova had disappeared.

Kerney gave the dispatcher a description of Robert, ordered a statewide APB, and suggested that the search should be concentrated in the Mountainair area.

"That's not going to be easy," the dispatcher said. "We've got blizzard conditions down there, Chief. Heavy snow and high winds."

"Understood," Kerney replied. "If Cordova is found, have him placed in protective custody on a mental hold. He's not a criminal."

"Ten-four."

As Kerney clicked off, Joe Valdez opened the passenger door and got in the unit. He had his jacket collar turned up and he rubbed his hands together to warm them.

"It's too damn cold, Chief."

Kerney turned the car heater up a notch. "Are you finished with the DA?"

Valdez snorted. "While Bucky was getting himself killed, the DA was busy doing a little dance on my head. He feels his office ethically can't take action against Springer and Cobb, since both have served as special prosecutors in civil cases."

"That's standard protocol. Who is he farming the case out to?"

"The attorney general's office. I think the decision was made before I even got there."

"Where are Cobb and Springer?"

"They've walked. I didn't even get a chance to lock them up. They're both threatening to sue for false arrest."

"Did the DA challenge the probable cause?"

"No, but he and his chief deputy went over everything with a fine-tooth comb. I had to produce all the evidence, including the videotape of Watson's confession."

"Did you keep copies of everything?"

"Multiple copies. I'm not going to let this case bite me in the ass."

"Did you get anything out of Cobb and Springer?"

"Not a damn thing," Valdez answered. "Know what I think, Chief? It's gonna be years before those two go to trial, if ever. In fact, I don't think there's even a remote chance they'll be indicted. Not with the potential star witness for the prosecution so conveniently dead."

Valdez put his hand on the door handle. "Gotta go. The AG wants to meet with me pronto."

"Do you want someone to go with you?"

Joe took a minute to consider the offer. "No thanks, but I'll call for backup if he starts busting my balls. So who killed Bucky Watson, Chief?"

"I don't know who pulled the trigger. But whoever he is, he's damn good at his job."

ROBERT TRUDGED through two feet of fresh snow down the side of the highway toward the village of Punta de Agua. Only the vague shapes of the mile-marker posts and road signs kept him headed in the right direction. He was off the plains and in the foothills, and wind-driven snow obscured everything. The road was buried by deep drifts and no cars had passed in either direction, not even a snowplow.

Cold to the bone, his feet felt frozen, and his side ached from the cracked rib. El Malo kept laughing at him inside his head. Everything felt heavy: his breath, his feet, the top of his head— even his eyes.

He walked on with his head lowered. When he finally stopped and looked up, he was in the middle of the village, across from a church. Robert remembered that the Evil One didn't like churches, but Jesus did. He walked to the church door and found it locked. A side door was also locked. Next to the stoop was a small pile of firewood. Robert picked up a stick, broke a window, and crawled inside.

Out of the wind and protected by thick adobe walls, Robert started to warm up a bit. He groped his way in the darkness to the altar at the front of the church and fumbled around until he found a candle. He lit it with a match and looked around. A woodstove stood against a wall in the middle of the sanctuary. He opened the firebox door and found that a fire had been laid. He put the flame of the candle against the kindling and sat down to watch it burn. The heat felt good against his face and hands.

He began to feel light-headed. Did he leave Nita's house because he did something wrong? Did he hurt her? He hoped not. But what happened?

Paul Gillespie would know, Robert thought as he curled up in front of the stove. Paul was always at Serpent Gate. He would go there in the morning and talk to him.

"HAS THE governor fired you yet?" Kerney asked as he joined Andy in his office.

"There's been nothing but ominous silence," Andy said. "Aside from the fact that Bucky Watson was assassinated, what else can you tell me about the shooting?"

"Not much," Kerney admitted. "But I'll bet Carlos Ruiz didn't pull the trigger this time."

"This time?"

"I've got him nailed to the Martinez murder."

"How so?"

Kerney told him about the Buick and getting an ID on Carlos from Ruben Contreras.

"We have to get to Ruiz somehow," Andy said.

"I agree. What's happening with the sanctions against DeLeon?"

"His assets are being frozen, his drug distribution network is shut down, and he's about to lose his diplomatic immunity. It may not bring him to his knees, but it will make him buckle a bit."

Kerney nodded. "The DA has kicked Springer and Cobb loose and passed the ball to the attorney general. Joe Valdez is with the AG now. He made need you to backstop him."

"The fucking politics never end," Andy said sourly as he watched Kerney head for the door. "Where are you going?"

"South."

"It damn well better not be Mexico again."

Kerney laughed. "Mountainair. Robert Cordova is missing."

"That crazy guy in the Gillespie murder case?"

"That's the guy."

Andy looked out the window. Freezing rain was pinging against the glass, and the neon lights from the bar down the highway, usually so bright, were just a shapeless blur. "Be careful driving," he said.

CARLOS HAD no doubt that he would be killed as soon as Kerney was dead. Since meeting Felix and Delfino at the airport, he'd been under close observation and never left alone. Whenever Felix looked at him, Carlos felt like he was a walking dead man.

He still retained his pistol in the shoulder holster, but it gave him no comfort. Any attempt to reach for it would be fruitless; Delfino would cut his throat before he could clear the holster. To survive, Carlos needed some kind of opportunity and a good deal of luck.

He drove the two men to the house where Kerney stayed, only to find an unoccupied state police patrol car parked in front of the residence. There were no cars in the driveway and lights were on inside the dwelling.

"Is that the gringo's police car?" Felix asked.

"No," Carlos replied. "He drives an unmarked vehicle."

"This is where you killed the wrong cop, is it not?" Delfino asked with a chuckle.

Carlos grunted a response as he turned the car around at the end of the lane.

"Where is the gringo, Carlos?" Felix asked.

"If he is not here, he's working," Carlos said.

"Then let us go to the place where he works," Felix said.

Carlos drove to the state police headquarters building and parked across the highway. Using binoculars, he found Kerney's official vehicle in the parking lot and pointed it out to Felix.

"We will wait for the gringo to leave," Felix said, "and kill him on his way home."

Within a matter of minutes, a fast-moving storm bringing wind-whipped, freezing snow made it impossible to see the police parking lot. At full speed the windshield wipers barely cleaned the glass, and visibility dropped to less than twenty feet.

"Is there no other vantage point we can use?" Felix asked in disgust as he took the binoculars away from his eyes.

"None that provides a clear view of the exits from the parking lot," Carlos replied.

"We cannot even see the parking lot, let alone who comes or goes," Felix said as he stared into the whiteout. "Get us closer. Cross the highway and drive past the building."

Carlos did as he was told, and in the vaporous light of the parking lot lamp they saw the empty space where Kerney's car had been.

"Go back to the house," Felix said in disgust. "We will kill him there."

Only the police cruiser was in the driveway when Carlos drove by. Felix directed him to park on the street and wait.

After an hour, with no sign of Kerney and the snow piling up, Carlos got anxious. "We will be stuck here if we don't leave soon," he said.

"We're wasting time," Delfino agreed.

"Where else can he be?" Felix asked Carlos.

"I do not know," Carlos answered. "He has no girlfriend, he sees no one socially, and he does not go to clubs or saloons. All he does is work."

"Check his dossier," Felix told Delfino.

"He investigated a cop killing in Mountainair recently," Delfino said. "Maybe he went there. Where is this place?"

"Southeast of Albuquerque," Carlos replied.

"You have a map?" Felix asked.

"In the glove box."

Felix got the map, unfolded it, and, using a pen flashlight, looked for the town's location. "It's not too far," he finally said.

"Let us visit Mountainair," Delfino suggested. "Judging by the name, I'm sure it's very picturesque."

"The roads could be very bad," Carlos said.

"You are here to drive us, not advise us," Felix snapped. "Delfino is right; it is better to search for the gringo than to sit here and risk discovery. If we do not find him, we will come back."

Carlos nodded, cranked the engine, and made a U-turn. Except for a few snowplows and sand spreaders that were busy clearing one lane in each direction, the highway out of town was virtually deserted.

• • •

THE BLIZZARD made Kerney's trip south unbelievably grueling. At times, he was forced to crawl along at ten miles an hour, and on several occasions his unit spun out on black ice without warning. Only the absence of traffic averted an accident.

In Estancia, he contacted the sheriff's department by radio and got directions to Nita Lassiter's house. He turned east into the teeth of the storm, and soon the car wipers were thudding against a rock-solid ice buildup on the windshield. He had to stop repeatedly and scrape the glass, while the storm raged around him, kicked along by gale-force winds.

The drive put him in a foul mood. Born and raised in the desert of the Tularosa Basin, Kerney didn't like snow much, and his aversion to it hadn't changed in spite of the years he'd lived in Santa Fe working for the police department.

He found Nita's house. Facing south, it had a wall of windows running the length of the structure. All the inside and outside lights were on, creating a lonely beacon that barely cut through the whiteout of the storm. It was the only sign of habitation he'd glimpsed since leaving the outskirts of Estancia.

Her four-wheel-drive truck was parked by the front door. He knocked and the door flew open. The look of relief on Nita's face dropped away as he stepped inside.

"I thought you were Robert," she said.

"You haven't found him?" Kerney replied as he unbuttoned his coat. He hung it on the rack in the small entryway.

"No. I have all the lights on in case he's nearby."

"He would need to be within a few hundred feet to see them. Have you searched outside?"

"Twice," Nita answered as she led him into a large room that contained a living area, dining alcove, and kitchen. "Everywhere," she added.

Kerney nodded and looked around. The house was passive solar with exposed adobe walls, insulated glass panels, a corner fireplace, and brick floors. Doors at both ends of the room led to bedrooms.

"I have people looking for him," Kerney noted, "although I doubt it will do much good in the storm. Let's hope he's found shelter."

Nita sank into a low-backed tufted leather chair that faced a sofa. "He put a pair of my underwear in the commode and rummaged through my bedroom dressers. I have no idea why he did it."

"Where have you looked for him?"

"I covered every back road between Estancia and Manzano, until the storm closed in and I couldn't see beyond the hood of my truck. We need to find him."

"In the morning," Kerney said wearily as he went to get his coat. The cold weather had stiffened his bum knee, and he had to force it to work.

"You can't possibly go back outside," Nita said as she followed him. "Stay here. I have a guest bedroom."

Kerney shook his head. "I can't do that."

"You looked exhausted."

"I'll be fine." Kerney slipped into his coat.

"Are you always so bullheaded?"

Kerney turned and looked directly into Nita's eyes. "Under different circumstances I would gladly accept your offer, Ms. Lassiter. But you are a confessed cop killer, and I'm the guy who busted you. Staying here tonight is not an option; it would be misconstrued."

"No one needs to know."

"My presence here is a matter of official record. Both the county sheriff's office and the state police dispatcher know exactly where I am."

"You're right; you can't stay."

"I'll get a room at the Shaffer Hotel in Mountainair."

"Will you at least call me when you arrive so that I know you made it safely?"

"I'll do that. Try to think of where Robert might be heading."

Nita nodded and forced a smile, but her eyes were worried.

"What's wrong?" Kerney asked.

"I don't want anything to happen to Robert."

"Robert is a survivor, just like you," Kerney replied evenly. "He'll be all right."

"Have you always been such an optimist?"

"I have my black moments every now and then."

"When was the last one?"

"The day I had to shoot you," Kerney replied.

Kerney's unexpected response shook Nita. "I'm sorry that happened. You must think I'm terribly weak."

"I think you're a woman who needs to get on with her life."

"In prison?"

"I hope not, Ms. Lassiter."

"It wasn't fair of me to say that."

"No harm done."

As soon as Kerney said good night and slipped out the door, Nita wanted him to come back. With all the constraints that existed between them, she knew he wouldn't. But she could sense Kerney's loneliness ran as deep as her own, and that left her feeling very sad.

13

Ugly things had happened in Robert's dreams, forcing him awake. Paul Gillespie's face floated through his mind. The face changed into *El Malo;* horns snaked out of his forehead like worms and his eyes turned fiery red and evil.

Robert opened his eyes, found himself in total darkness, and scrambled to his feet. He could feel the pressure of the walls and ceiling gripping him—pushing him down—and his heart pounded in his chest.

He ran, stumbled against something, groped his way toward a current of cold air that blew against his face, and found a broken window. He crawled out, fell on his knees, and ran until a pain in his side forced him to stop.

Gasping for air, he turned and looked back. The setting moon behind the church made the spire look like a dagger stabbing the sky. He shivered in the cold, but the tension in his body lifted, and he felt better now that he was outside. Then the voices returned.

He could only use his right thumb to plug his ears; somebody had put a plaster cast on his left arm. He tried to rip the cast off, but the plaster was too hard and thick. He gave up and started walking down the road. Snowdrifts buried the road and covered all but the tops of the fence poles along the highway.

Somewhere, Robert had gotten a new coat, and it felt warm. But the air was frigid and his feet were cold. He looked down at the boots that flapped against his ankles, wondering where they had come from. As he walked, snow seeped over the boot tops, soaked his feet, and made it hard to move. He stepped carefully to keep the boots from coming off in the snow.

There was no traffic on the road. Everything was silent and still. He stuck his thumb out as soon as he heard the sound of an engine and the scrape of a plow on the pavement behind him. An orange highway department snowplow slowed to a stop. Robert got in.

"Did you go off the road?" the driver asked. "I didn't see your car."

"No, I'm just walking." Robert stared at a pack of cigarettes on the dashboard. "Got a spare smoke?"

"Help yourself."

Robert grabbed a cigarette and lit it.

"Looks like you got banged up a little," the man said, eyeing the cast on Robert's arm and his missing teeth.

"Got in a fight," Robert replied, thinking maybe it was true. "No big deal."

"Where are you heading?"

"Mountainair."

"I can take you as far as the maintenance yard in town."

Robert nodded. "That's cool. Got any coffee there?"

"The pot is always on." The driver dropped the transmission into gear, lowered the blade, and began plowing his way toward Mountainair.

Robert puffed on the cigarette and tried to concentrate on where he was supposed to go after he got to town. Nothing registered. The voices were gone, replaced by a noise like radio static.

Close to town, with the sun just up and the glare off the snow bouncing into the sky, a state police car passed them. Robert turned his head to follow the car, thinking that if he got out and waited, the cop might come back and take him to jail. He shrugged off the thought and snorted. Cops were assholes.

The driver gave him a strange look.

Robert bummed another cigarette and stared out the window. He liked the way the snow covered everything and made things look clean. His feet started to hurt as the driver turned into the maintenance yard. It felt like somebody was sticking pins into his toes.

He jumped out of the truck and went with the driver into the empty office.

"Got any rubber bands?" Robert asked.

The driver rummaged through a desk drawer and held out a handful. Robert pulled them over his boots. Maybe they would help keep the snow out.

"What happened to your laces?" the driver asked.

"I don't like them."

The driver filled his thermos, gave Robert a cup of coffee, and went outside to load sand into the truck's spreader. When he returned the hitchhiker was gone.

•   •   •

NITA FOUND Kerney sitting in the Shaffer Hotel dining room picking over a light breakfast. The room was full of railroad workers just in from a night of clearing a freight derailment at Abo Pass. Snow and mud had been tracked into the room, and small brown puddles had formed under the tables where the workers sat.

Nita dropped her coat over the back of an empty chair and joined Kerney at the table. "Good morning," she said.

"Morning," Kerney answered, inspecting her outfit. She wore insulated boots, jeans, and several layers of sweaters. "Going somewhere?"

"With you," Nita replied.

"That's not possible."

"Do you want to waste time trying to find your way to Serpent Gate, or do you want to get there in a hurry?"

"There are a lot of other places Robert could be," Kerney said.

"I've already looked everywhere else."

"Then I'll start at Serpent Gate."

"It's not that easy to get to. Do you have a four-wheel-drive vehicle? It's going to take one to get in."

"No, you're not going."

"Then I'll go by myself," Nita said as she started to rise.

"Hold up."

"Robert is out there, and I'm going to find him if you won't."

"Why are you so sure he's there?"

"Can't you figure it out? What happened to me—and Robert—took place at Serpent Gate. He's always gone back; I never have."

Before Kerney could respond a patrol officer entered the room and walked quickly to the table. He gave Nita a questioning glance and a tight nod before addressing Kerney.

"No luck so far, Chief," he said. "I covered all the major roads in a ten-mile radius."

"Robert may come here," he said as he laid some bills on the table to cover the meal and the tip. "Pick him up if he shows. Don't scare him off. He doesn't like cops much. I'll be on my handheld radio if you need me."

Kerney stood up, took Nita's coat off the back of the empty chair, and held it out. "Let's go to Serpent Gate."

CARLOS TRIED to act cordial and relaxed with Felix and Delfino, but his attempts at small talk were rebuffed. He drove through the night while one man slept and the other stayed awake, watching him. Even when he had to take a piss along the side of the road, he had company. When he suggested a meal stop, the idea was rejected. Carlos had to come up with a plan to save himself, and soon.

The blizzard had made travel almost impossible. Felix had ordered him to take the interstate in the hopes that the road would be in better condition. But south of Albuquerque the highway became a nightmare, and Carlos missed the exit to Mountainair because of a fierce whiteout that obliterated the road signs. When he got back on track, it took hours to travel fifty miles to Mountainair.

Carlos drove into the village with a low sun in his eyes. It wasn't much of a town from what he could see: a cheap motel or two, boarded-up businesses, a school, and a main street that sputtered to a stop after two long blocks.

"I need some coffee," he said to Felix as he slowed to let a crazy-looking man with missing teeth scurry across the street, the coat draped over his shoulders flapping in the breeze.

"We'll get some to go," Felix said. "I saw a sign for a hotel restaurant. It should be on the right, a block down."

Carlos made the turn and saw the man in the flapping coat run across the road toward an abandoned warehouse next to some train tracks. In front of the hotel, a man, woman, and a cop came out the front door.

Carlos accelerated. "That's Kerney," he said as he passed the trio in front of the hotel. He went around the block and returned in time to see Kerney and the woman pull away in a pickup truck.

"Are you positive?" Felix asked.

"Completely."

"Don't follow too closely."

The cop paid no attention as Carlos cruised by. Carlos let several vehicles pass him, but kept the truck in view. The road had been sanded and plowed, but black ice slowed traffic. Several miles beyond the village, Carlos topped out at the crest of a hill and panicked. The pickup was nowhere in sight. He started scanning for the truck off the roadway.

"You've lost them," Felix snapped.

The highway divided a slender valley cut by wandering arroyos that gradually opened to a large pasture. To the south, a half circle of hills hid the mainline railroad tracks from view. Fresh tire tracks entered a ranch road.

Carlos squinted against the glare of reflected sunlight on the snow and caught sight of the truck traveling toward the hills.

"There," he said, pointing.

"Follow," Felix ordered.

At the gate to the ranch road, the car lurched to a stop in the middle of a snow-filled ditch. Carlos tried backing up, and the wheels spun without grabbing. He got out to take a look and Delfino joined him. The rear wheels were deep in snow to the top of the hubcaps.

"We'll have to dig the car out," Carlos said.

"Leave it here," Delfino replied. "Open the trunk."

Carlos unlocked the trunk and watched Felix and Delfino slip backpacks over their shoulders.

"Let's go," Felix said to Carlos.

"I'll wait here," Carlos replied.

"Move," Felix said, stepping out to take the lead.

"The police will notice the car."

"Today it is just another stranded vehicle in a snowbank," Felix replied. "Let's go."

The sun gave no warmth and the glare off the snow was intense. Carlos followed Felix while Delfino stayed behind him. They walked single file at a fast pace in the ruts left by the truck. Behind him Carlos could hear the even breathing of Delfino close at hand.

Wind gusts seared against his face, his breath froze on his mustache, and his sunglasses fogged up. On the back side of the hills, the road dipped under a double set of train tracks. At the top of a rise beyond the tracks, Carlos spotted the pickup.

Felix saw it also. He holstered his handgun, took off the backpack, and removed an Uzi submachine gun. Delfino did the same.

"Take Carlos to the trestle and wait for me," Felix ordered Delfino. He left the road and started a loop in the general direction of the truck.

From the trestle Carlos and Delfino watched Felix approach the truck. He checked the bed and the cab, returned to the tailgate, crouched down, and signaled them to approach. With Delfino at his side, Carlos trotted to the pickup. Beyond he could see two figures moving toward a low ridgeline.

"Get down," Felix said.

Carlos ducked behind the tailgate.

"How do you want to take them?" Delfino asked.

"From both flanks," Felix said. The figures up ahead were small dots against a white backdrop. "Carlos, you go with Delfino."

Carlos took out his handgun, glancing at Delfino for a reaction.

"Take the point," Delfino said.

Carlos broke trail through the crust of snow, his legs sinking into drifts up to his knees, slowing his pace. He looked back once; ten steps behind, Delfino had the Uzi pointed directly at him. He scanned the left flank for Felix; he was nowhere in sight.

Carlos was a sitting duck. All he could do was keep moving.

FROM INSIDE the old grain warehouse, Robert watched the cop in the squad car. The man just sat in the cruiser with his engine running, tailpipe exhaust billowing like frost in the cold morning air. Robert knew if he went to the hotel, the cop would beat him up, just like Ordway had.

He didn't know what to do. Seeing Kerney and Nita together had left him with a mean, jealous feeling, and his head felt full of hissing snakes. He had to get away and never come back, but where should he go? He went out the rear of the warehouse and scrambled down a small embankment to the train tracks. Behind him stood the old train station. Maybe east, he thought, to Texas.

The hissing snakes whispered Paul Gillespie's name in his ear. He would go west to Serpent Gate.

He hurried down the tracks to the underpass. The cop never saw him. Cops were stupid—too dumb to realize that the train tracks were highways, just like roads, only better.

The cast on his arm banged against his broken rib as he ran, but the pain didn't bother him. He laughed until cold air rushed into his lungs and made him cough.

THE SNOW at the top of the rise was too deep for the truck, so Nita and Kerney pushed ahead on foot. The storm had erased any footprints or tracks. Kerney scrutinized every drift they passed for telltale signs of Robert. He saw nothing. If Robert's body was nearby, it wouldn't be found until the first good thaw.

The raw Arctic wind kept the temperature well below freezing, and the branches of the piñon and juniper trees cracked like gunshots as they snapped under the weight of the snow. Each step they took broke trail in the frozen crust, and they were knee-deep in drifts. Nita didn't tire or falter, but Kerney had a hell of a time with his bad knee. The tendons and few remaining ligaments ached every time he pulled the leg free to take another step.

The ridge ran at a right angle to the hills. At the top, Nita held them up. Without warning, the ridge sheared off, revealing a granite monolith standing in the middle of a narrow gorge. A rockfall closed off one end, and the only approach seemed to be through a shallow arroyo that ran up to the ridge.

Kerney guessed the monolith to be fifty feet long and ten feet away from where he stood. He looked into the shadows and waited for his vision to adjust. Fifteen feet below the drop-off, a slender ledge ran along the length of the monolith. Above the ledge, at about the chest height of a small man, a duplicate of the serpent on Pop Shaffer's fence had been chiseled in the stone. It was surrounded by images of birds, fish, and other symbols, including a horned demon.

"How deep?" Kerney asked. The snow in the gorge stopped at the ledge of the monolith.

"Less than twenty feet. Do you think you would have found it on your own?"

"I probably would have fallen into it," Kerney said. "What's on the other side?"

"More rock art and lots of rattlesnakes in the summer," Nita answered. "It gets good sun, and the snakes like the heat. I don't think Robert's been here," she added.

"We'll poke around anyway."

The wind died down and Kerney heard crunching sounds from behind. Out of the sun, two men were coming straight at them. Another man flanked them, cutting off any retreat. He saw weapons in their hands, and without thinking he pushed Nita over the ledge and jumped with her as the men opened fire. He crashed into a snow-covered shrub, branches whipping his face, and landed in a heavy cushion of snow.

He scrambled to the ledge of the monolith, grabbed Nita by the hand, and pulled her to him.

"Move," he hissed, freeing his handgun. "Get to the other side, out of sight."

Nita gave him a petrified look. He pushed her to get her started. Automatic rounds sprayed the gully as he turned the corner. Nita was off the ledge, standing waist-deep in a drift.

"What is it?" Nita asked. "What's happening?" It was all she could think to say.

"Don't talk."

The gorge was wider on the back side of the monolith, where the arroyo had eroded the ridge. Kerney heard the thud of two men dropping into the gorge, and looked for cover. Below the ledge circling the monolith was a crevice large enough for one person. He yanked Nita by the hand, forced her down, and shoved her into it.

"What are you doing?" she whispered.

"Curl up in a ball and be quiet," he said. "I'll come back for you." He pushed her knees to her chest and piled snow over her, trying to make the mound look as natural as possible.

He held his breath and listened. Nothing. Three men were coming at him from front and back, and there was no place to hide.

The mound covering the crevice was in deep shadows. Maybe they wouldn't spot Nita; maybe she could survive.

A small conical cedar tree stood at the far end of the monolith, where sunlight had yet to reach. Kerney eyed it. About the height of a man, the tree would be the first thing a shooter would see coming around the front end of the monolith.

Kerney took off his coat, went to the tree, wrapped the garment around it, and buttoned it up. At a quick glance, it might pass for a standing man. With his back against the monolith, he hunkered down and waited, listening for footfalls in the crusted snow, scanning left and right. He saw a long shadow flicker on the snow beyond the cedar tree. The shadow appeared again as the silhouette of a man.

Automatic fire ripped through Kerney's coat. When the man stepped into view, Kerney shot him twice in the chest, checked his flank, and ran to the snow-filled arroyo that sliced into the side of the ridge. With any luck, he could belly-crawl to the top of the ridge without being seen, and swing behind his pursuers.

DELFINO KEPT Carlos in front of him as they moved slowly along the ledge of the monolith, following the tracks left by Kerney and the woman. He stopped at the sound of Felix's Uzi and the two answering shots that followed. He waited for Felix to fire again. All was silent.

"Something's wrong," Delfino said. He dropped off the ledge, stepped past Carlos, and chanced a quick look around the corner. He spotted Felix's prone body near a coat wrapped around a tree. There was no sign of the gringo or the woman.

"Felix is down," Delfino said, turning the corner.

Carlos followed and stopped by a mound of snow that filled a small crevice under the ledge. Ahead, Felix sprawled on his back, not moving, the Uzi clutched in both hands.

"He's dead," Carlos said.

"We can still cut them off," Delfino replied. "They must be up ahead. Go back the way we came, and circle around."

Delfino glanced down and saw only one set of footprints in the snow—Kerney's tracks. Where did the woman go? Before he could look to find her hiding place, Carlos shot him in the back of the head.

Smiling, Carlos picked up Delfino's Uzi, holstered his pistol, and retreated. Now that the odds were even, he would follow Delfino's advice, backtrack around the monolith, find Kerney, and kill him.

KERNEY WINCED when he heard the pistol shot. He cursed himself for leaving Nita behind, reversed his crawl, and scanned from low to high ground as he moved down the arroyo. The sun was higher in the sky, but the monolith cast a fat shadow, and he could clearly see only the dead man by the tree, where his bullet-shredded winter coat flapped in a light breeze.

As far as he knew, two more men were still in the gorge, setting up a cross fire, which would be the smart thing to do. The arroyo gave him cover only if he stayed prone and low. He wanted to get up and make a dash to Nita. He forced himself to wait. The men stalking him controlled the action. All he could hope to do was counterpunch and survive.

Cold and soaked to the skin, he burrowed into the snow and tried not to shiver.

CARLOS WORKED his way slowly and quietly through the snow until he reached the end of the monolith. Darkness still lingered in the constricted ravine, but the sun was in his face every time he glanced up.

He took one more look at the ridgetop, and a snowball hit him in the face. He squinted into the sun, and started firing the Uzi at the moving shape above. It vanished before he could focus on it. He stepped forward to fire again and a bullet tore through his stomach and shattered his spine. He took another bullet in the chest as he fell.

Carlos hit the ground and Kerney ran in a low crouch, zigzagging past the dead man by the tree, waiting for bullets to tear into him. He made it to Nita's hiding place and found another man with the back of his skull blown open, the snow around his head icy pink.

He dropped his handgun, dug into the mound with both hands, and pulled Nita out of the crevice. She was pale, shaky on her feet, but unhurt.

"My God," she said, staring at the body. She started to cry.

"Not now," Kerney said sharply. "Robert is out there somewhere. Find him."

She nodded and began to move. Kerney left her and went to check on Carlos.

Carlos lay on his back staring into the sun until a shadow passed over his face. He felt the Uzi being pulled from his hands. He blinked and saw Kerney leaning over him.

"You're a hard man to kill, gringo," he said.

"You're dying, Carlos."

"I was going to die today, anyway."

"Is that why you killed one of your partners?" Kerney asked.

Carlos nodded and coughed up blood.

"Where is Nick Palazzi?"

"He fucked up, just like me. DeLeon had me kill him."

"And Amanda Talley, did you do her, too?"

"I never killed such a beautiful woman before."

"Where's her body?"

"No more body. Gone."

"What about Gilbert Martinez?"

"I thought it was you, gringo. I really wanted you dead."

"You've been a busy boy, Carlos."

Carlos gurgled once and died.

"Did you kill them all yourself?" Robert asked.

Kerney wheeled to find Robert and Nita at his side. Frozen snot hung from Robert's nose. He wiped it away with a sleeve.

"No," Kerney answered.

"Did you kill one of them, Addie?" Robert's eyes were jumpy and big as saucers.

Nita stiffened as though she'd taken a body blow. "No."

"Yes, you did," Robert said, inclining his head. "I saw his body over there. You killed the motherfucker."

Kerney eyed the crazy grin on Robert's face. "Do you need a ride to jail, Robert?"

Robert nodded.

"Let's go." Kerney led Nita and Robert away from Serpent Gate.

14

Kerney drove to the highway and found a car blocking their way through the ranch road gate. He keyed the handheld radio, made contact with the state police officer he'd left at the Shaffer Hotel, reported the shoot-out, and requested a tow truck.

"Send a snowplow also," he added as an afterthought. "We'll need the road cleared to the crime scene."

"And an ambulance," Nita said as she dropped Robert's boots on the floorboard.

Robert was in the back of the extended-cab. Kerney looked over his shoulder. Robert's feet were badly frostbitten.

Kerney relayed the message.

"Get me some snow," Nita said.

He got out of the truck and passed handfuls of snow to Nita, who rubbed it on Robert's bare feet. Robert howled, kicked wildly, and tried to fight his way out of the truck. Kerney popped the driver's seat forward on its tracks and pinned Robert down while Nita finished the job.

"How bad?" he asked.

Nita answered with a wary shrug.

The ambulance arrived with the state police unit. Kerney carried Robert to the vehicle. He struggled fiercely as Kerney put him on the gurney. It took all of his strength to hold Robert while the paramedics strapped him into the restraints.

Robert screamed in protest.

The ambulance pulled away for the trip to Albuquerque just as a tow truck arrived. Kerney looked around for Nita. She was in her 4 x 4, behind the steering wheel. He walked to her and she rolled down the window.

"Did you hear what Robert said to me?" she asked, without looking at Kerney. Her eyes were fixed on something—or nothing—outside the windshield.

"I may have missed it."

Nita kept looking away. Her hands gripped the steering wheel and her knuckles were white. "He said he raped me."

"He didn't mean anything by it."

"I think he believes it."

"Gillespie left a lot of victims behind."

"Addie is going to come and live with me, at least until my trial is over," she said without emotion.

"That's good." Kerney watched the officer guide the tow truck into position behind the car.

Slowly Nita switched her attention to Kerney. Her eyes were empty. "Do I have to stay here?"

"You can leave as soon as the way is clear," Kerney said.

"Who were those men?"

"Killers hired by a Mexican drug lord. They were after me, not you."

"Have you killed men before?"

Kerney didn't reply. The rear wheels of the car were off the ground. The operator stopped the winch, got in the truck, and pulled the vehicle out of the way.

"It's not a good feeling, is it?" Nita added, directing the question to herself.

Kerney answered anyway. "It never is, and never should be."

"Can I go now?" Nita asked.

Kerney nodded. A highway department snowplow came over the hill and stopped at the side of the road.

Nita smiled stiffly. "I guess I'll see you in court someday, Mr. Kerney."

"Someday you will, Ms. Lassiter."

Nita drove away and the patrol officer brought Kerney a jacket to wear. He put it on and went to the cruiser to get warm, while the officer talked to the snowplow operator. The driver dropped the blade and started the truck down the ranch road.

Kerney thought about the three dead men in the snow, and about Nita, Robert, Addie, Paul Gillespie, and Serpent Gate. He wondered if Robert would ever go back there again, and if Nita would be able to leave it behind for good.

THE MORNING after the gunfight at Serpent Gate, Kerney found his way to a new residential subdivision off Airport Road. The houses were pueblo-style one- and two-story structures on small lots. He parked at the curb in front of the Martinez family home.

Gilbert had only recently bought the house and moved in. It had yet to be landscaped, and snow covered the raw patch of land surrounding the house. Railroad ties were stacked against the side of the garage. Kerney wondered, now that Gilbert was dead, who would build the flower beds and plant the trees and shrubs when warm weather returned. The thought made his gut feel like a lead ball.

He got out and rang the doorbell.

Sandra Martinez, Gilbert's widow, used the partially open front door as a barrier, and studied the stranger standing on the porch.

"What is it?"

She had dark, intelligent eyes, a grief-filled face, and spoke in a drained voice.

"Mrs. Martinez, I'm Kevin Kerney."

Sandra's hand tightened on the doorknob. She forced back a response, while the man who should have been killed instead of her husband looked at her.

"Is there anything I can do for you or your family?" Kerney asked.

"No," Sandra said. "Thank you for stopping by." She closed the door in his face.

Kerney hesitated before ringing the bell again. After a minute, it grudgingly opened.

"Mrs. Martinez—" he said.

Sandra raised a shaky hand to cut him off, and her breath caught in her throat. She swallowed hard. "I know you came here with good intentions."

"I liked and respected your husband very much."

She forced a thin, dry smile. "Gilbert liked you, too."

"I feel responsible for your loss."

"You may be responsible, but you can't make amends for it, can you?"

"No, I can't."

"Then there's nothing more to say." She slowly closed the door again.

• • •

ANDY STUCK his head inside the conference room and found Kerney pecking away at the keyboard of an old computer that he'd scrounged from supply.

"Paperwork?" Andy asked.

"I'm just finishing up."

"I can get you a new computer, Kerney. All you have to do is ask."

"This one will do for now." Kerney hit a function key. The printer whined as it fed a sheet of paper into the rollers.

"DeLeon has left Mexico," Andy said.

"Where is he?"

Andy shrugged. "The Mexican authorities say they don't know. And if they do, they aren't telling. They did identify the two hit men DeLeon sent after you."

"So quickly?"

"Both were former federal intelligence agents cashiered for being on the cartel's pad. They're wanted on multiple murder charges. It seems they assassinated a judge, a prosecutor, and a district police commissioner in Chihuahua."

"Nasty boys."

"The Mexican government is sending you a citation."

"I don't want it," Kerney said gruffly. The printer spit out a sheet of paper. Kerney plucked it out of the tray and gave it to Andy.

Andy read it. It was an official request to award the police medal of valor posthumously to Sergeant Gilbert Martinez. "Would you like to make the presentation to Gilbert's widow?" he asked.

"That's not a good idea."

"Stop blaming yourself, Kerney. What happened to Gilbert wasn't your fault."

"That's not the way Sandra Martinez sees it."

Andy studied Kerney's face and decided to drop the subject. "Are you planning to stick around for a while? I've got six major cases I need you to bird-dog. And I don't want you creating a vacancy Vance Howell can fill."

Kerney cracked a small smile. "You think the governor would dump Howell on you if I left?"

"In the blink of an eye."

"Are you catching any flak from Springer?"

"Not yet. The department has gotten too much good press lately. But the word is out on the governor's staff that I'm insubordinate and not a team player. My reputation is getting as bad as yours."

"I've worked hard to build that reputation, Andy. Don't butt in on my turf. Are you going to stick it out?"

"Hell, yes, I am. I took this job because I wanted to do some good. I need you to watch my back while I push my budget through the legislature."

"Do you think Springer might torpedo the budget as a payback for busting his nephew?"

"That thought has crossed my mind."

"I'll think about staying around for a while."

"Good deal," Andy said.

"But I need a few days off for personal business."

"Take as much time as you need," Andy said from his door. "I'll see you when you get back."

On the conference table was a box of five hundred freshly printed business cards that had arrived in the mail. Kerney hadn't asked for the new cards—probably a clerk had automatically ordered them when his promotion had been posted.

He took one card from the box and slipped it in his wallet.

•   •   •

AN ENTIRELY different climate greeted Kerney in Mexico. Even in the late afternoon, the day was warm, the sky a rich blue, and a dry breeze from the open truck window felt good against his face.

He drove the highway south of Juárez, and passed the turnoff to DeLeon's hacienda without stopping. Since his only other visit, the access road had been paved and an electronic security gate barred entry. Probably DeLeon's restoration of the hacienda was complete. Kerney looked forward to seeing it.

He traveled past a long sweep of hills that blocked the Rio Grande from view, and took a dirt road that led to a constricted *bosque* along the river. He parked out of sight from the highway, got his gear, and started walking.

The brown, slow-moving river sucked up the fast-fading light, giving back no reflection, and it stank with a foul combination of human and industrial waste. On the Mexican side, there were holes cut in the twenty-foot-high chain-link border fence big enough for three men to pass through side by side.

The *bosque* gave out where the river carved through some hills, and Kerney hiked up a rock-strewn incline. He reached the top as the last rays of a setting sun dimmed to dusk. Below, the *bosque* reappeared, not very wide, but thicker than before. The hacienda stood nestled against the side of the hill with a view that took in the sloping river valley.

DeLeon had brought the estate back to life, and the hacienda with its long, two-story sweep looked grand. Plastered mud brown with small shuttered windows that marched along the wall on either side of massive center doors, it resembled a fortified citadel.

When Kerney had last seen it, the building had been nothing more than an adobe shell sitting above an old basement hollowed out of the hill.

As the dusk turned to night, Kerney slipped a night-vision

viewer out of the pouch. He scanned the hacienda for signs of activity and saw nothing. All seemed equally quiet at the outbuildings, including the small chapel and a circular stone granary that soared like a watchtower next to the hacienda.

After an hour of watching, headlights came into view on the access road and a car parked in front of the hacienda. It was a Chihuahua federal police unit. Two uniformed officers got out, and one checked the hacienda while his partner rattled the locked chapel door and walked out of sight around the side of the building. No lights came on inside the hacienda.

After completing the building security check, the cops drove down a gravel road that led to the *bosque*, spotlighting the old stone foundations and rock fences along the way. Finished with the patrol, they left on the access road.

Kerney waited an hour and a half until the officers came back and completed another tour. He put the night-vision viewer away, and trotted to the side of the hacienda. Under a portal, arched lead-glass doors opened onto the patio. Kerney inspected the doors with a flashlight and found alarm sensors attached to the glass.

He backtracked to the chapel and checked for a rear entrance. There was none, but small stained-glass windows showing the stations of the cross ran the length of the building on either side. The windows were wired to the alarm system.

Kerney figured DeLeon had something valuable inside the chapel—like maybe a priceless religious statue.

He had no way of knowing where the Mexican cops might be stationed. They could be at the access road security gate, or checking on another *jefe*'s mansion some distance away.

It would have to be a smash-and-grab affair. To do it right, he needed to be in, out, and gone in a few minutes. He could make it if he pushed his bad knee to the maximum and got lucky inside the hacienda.

He picked up a rock, broke a chapel window, and hauled himself inside. The alarm was silent, but intrusion sensors mounted near the ceiling blinked rapidly. His flashlight beam illuminated the Lady of Guadalupe statue on the center of the altar. Kerney grabbed it, kicked open the chapel door, put the *bulto* on the outside step, and sprinted to the hacienda.

He blew a hole in one of the glass patio doors with his nine-millimeter, unlocked it, and did a fast-and-dirty search, sweeping his light quickly over the walls of each room. He found the sheathed U.S. Cavalry sword above the mantel in the billiard room. He took it, left his business card on the mantel, and ran like hell, retracing his steps.

He snatched the *bulto* from the chapel step at a dead run, and sprinted for the hill. He could hear the sound of a fast-approaching vehicle. He didn't stop running until he was on the back side of the hill. He jogged to the cover of the *bosque* before slowing to a walk. Sharp jolts of pain ran up his leg.

Kerney smiled in spite of the pain as he glanced at the statue and sheathed sword in his hands. It was, at best, a small victory over DeLeon. But he knew it would sting him.

ANDY HELD a brief press conference as Kerney watched from the back of the room. He said a few words about the return of the *bulto* from an anonymous source, and presented the statue to a museum official who gushed in appreciation while the video cameras whirled and reporters scribbled in their notebooks.

Kerney slipped away before the reporters started asking questions, and went to pack the sword and scabbard for shipment.

The sword had a three-quarter-inch blade, a gilded brass hilt, a grip wrapped in twisted wire, and a gold-lace strap attached to the handle. The nickel-plated scabbard had a mounting of gilded brass. It was in mint condition.

Kerney would mail the sword to West Point, where the other military artifacts found on the missile range were on permanent display. He packed it carefully and included a note returning the items with the compliments of Major Sara Brannon, the army officer who had worked with Kerney on the smuggling case.

Kerney had been thinking a lot about Sara lately; they had a long-standing date to meet when she returned from her tour of duty in Korea in late spring. It felt like a long time away.

Andy came in as he licked the shipping label and stuck it on the package.

"What's that?" he asked, tilting his chin at the package.

"Just a memento I'm sending off on behalf of a friend," Kerney said as he picked up the package. "I have to visit someone. I'll see you later."

Kerney stopped in on Joe Valdez before leaving headquarters. Joe was busy boxing up files. He stretched packing tape over the top of a carton and sealed it shut.

"That's it, Chief," Joe said. "Every shred of evidence on Roger Springer, Sherman Cobb, and Bucky Watson is in these boxes. I have to deliver it to the AG this afternoon. The case is out of our hands."

"How far did you get on the money laundering?" Kerney asked.

"Pretty far," Joe answered. "Bucky liked to use DeLeon's money instead of his own whenever possible."

"How about for political campaign contributions?"

"Bucky made some big contributions to the governor's campaign, but I didn't track the source."

"Would you do that for me before you take the files to the AG?"

"What are you looking for, Chief?"

"I'd like to know if Bucky gave DeLeon's money to the governor's reelection committee."

"What difference would that make? Unless we could prove the committee knew the money was tainted, no crime has been committed."

"That's not what I'm after, Joe," Kerney said. "Do it on the QT."

"Whatever you say."

"Thanks."

After Kerney left, Joe got his penknife out and started opening the taped cartons, wondering what kind of political game the deputy chief was playing. He decided he didn't want to know.

Robert had been transferred from the hospital in Albuquerque to the Las Vegas Medical Center. Kerney found him in one of the cookie-cutter-modern treatment cottages behind the original nineteenth-century building once known as the New Mexico Insane Asylum.

The cottage consisted of a combined dayroom and dining area with private cell-like sleeping quarters that branched off from a semi-circular core. In spite of the white walls, sunlight from skylights and windows, and the numerous game boards and magazines scattered about, the cottage had a grubby, neglected appearance.

Robert sat in a plastic chair facing a television set, watching a religious program on a Christian station. A pair of crutches rested against his leg, and his feet were wrapped in bandages.

Kerney sat down next to Robert, who gave him a dismissive look and turned his attention back to the set.

"How are you, Robert?"

"Jesus cut off all my toes," he said, keeping his eyes glued on the screen.

"Jesus did that?"

"He cut them off for raping my daughter," he said matter-of-factly.

"That's pretty harsh."

"Jesus knows what he's doing," Robert said instructively. "You should know that."

"I hope he does."

"Do you love Jesus?"

"Everybody should," Kerney answered.

"That's right. Are you a doctor?" Robert asked, searching Kerney's face.

"No, my name is Kerney."

"That's a funny name."

"Don't you remember me?"

"I never saw you before," Robert said as he switched his gaze back to the television.

Kerney stayed until it was clear Robert had nothing more to say.

DeLeon's forty-million-dollar yacht was anchored just outside the bay of the coastal city of Manzanillo. Enrique watched the wake of the approaching boat cut through the Pacific Ocean before moving to the shade of the canopy on the foredeck.

DeLeon used Manzanillo as a transfer point for cocaine shipments from Columbia and Ecuador. The product came in by ship to be off-loaded at the dock into waiting trucks. This arrangement was possible because DeLeon had made the local police commander and his immediate assistants wealthy men.

The boat came alongside, and within minutes Brigadier General Sergio Garcia Perez, deputy chief of Mexican intelligence, was on deck.

"Señor DeLeon," General Perez said with a wide smile. "I am delighted to see you again."

"It is good to see you, General," Enrique replied. "Join me for a drink." He motioned for a mess boy, who came, took the general's order, and returned quickly with a wineglass.

"How can I assist you?" Perez asked from his deck chair.

"I understand you have an agent who is expert at arranging accidents that do not raise suspicion. A Cuban expatriate, I believe, fluent in English and trained by the Americans."

Perez masked his surprise. Few people outside the Mexican intelligence community knew of his Cuban asset. "That is correct."

"Would it be possible for me to utilize his services?" DeLeon inquired. "Anonymously, of course."

"Perhaps," Perez said cautiously. "Who is the object of your concern?"

"An American police officer in New Mexico." DeLeon held out Kerney's dossier.

Perez paged through the dossier and scanned the photograph. This was the man who had killed two of his former agents in a shoot-out north of the border. A deep background check would be necessary before Perez would make a commitment; no ordinary policeman could take out two highly skilled operatives so easily.

"If I agree to your proposal, when would you like this accident to occur?" Perez asked.

"Only when you are sure there is no risk to you and there is no chance of failure," Enrique replied, getting to his feet. "But come, other than your fee, we have talked about business long enough. I have had a meal prepared I think you will enjoy."

As KERNEY looked on, Andy read through Joe Valdez's report on Bucky Watson's political campaign contributions to the Committee to Reelect the Governor.

"So the committee got dirty money from DeLeon through

Watson," Andy said, dropping the last sheet of paper on his desk. "Over seventy-five thousand dollars. That's quite a contribution."

"I'm sure they didn't know the source of the money," Kerney said. "But it might upset the voting public if word got out the family values candidate got reelected with the help of a large donation from the Mexican drug lord responsible for the murder of two police officers and a multimillion-dollar theft."

Andy put the report in order and locked it in his desk. "I think I'll hold on to this for a while."

"Good idea."

"We might just get the funds for expansion the department needs next year." Andy leaned back in his chair with a satisfied look on his face.

"Wouldn't that be great?" Kerney replied.

"BUT YOU can stay here as long as you like," Fletcher said.

"I can't keep bunking with you forever," Kerney said with a shake of his head. He stuffed the last of the shirts into a canvas carryall and zipped it closed. "Besides, I'm only moving six blocks away. We'll be neighbors."

"You're a workaholic. I'll never see you."

"I may not be working at all." Kerney went to the closet, took sweaters off a shelf, and dumped them into a plastic bag.

"Are you leaving the state police?"

"I haven't decided."

"What kind of place have you rented?" Fletcher asked.

"It's a furnished one-bedroom with a fireplace and patio."

"Does it have charm?"

"It will do for now," Kerney replied.

He got his shaving gear from the bathroom and looked around. All of his possessions were packed; it would take no more than two or three trips to his pickup truck to move out. He needed to spend a little money and buy some things. Pots, pans, plates—that sort of stuff. Maybe even a television.

"I'm going to load up," he said.

"I'll help you carry your things out."

Fletcher followed him outside, lugging the large plastic bag. A truck pulled into the driveway and a woman got out. She stuck her hands in the pockets of her leather jacket and walked quickly to Kerney. Close up, Fletcher found her quite attractive.

"Ms. Lassiter," Kerney said. He took the plastic bag out of Fletcher's hand and put it in the bed of the pickup. "What can I do for you?"

Nita looked at Fletcher and hesitated. "It's nothing official."

"Are you sure you want to talk to me?" Kerney asked.

"Yes, just for a moment. Please."

"I'll get the carryall," Fletcher said, stepping off toward the guest quarters.

"What is it?" Kerney asked.

"The DA has offered my lawyer a plea bargain—voluntary manslaughter. I'd serve a reduced prison sentence."

"What did Dalquist say?"

"He doesn't want me to take it. I wanted to know what you thought."

"I'm not a lawyer, Nita."

"That's why I'm asking."

"If it were me, I'd go to trial. There's no way I'd agree to be locked up in prison, under any circumstance."

"Think I can win?"

"You've got too much to lose not to try."

"Thank you, Kevin."

"Call me Kerney. Most of my friends do."

Fletcher returned in time to see the woman lean close to Kerney with her hand on his arm and say something he couldn't hear.

Kerney reached out and squeezed the woman's shoulder. She kissed him on the cheek and hugged him before breaking away and giving him one last, long look. She walked slowly to her vehicle and drove away.

"Why would you let an attractive woman like that walk away?" Fletcher asked. "She didn't seem to want to leave at all."

"I know where to find her, and I have an open invitation to visit, if things work out," Kerney said, taking the carryall from Fletcher. "Besides, timing is everything."

"How true."

Kerney smiled. "I'll see you later, Fletcher."

"Dinner here, next Tuesday night," Fletcher suggested.

"It will be my pleasure."

ABOUT THE AUTHOR

Michael McGarrity entered law enforcement in his forties as a deputy sheriff for Santa Fe County. He established the first sex crime unit in the Santa Fe Sheriff's Department and led it to award-winning status, personally breaking many of the unit's most difficult cases. He has also worked as an instructor at the New Mexico Law Enforcement Academy and as an investigator for the New Mexico Public Defender's Office. His previous novels are *Tularosa* and *Mexican Hat*. He lives in Santa Fe, New Mexico.